hidden
truths

USA TODAY BESTSELLING AUTHOR

K WEBSTE
NIKKI A

My life was easy, simple, fun.

Light.

Until I got wrapped up with the wrong people.

Nothing but a piece of property to pay for the sins of my father.

I'm to be married off to a handsome monster.

I see his truths every day, and it's hard not to fall for the enemy.

He won't let me escape, but I'm not sure I want to.

I wanted to marry for love, but it looks like love is a lie.

To our readers, thank you for continuing
to trust us with your hearts.

hidden *truths*

chapter
one

Kostas

THE DARK BLUE WATERS OF MIRABELLO BAY ARE calm this evening. Unlike the storm brewing inside me. Where the sea before me shimmers in a serene way beneath the moonlight, the one I hold claim to is raging.

Skoulíki.

I lift my tumbler to my lips and sip the ouzo, relishing the burn that races down my throat when I swallow. It only adds fuel to the anger flickering inside me, threatening to spread like wildfire. When my wrath has been unleashed, men who wrong me—who shit on the Demetriou name—get burned.

Someone clears their throat. Just once. Quietly. A reminder to move the fuck on.

Yes, Father.

Reluctantly tearing my gaze from the bay, I regard my new guest with cold, barely contained contempt. A *skoulíki* in our rich, fruitful soil. A man so slimy and dirty, I can barely look at him. He doesn't belong here, tainting the exquisite room he's sitting in.

Niles Nikolaides.

Nothing but a filthy worm in dire need of being plucked from the dirt and fed to a fucking bird. Ignoring the piece of shit who's sitting uncomfortably in a leather armchair, with all eyes on him, I skim my gaze around the room. They're all waiting for me to make a move, especially Father.

The move I want to make is to grab Niles by the throat and throw him off the goddamn balcony. Too easy. Too fucking easy for a man like him. A man who has been stealing from right under our noses. Allowing passage into Thessaloniki without paying the Demetriou tax.

"You think because we are in Crete we don't see what it is you're up to at our port?" I ask, my tone icy and condescending.

Niles clenches his jaw and sits up, shaking his head. His good looks won't help him in a room full of men who hate him. And while my father has never come out and stated why, I can see pure hatred for Niles flickering in his hazel eyes.

Father leans back on the leather sofa, and a small smirk tugs at his lips. He's enjoying seeing Niles in the hot seat, the center of my thunderous attention. Beside him, my brother, Aris, grins. While forcing Niles to squirm some more—like the worm he is—as he waits for me to continue, I study my brother.

Aris is so different from Father and me with our dark hair, calculating eyes, and permanent scowls.

Ezio Demetriou and I could pass for brothers rather than father and son. It's Aris who stands out with his golden skin, light brown hair, and playful brown eyes. He is soft to our hard. Warm to our cold. Weak to our strong. Aris is my mother made over, much to my father's disappointment.

"Sir," Niles starts unwisely.

I sear him with a glare. "You are here to listen, *fíle*." *Friend.*

Aris snorts, earning a sharp look from our father. We all know Niles is no friend.

Motioning with a quick flick of my fingers, two of my most trusted men approach from the shadows of the room. They're dressed in black suits, hiding enough weapons to take out a small army beneath their jackets. Adrian and Basil are the largest men in this room. Imposing, threatening, cruel. All it takes is one nod of my head and they'll drag Niles, the *skoulíki* from Thessaloniki, to the *kelári* for a proper punishment. A punishment extracted with his blood. He must sense the violent storm churning in my eyes because he does what they all do.

Spews more bullshit.

"I can make this right, Kostas," Niles pleads, eyeing Adrian and Basil warily. "I was in a bad place. Everything is better now. Think of it as a loan."

Ignoring him, I walk over to the table where the expensive bottle of ouzo sits and refill my glass. I pour two fingers' worth of the clear liquor into the glass of ice and then splash in some water from a decanter. Like oil trying to mix with water, the ouzo becomes cloudy, but never truly mixes. I give the tumbler a shake before draining the glass and setting it back down.

"*Ena macheri*," I demand coolly to Basil, holding out my hand.

Basil pulls a sharp Benchmade Nimravus knife from inside his jacket. At just four and a half inches, it's small enough to conceal, but long enough to do lethal damage. Niles knows this because he starts shaking his head.

"No, Kostas, listen," he pleads. "It was all part of my plan. To get into better graces with the Demetriou name."

I take the knife from Basil and study the pointy tip of the blade. "Explain how *you* taking *our* taxes and keeping them for yourself, when it is *us* who allows the ships passage into the ports, gets *you* into good graces with *us*." I dart my gaze to my brother. "Aris may be the numbers whiz here, but I must say, even I know something isn't adding up."

Niles, known for his killer smile and charm, pales as a frown wrinkles his brow. He ages ten years before me. His green eyes that usually light up with a calculating glint have dulled. A man knows when death is knocking on his door. He may not want to answer, but we're fucking here whether he likes it or not.

The negotiator slides back into the pilot seat as Niles's eyes light up with their usual devious glow. "The numbers didn't add up when you started tripling the taxes I owed a decade ago," Niles says without meeting my father's barely hidden murderous stare. "And yet I didn't argue. I paid my dues to the Demetrious."

Father's eyes narrow and a vein jumps in his neck. Aris frowns, shooting me a questioning look. It's rare for my father to show emotion. He hates Niles. Always has. It's always been clear to me, although I've never understood why. Nor have I asked.

Niles is smarmy.

That's enough for me to have my father's back.

"Your point?" I demand in a bored tone, picking at my nail with the tip of Basil's knife. "I feel as though you're unsuccessfully trying to make one."

"My point is I've been paying more and more over the years without argument. The taxes I collect on your behalf at the port are being underutilized. All I did was gain new contracts. I didn't take from your current ones." His face breaks out in a grin, as though his new reasoning will somehow save him from my wrath.

"The territory still belongs to us," I snap, no longer able to keep my fury on a leash.

Aris smirks at my outburst, while Father's brows furl together in an irritated way.

Sorry, Father, but this prick is pissing me off.

Taking a deep breath, I regain some composure before I speak again. "The territory is *ours*. Therefore, new contracts are *ours*. That fucking means new taxes are *ours*."

"And you'll get your money," Niles lies smoothly. "You always do. I've simply invested it in other ventures. When I earn it back, which is soon, you'll be paid back for the taxes. Plus interest."

I can tell Father wants to take over. He doesn't like that I'm allowing Niles to continue to plead his case. The worm needs to die.

"What are these other ventures?" I ask, ignoring the anger rolling from my father in waves.

"Mostly trafficking," Niles says, his green eyes flaring with wickedness. "Of the human variety."

My stomach roils in disgust. Not because of what he's chosen to traffic, but the fact he's allowing these vermin to pass through our ports. The Demetrious aren't the mafia or cartel. No, we're a dominant crime organization. Masters of power, influence, and wealth. We manipulate it to our advantage without having to scrape the bottom of the barrel ever.

Niles lives there.

In the dirty, dank bottom with all the other worms.

I want to fucking drown him.

"Basil," I boom, no longer interested in speaking with this lowlife. "Take him to the *kelári*." I point the blade at Niles. "I'll finish this conversation when we're alone." And when I'm cutting his useless tongue from his mouth.

Father rises from the sofa, giving me a subtle shake of his head. Aris sees and lifts his brows in surprise. To any other man, this is nothing. To our family, it's a crushing blow.

He's undermining my authority.

My father doesn't like my choice to kill him.

Rather than arguing with my father—something Aris would do—I clench my teeth and take a step back to give him the limelight. White-hot fury blazes inside me. Why doesn't he want this asshole dead tonight? He fucking stole from us. Lied to us. Whatever decade long hard-on for punishment my father has against Niles is getting old. It goes against everything he's taught me.

Loyalty is everything.

Niles is far from loyal. He's as disloyal as one can get. The motherfucker has blatantly admitted to stealing from us for his own agenda. Any other fool would be in the *kelári*, paying for his crimes with flesh and blood and screams.

Not Niles.

Never Niles.

Why do you keep him around, Father?

"Take a walk with me," Father tells Niles. "You too, Kostas."

Aris's jaw clenches at being left behind. As he should be. The men are talking. Niles rises, his green eyes darting between my father and me in confusion. When my father walks out onto the balcony, Niles and I follow suit. I close the door behind us and inhale the salty sea air.

Father leans against the balcony wrought iron railing and regards Niles as though he is a fungus. A fungus he's devoted his life to trying to destroy. Not kill, destroy. I've observed my father enough to learn to read his eyes. He says very little, but his eyes are telling if you're watching. He enjoys ruining Niles, but never ending him.

"You owe our family something far more valuable than your worthless life," Father tells him, his voice cold and cruel. "Do you agree?"

Niles, clearly eager to save his ass from death, nods emphatically. "I do. I'll get you your money. Soon, Ezio."

Father's nostrils flare, his only tell at how disgusted he is to have to deal with Niles. "Money is of no issue. It's a way we control people like you." He sneers. "What I want is priceless to a man like you."

Niles frowns, and his body stiffens. "And what is that?"

When Father glances my way, his eyes quickly assessing me, a cold chill numbs me to my bone. I don't like feeling as though I'm a pawn in this game. I'm a power player. I own the fucking board right along with my father. His telling eyes state otherwise.

"Pérasma Hotel & Villas could use a little sunshine," Father says, smirking at Niles. "I know my son could use a little warmth."

Our Greek resort that's a gateway to the Aegean Sea is known for its warm, picturesque location. While we may run darker business under our bright resort face, it's never for a lack of sun. My father is talking in riddles and it infuriates me. We're practically partners, and whatever game he's been playing with Niles for years, I'm not on his team. It's man against man, and I'm simply a weapon to be used.

Niles sucks in a sharp breath. "No."

Father's brow lifts high up his forehead. "No?"

No is not in Father's vocabulary. I learned that from an early age.

"I, uh," Niles stammers. "You know that's unfair."

The malevolence in my father's eyes is enough to have Niles taking a step back. "Life is unfair," Father tells Niles. "But at least you'll have one. I believe this is the best you could ever hope for."

And like a worm caught in a hawk's beak, Niles squirms with unease.

He'll devour you one day.

One simple nod is all it takes from Niles to seal their deal. Niles Nikolaides will live to see another day because he just negotiated something that is clearly very important to him.

Fucking fool.

chapter
two

Talia

"**W**HAT'S HERE? A CUP, CLOSED IN MY TRUE love's hand?" I pluck the metal tumbler out of Alex's still hand and bring it to my nose, sniffing the contents. "Poison, I see, hath been his timeless end. O churl! Drunk all, and left no friendly drop to help me after?"

I drop to my knees on the hardwood floor and bow my head in a position of prayer. Tears prick my eyes as I glance up at the man before me, lying still in the tomb. "I will kiss thy lips. Haply some poison yet doth hang on them to make me die with a restorative."

Crawling into the tomb with Alex, I snuggle up next to him and place a soft, chaste kiss to his lips. His tongue darts out playfully, and I have to stifle a laugh. "Thy lips are warm!"

From a distance, a masculine voice calls out, "Lead, boy. Which way?"

"Yeah, noise?" I ask no one. "Then I'll be brief."

Reaching over Alex's body, I find his dagger and pull it out. The silver metal glistens in the light. "O, happy dagger!

This is my sheath." With tears trailing down my cheeks, I stab myself in the stomach and let my body fall limply against Alex's.

With my eyes closed, I lie in the tomb, listening as the guards speak around me, trying to figure out what has happened. Next my mother and father enter. My mother screams and cries and begs for answers, while my father demands to know what's happened. Alex and I continue to lie still while the friar explains everything from our love, to our death. My parents cry and mourn the loss of their daughter.

And then the prince speaks. "A glooming peace this morning with it brings. The sun, for sorrow, will not show his head. Go hence to have more talk of these sad things. Some shall be pardoned, and some punished. For never was a story more woe than this of Juliet and her Romeo."

The curtains close, and the auditorium booms with applause.

"You are such a beautiful Juliet," Alex says, lifting onto his forearms and caging me in.

"And you are a handsome Romeo," I say back.

Alex's lips curl into a boyish grin. His face comes down, about to kiss me, but before our lips meet, we hear, "Not now! Not now! Out! Out!" Professor Marino chides. "We have curtain call! Come!"

Alex steps out of the tomb first and then helps me to my feet, lifting and setting me down. "Later," he murmurs into my ear. Blush creeps up my neck and cheeks, heating my skin.

We form a line, and the curtains open. Everyone bows and curtsies, and the applause starts up once more. My eyes dart across the people and land on my family. My mom's face splits into a huge smile. Our eyes meet, and she mouths, *I love you.*

I love you more, I mouth back.

My eyes land on my brother next. With his fingers between his lips, he's whistling so loud, the sound overpowers the applause. My eyes roll of their own accord, but deep down, I'm happy to see him here. When I was ten, and he was fifteen, our parents divorced. I moved to Rome to live with my mom and her parents, but my brother, Phoenix, stayed with our father in Thessaloniki. I hate the distance between us, but there was no way of going around it. I wasn't about to stay in Greece without our mom, and Phoenix couldn't leave. Running the family business with our father was never not an option.

My eyes leave my brother's and roam over to my stepdad, Stefano. Then, I smile when I see my grandfather and grandmother, Emilio and Vera, still affectionately referred to as Nonno and Nonna. They're all clapping and beaming with pride.

The curtain closes once again and everyone cheers. "Magnifico!" Professor Marino exclaims. "What a wonderful way to end the semester. Go now and greet your families. I will see all of you in August. Enjoy your summer…but not too much." She winks playfully, and we all laugh.

"Come," I say, grabbing Alex's hand. "I can't wait for you to meet my family." I already know his family isn't here. His parents live in the States and weren't able to fly over. Instead, Alex will be visiting them this summer, and he's invited me to join him.

"Talia!" My mom wraps me in a hug and kisses my cheek. "There was no Juliet better than you." She pulls her face back and frames my cheeks. "You did a marvelous job."

"Thank you, Mom."

"Talia, you did a wonderful job," my grandfather says. "You both did." His eyes flicker from me to Alex, and I take that as my cue to introduce Alex to everyone. "Alex, this is my family. My mom, Melody, my stepdad, Stefano. This is my brother, Phoenix, and my grandparents, Emilio and Vera."

Alex gives my mom and grandmother a kiss on their cheeks and then shakes each of the guys' hands. "It's a pleasure to meet all of you."

"Oh, you are American," my grandfather states when he hears Alex's American accent, even though he already knows as much. I've spoken to my family several times about Alex since we met in our Performing Arts class this semester when he transferred here to study abroad for his last year and a half of college.

"I am, sir," Alex says. "Italian-American. I came here to learn about my roots."

My grandfather gives him a nod of approval. "Will you be joining my granddaughter this summer?"

Alex gives me a confused look. I haven't told my family that I've decided to join Alex in the States instead of spending my entire summer at home like I usually do.

"Actually, I'm going to Chicago with Alex for the first half of the summer," I admit.

Nonno's lips turn down into a frown as I knew they would, but it's my mom's face I'm more concerned with. Her brows are knitted together, and her lips are pursed. I know I shouldn't have sprung this on her, but it was last-minute. I only found out a few days ago and felt it would be best to tell her in person. Aside from my one week with my father at the end of every summer, my vacations are always spent with my mom. She's my best friend, and moving to Florence to attend school was one of the hardest decisions I've had to make. Living three hours from her hasn't been easy.

"I'm sorry, *cara mia*, but that won't be possible," my mom says. "You've been summoned by your *father*." She spits out the title like it's a curse word. She doesn't talk about why she and my father divorced, but whatever happened, I know it was bad because even after all these years, she still refuses to see or talk about him.

"What? No!" I shake my head in confusion. "I always visit him the last week of the summer. You know this."

"Why am I just now hearing about this?" Nonno asks, his voice filled with concern.

"I only just found out last night," Mom explains. "Your brother will be taking you back with him."

"So, that's why you came?" I hiss, choosing to hide my hurt with anger. "Not to see my final performance, but to drag me back to Thessaloniki?"

"I came here to watch you," Phoenix says slowly, "but yes, I also came to escort you to Dad."

"I'm not going." My chin lifts in defiance and my arms cross over my chest. "I'll see him at the end of the summer like I do every year. Besides, I already purchased my plane ticket to Chicago."

"*Cara mia*, why don't we discuss this in private?" my mom suggests. Her tone hints she's trying to be polite in front of Alex, but the way she quirks one brow up tells me there will be no discussion.

Whether I like it or not, I will be going with Phoenix to visit our dad.

We go to dinner as planned, but the entire meal is filled with tension. Everyone is being polite, but there's a giant elephant in the room. When dessert is served—my favorite, crème brûlée—I finally address what nobody wants to talk about. "Why am I going to visit Dad now?"

"I'm not sure," Phoenix says. "I've only been told to bring you to him."

"And if I refuse to go?"

Phoenix hits me with a *don't make this difficult* glare. "You don't have a choice."

"Mom," I plead. She always has my back when it comes to my father. If anyone can keep me from having to go, it's her.

"I told you we would discuss this later," she says, taking a bite of her dessert.

"I have to take her from here," Phoenix says.

My mom's eyes widen. "Now? I thought we could return home first."

"We're flying out of Peretola," he states. "The plane leaves at seven o'clock."

"Maybe I can go first and then you can follow after," Alex suggests, ever the peacemaker.

When we met, I was arguing with another student about a performance we were working on. She felt I was being too dramatic for the character, and I felt I wasn't being dramatic enough. Alex walked over and played mediator—agreeing with her instead of me. Afterward, he introduced himself, to which I gave him the cold shoulder, upset he didn't agree with me. He laughed and told me he would never be anything but honest with me, and he's been a part of our group ever since. What started out as friendship eventually grew into more, and about two months ago, we made our relationship official. He's sweet and thoughtful and caring, and I can see a future with him.

"I wanted to go with you," I whine, annoyed that once

again my father is messing up my plans. This is just so typical of him. He is such a mess, and it always spills over onto his family. Last summer I made plans to visit Cambridge with some friends. We set up our flights and made our hotel reservations, but because my father had issues with his business, he had to push my trip to visit him back, and I couldn't go to Cambridge.

"Go see your dad, and once you're done, we'll transfer your plane ticket over so you can fly from there to Chicago," Alex says. He reaches his hand under the table and squeezes mine gently.

"Can I do that?" I ask Phoenix.

"I don't see why not." He shrugs then glances at his watch. "We really need to get going, though."

"I haven't had time to pack."

"I've been told it will all be handled," Phoenix says.

"How long is the flight?" Alex asks.

"Five hours," I say, slumping into my seat, frustrated. I'm twenty-one years old. My dad shouldn't be able to dictate my life anymore. And if I were more of a bitch, I would put up a fight. But it's just not worth it to argue. Growing up, I've witnessed on more than one occasion the way he treats those who argue with him. The last thing I want is to get on his bad side. My father and I have a weird relationship. When I was younger, I was his little girl. His *sunshine*. But once my parents divorced, it was as if I was made to choose sides. And I chose my mom's. Ever since then, our relationship has become strained. He's changed so much over the years. He used to be a man I could go to with my problems, but over time, his own problems have taken over his life, leaving little to no room for me. I miss him and hate him and love him all at the same time.

"Call me as soon as you arrive." Alex presses a soft kiss to my lips. "The time will fly by and soon you will be in Chicago with me. I can't wait to show you around."

Everyone stands and exchanges hugs and kisses. Reluctantly, I go with Phoenix, while my mom and grandparents head back to Rome, and Alex heads back to his apartment to pack for Chicago.

The town car takes us to the airport, but where I expect us to be dropped off so we can check in and go through security, we're instead driven around the back and onto the tarmac.

The driver pulls up to a huge sleek silver plane. Across the tail reads Global 8000 with a large letter D across the side.

"We're flying on that?" I ask, confused. There's no way our father can afford a seat on this plane, let alone chartering it to pick me up.

"It was given to us on loan," Phoenix says, stepping out of the car and then taking my hand to help me out.

We are greeted by two pretty flight attendants who hand us each a glass flute filled with champagne and welcome us on board. The captain and co-captain also introduce themselves and let us know we'll be taking off shortly. As we walk through the plane, I am stunned by the extravagance and luxury that fills the inside. Gray leather seats line the entire left side with a large flat screen television hanging on the wall. The right side has several recliners with glossy mahogany tables separating them. If it weren't for the circular windows, I would think I was standing inside an expensive apartment.

"If you need to take a shower or wish to take a nap, there's a bedroom and full bathroom in the back," one of the attendants informs us, and my jaw drops. There's an entire bedroom on this plane?

"Phoenix," I hiss, pulling him to the side. "There's no way Dad can afford this."

"I already told you it's on loan." The way he says it sends a shiver racing down my spine.

"Nobody *loans* something like this for free! He couldn't even afford the home we grew up in anymore and had to sell it!" *Something is going on here…*

Just as Phoenix is about to say something, the captain comes over the intercom and asks that we have a seat and buckle in since we'll be taking off in five minutes. "The skies are clear, and the flight to Heraklion will be four hours and nine minutes."

"Heraklion?" I shriek. "Isn't that in…Crete?"

Phoenix sits on one of the leather couches and nods. "Yes, have a seat."

"No! I thought you were taking me to Thessaloniki. What the hell is going on?" My eyes find the door where we came from and see it's already shut.

"You can't leave," Phoenix says, reading my thoughts. "They're not going to open it now. We're about to take off. So, please, just sit."

"First tell me why we're going to Crete."

Phoenix sighs. "Dad is visiting with the Demetrious, a family he does business with. They own the ports Dad rents from. He's requested for us to come and join them."

I drop onto my seat with a huff. I can tell by the way Phoenix is answering my questions, he either doesn't know much or he's purposely being vague. Either way, it doesn't take a rocket scientist to know whatever is going on can't be good.

Once upon a time, my mom said our dad used to be successful, but greed got to him, and little by little he got in over his head. Every time I visit him, his homes get smaller. His clothes become more ragged. The restaurants we go to aren't as expensive. He's sold his yacht and no longer has a driver. Instead, he drives a cheap American car.

He always tells me it's just a minor setback and everything is going to be okay, but I've learned over the years, my dad is a pathological liar. I've begged him to get out of whatever he's in, but he won't. I don't know exactly what he does for a living, or what Phoenix does by his side, but I've overheard my grandfather and mom talking enough to know whatever they're doing isn't exactly legal.

"You know this can't be good, right?"

Phoenix doesn't agree or disagree. "Why don't you take a nap in the bedroom? I imagine you've had a long day."

We arrive in Crete four hours later, and waiting for us is a black limo. I took Phoenix up on his suggestion and slept the entire flight, so now I'm wide awake. *Should be a fun, sleepless night...* The drive to wherever we're going takes about an hour. I text Alex to let him know I've arrived safely, and he texts back he'll call me once he's settled in Chicago.

Because it's almost midnight, everything is dark outside, making it hard to see. It's not until we pull up to a large wrought iron gate, which reads Pérasma Hotel & Villas, that I can finally make out what's around us. As the limo drives down the windy road, I take in my surroundings. Palm trees line each side of the road until we get to the front of the hotel. My God, it's gorgeous! The entire front is lit up with soft honey-colored lights. The split-level buildings are white and sleek with large picture windows. It's the perfect combination of chic and contemporary.

The driver opens my door and helps me out, and the first thing I smell is the salt water. We must be near the beach.

"It's late," Phoenix says, eyeing his phone. "I've been told there are rooms waiting for us, and we'll meet up with Dad in the morning."

"I don't have clothes," I remind him as we step up to the front desk.

"Good evening," a brown-haired petite woman says sweetly. "You must be Talia and Phoenix Nikolaides."

"We are," Phoenix says, hitting her with his best smile that always has women turning into disgusting piles of goo at his feet. My guess is within an hour she'll be in his room *personally* turning down his sheets. Gag!

"Great, we've been expecting you. Everything you will need, including clothes and toiletries, is in your rooms. If there is anything that isn't to your liking, please call the front desk and we will get it for you. Breakfast will be served at ten, and it will take place on the first floor in the banquet hall." She hands us each a card and explains how to get to our rooms. The way she holds on to Phoenix's card for an extra second doesn't go unnoticed. I seriously hope our rooms don't share a wall. If I have to listen to him screwing her all night, I will lose it.

As we walk down the wooden pathway she told us to take, my head moves from left to right, taking everything in. The hotel is literally sitting on the side of a cliff overlooking Mirabello Bay. I've seen this area in pictures but never in person. It's absolutely stunning.

As we continue to walk to our building, I notice the hotel is split into several areas—each having its own pool, restaurant, and pathway that looks to lead down to the water. I wonder if I'll have a chance to check it all out while I'm here. I'm not happy about being here, but if I'm going to be forced to be somewhere, at least I can enjoy the sights. While Thessaloniki is on the water, it's nothing like Crete. The water isn't as pretty as it is here, and the entire area smells like fish because of the ships bringing in loads from the sea.

We arrive at our building, and Phoenix tells me to get some sleep before heading into his room. Using my card, I place it over the black circle on the door and a lock clicks open. I enter the room and am almost knocked on my ass by the sheer luxury of my suite…no, not a suite, it's more like a home! The extravagant king-sized bed sits catty cornered with plush white sheets trimmed with gold and matching pillows fluffed on top. I open the large cherry wood armoire and spot several gorgeous dresses. The tags indicate they're all my size and expensive brands. I open a drawer and find various bras and panties, all with tags on them—again in my size. The next drawer contains silky pajamas in several different colors. The material glides through my fingertips.

I step into the bathroom and find a huge egg-shaped freestanding spa tub and a shower that could probably fit ten people inside. The walls, floors, and counters are all various shades of onyx, gray, and white marble.

Walking past the bed, I step up to the large window that makes up the entire west wall. It's too dark to see much of anything, but I can almost make out the water down below.

Sitting on the end of the bed, I lie backward onto the mattress and am swallowed up by the comfy down blanket. I've been raised in homes with wealth. When I was little, before my father began his descent, and then when my mom married Stefano, I grew up in expensive homes. Have been given all of the luxuries life has to offer. I attended one of the best private schools in Italy—my university tuition costs more than most make in ten years. But lying here in this bed, thinking about the plane I was brought here on, and glancing around at the furniture and décor and clothes that surround me, I realize I've never experienced this level of wealth.

None of this makes any sense. I've visited my father every summer for the past eleven years, and every time, his situation was worse. I expected to be taken to him in coach on a shitty plane and then driven in by cab to whatever apartment he's living in now.

Knowing there's no way I'll be able to fall asleep right away, I decide to go for a walk. I should probably tell Phoenix, but then he'll just tell me no or insist on tagging along. Plus, he's probably already getting it on with that woman from the front desk.

After changing into a pair of shorts and a flowy top, I grab my phone and room key and put them in my back pocket. I take the wooden path down a little ways until I come to a bridge that forks. Under the bridge is flowing water and what appears to be different kinds of fish. I go left and it leads me to a courtyard that's filled with beautiful outdoor daybeds with plush mattresses and pillows. I walk a little farther and find several mocha-colored whicker sectionals in the shape of half-moons. I imagine during the day people come out here and lounge out, reading a good book or even taking a peaceful afternoon nap.

I'm about to sit on one of the sectionals when I notice the exquisite stone fountain in the center of the courtyard. "Bernini's *Rape of Proserpina*," I say out loud.

"You know your art," a masculine voice says.

I turn to find a gorgeous man standing in front of me. He's dressed in a pair of khaki shorts and a white button-down shirt, his sleeves rolled to his elbows, exposing a hint of tattoos. It's hard to tell in the dark, but his hair appears to be a dark shade of brown. At one point it looks like it was gelled neatly, but now it's messy as if he's been running his fingers through it. He's sporting a pair of brown leather Sperry boat shoes. He's the perfect mix of casual meets elegance.

"It's a rather controversial piece," I tell him. It would be hard to major in art and not know about a piece like this. One of my favorite classes I've taken was Classical mythology.

"Some say controversial, some say exquisite." He shrugs, taking a step forward.

"If you can call rape exquisite."

Stepping closer, the gentleman flashes me a brief wicked grin, and I'm able to get a better look at him. His hair is in fact the color of creamy hot chocolate on a cold day. His eyes are a beautiful shade of hazel, but they're hard. Unforgiving. One side of his mouth is quirked up into a smirk I imagine has women falling at his feet. Hell, it almost has me falling. *Almost.*

"That's one way of looking at it."

"That's the only way," I argue.

The gentleman raises his hand to his face and strokes his stubbled chin. "The scene screams of passion, frenzy, a mixture of tenderness and harshness. It's the climax of the moment. They're teetering between hate and love." Hmm… so he believes *that* version of the story.

"She's trying to get away. She's pushing at his face, begging him to let her go."

"Or maybe she's just scared."

"Exactly," I say, now confused. Wasn't he just disagreeing with me?

"Scared of wanting him," he clarifies. "Scared of what she might feel. She wants to hate him, but she still *wants* him. What's that saying?" He tilts his head to the side slightly and smirks. The simple gesture makes him appear even more handsome. "There's a thin line between love and hate."

"How cliché." I roll my eyes, annoyed that he's trying to turn a serious work of art into an erotic sexual experience. "There's nothing passionate about this piece. It's about a god kidnapping a woman and forcing her to be his wife."

The gentleman barks out a harsh laugh. "If she didn't want to remain with him, she wouldn't have eaten those seeds." He steps another few feet toward me, until he's so close I can smell his cologne. It's fresh and masculine with a hint of danger. My heartbeat becomes erratic, suddenly remembering I'm on this island and standing here with a man I don't know in the dark of the night.

"Have you ever been in love?" he asks without giving me a chance to respond to his last statement.

His question throws me off for a second, but then I nod, thinking of Alex. We haven't exchanged the words, but I believe I'm falling in love with him.

"And this person you've loved, have you ever been mad at him? Hated him?"

My eyes lock with his, and I imagine I give him a look of confusion because he doesn't wait for my answer but instead continues to speak.

"Hate and love are shared passions. They pull you in and

take over your body, your heart, your mind. They are both powerful emotions. It's why some say the best kind of sex is hate sex and the next is make-up sex." He smirks darkly, and my stomach knots. "The first is two people who've built up anger festering inside of them, which turns into passion and arousal. The second is two people who are still mad at each other but are trying to forgive one another. The anger still runs through their veins, but the love and forgiveness is slowly seeping in."

He nods toward the statue. "That is the perfect depiction of hate and love mixing."

I hear what he's saying, but I can't imagine having sex with someone I hate and enjoying it. That's why it's called making love. You're supposed to be with the person you love.

"Have you ever been in love?" I ask, turning his question around on him.

"No," he states matter-of-factly. "But I've had plenty of hate sex."

I turn my eyes back to the statue, but I can't see what he's saying. The man is forcing her into his clutch, while she's pushing him away. I just can't imagine at any point she would enjoy being with him.

"If you've never been in love then how do you know how it feels? How can you compare love to hate?"

"I've witnessed it firsthand. Read about it. You don't have to be in love to recognize what it looks like. To understand it."

He makes a valid point, but I still don't agree with his analysis. "I guess we'll have to agree to disagree." I shrug noncommittedly. "It's late, and I have an early morning, so I better get back to my room."

"I never got your name," the gentleman says.

"No, you didn't."

His shoulders shake up and down in silent laughter, but he doesn't say anything else. I turn and walk back toward my room, unable to get what he said about the sculpture off my mind. Just before I get back to the building where my room is, I decide to take a detour. This hotel is like nothing I've ever experienced, and I'm curious if there are any other statues or décor like the one in the courtyard.

I take a left and head down a wooden walkway. A few people are walking in various directions. A couple holding hands. A group of people laughing and talking. As I continue in my direction, I hear the light thumping of bass. I follow it until I get to a well-lit area. There's a pool and wet bar, where at least a dozen people are lounging around. Some are swimming, and others are sitting along the edge of the pool. A few people are sitting on the stools in the water at the bar, having a drink.

Opening the gate, I step inside and head to the back of the bar, the one on land and not in the pool, to grab a drink. Maybe it will help me wind down and get some sleep.

"What can I get you to drink?" the bartender asks, and it's then I remember I don't have any money on me since I left my purse in my room.

"I didn't bring any money. Is there any way you can charge it to my room?"

"I got this," a gentleman says. He gets off the stool and walks around behind the bar. The first thing I notice is he's shirtless and has several intricate tattoos along his chest. My eyes glide down to his perfectly sculpted abs, but I can't see any farther because of the bar being in the way.

When my eyes ascend and meet his, I notice they're a dark brown and match his hair. Both the color of espresso.

What's up with these sexy men on this island? Unlike the guy I spoke to about the statue, this guy's smile is less deviant and more playful. His eyes, even though the color is dark, don't *scream* dangerous, but instead scream light and laughter. Quite the contradiction.

"What's your poison?" he asks, holding up a bottle of alcohol in each hand.

"White wine, please."

He tilts his head to the side, reminding me of the gentleman from earlier, and groans. "Bo-ring."

A giggle escapes my lips, and I shrug, sitting on the stool he just got up from. "I know, but it's been a long day and I'm hoping to get some sleep soon."

He grabs a wine glass and pours me a drink. When I take a sip, I notice it's light and fruity. "This is delicious."

"Santorini. It's the best."

I take another sip and have to agree.

"So, what brings you to Pérasma?" he asks, popping a cap on a beer and taking a long gulp.

"My father…he's *summoned* me," I say, trying, and failing, to withhold the annoyance in my tone.

The gentleman's brows rise, but he doesn't say anything, so I continue.

"I have no clue how he can even afford to stay here, but I guess I'm going to enjoy it while I can, since I have no choice."

I take a long sip of my wine and enjoy the coolness as it descends down my throat.

"And you?" I ask in return. "Do you work here?" He must be in close with the place to be allowed to get behind the bar and serve me.

"Something like that." He winks playfully then pours

some more wine into my glass. "I was just about to go for a swim. Would you like to join me?"

I glance down at my outfit. "I don't have a suit." A yawn escapes me, and I cover my mouth with a giggle. Clearly, the wine is already doing what I was hoping it would do. "And I have an early morning," I say, repeating the same thing I told the other gentleman a little while ago. "Some breakfast with my dad and brother."

Standing from my stool, I down the rest of the wine in the glass. "Can you charge the wine to my room? I'm in four-nineteen."

His eyes widen a fraction, and then he grins. "It's on the house."

"Oh, okay. Thank you. Maybe I'll see you again during my stay…"

"Maybe."

I wake to the sound of knocking on my door. I glance at my phone and it reads nine thirty. And then it hits me, we're supposed to meet for breakfast at ten. Shit! I overslept. When I got back to my room last night, the wine knocked me out and I never set my alarm.

"Coming!" I yell. I swing the door open and Phoenix is standing there in a black three-piece suit.

"Wow, look at you. I thought we were just meeting Dad for breakfast." I step back so he can enter.

"It's more of a business meeting. We're meeting with the Demetrious. I told you about them yesterday." He's right. He did. I just forgot. "They own this hotel…well, really this island. Go get ready," he instructs. "They don't do well with tardiness."

"Since when do I attend business meetings?" I ask, snagging a simple floral dress from the armoire. Then I pull the drawer open and grab a matching set of white lace bra and panties.

"Since now, I guess. Go. Shower."

After taking a quick shower and blow-drying my hair just enough so it's not soaking wet but hanging in loose waves, I get dressed. I find various pairs of shoes in the closet, from heels to flip-flops, and decide on a cute pair of wedges.

"Ready?" Phoenix asks from the living room. "It's two minutes till ten."

"Yes, sorry!" I grab my phone off the nightstand but realize I don't have anywhere to put it, so I grab my purse, stuffing my phone and room key in it.

"Let's go."

We walk down the long pathway, back toward the courtyard. As we pass the statue from last night, I think back to my conversation—more like debate—with the gentleman. How he can see anything other than a woman scared and trying to escape a man who is kidnapping her is just crazy. Passion doesn't stem from anger. It stems from love. I can't imagine having sex with someone I don't love, let alone with someone I hate. While the majority of my friends enjoy hooking up, I've never seen the appeal. Sex should be intimate with the person you love and trust and want to spend your life with. It shouldn't be casual, and it definitely shouldn't be done out of anger.

We enter the building and there's a hostess waiting at the door. "Good morning, Mr. and Miss Nikolaides. Everyone is already inside."

I'm taken aback for a moment that she already knows who we are.

"Thank you," Phoenix says.

We walk past the hostess stand and enter the dining room, and standing around the table are several men. The first one I spot is my dad, dressed in a suit similar to Phoenix's. My initial thought is maybe, for the first time, he's actually gotten himself together. But then his eyes meet mine, and I see the stress and nervousness in them, telling me nothing has changed.

He cuts across the room and pulls me into a tight hug. "My sunshine," he murmurs, and my heartstrings tug at the nickname he gave me when I was little. He used to tell me I was the light in his darkness. "I'm so sorry. Please forgive me. Please," he begs.

"What?" I ask, confused. "Forgive you for what?" What's going on here? Why is he begging me to forgive him? "Dad, what did you do?"

I pull out of his embrace and glance around the room. I'm shocked by what—or I guess, I should say *who*—I see. The gentleman from last night. The man I argued with over the statue. He's standing there, no longer dressed casual, but in a suit. Unlike the suits my brother and dad are wearing, which give off a formal vibe like one would wear to a dinner party, this man's screams power and wealth. His hair is gelled perfectly in place, and his eyes… How can eyes so light appear so dark? His jaw is ticking as he stares back at me, as if the simple fact of me existing offends him.

"And so we meet again," another voice says, tearing me away from the scary gentleman. *The man from the bar.* He, too, is dressed to the nines, but even in a suit, he appears playful and happy. It's almost hard to take him seriously.

"Dad, what's going on?"

chapter
three

Kostas

I DART MY HARD GAZE TO MY FATHER, WHO REFUSES TO look my way. His entire focus is on Niles and the woman. A satisfied smirk plays on his lips. I want to drag my father out of the room and demand answers. What the hell kind of beef does he have with Niles that he'd rope the man's family into this as well?

Aris's brown eyes meet mine, questions dancing in them. As though I have the answers. I don't think Father would convince Niles to bring his family here just to kill them, but this whole thing feels out of my depth. At this point, I'm not sure what my father is capable of.

Killing people is a dirty necessity.

Killing people who've fucked you over is imperative.

Niles and his son, Phoenix, by default since he's his right-hand man, have stolen from the most powerful family in Greece. They need to pay. They *will* pay.

But the woman?

Glittering blue eyes. Sexy, wavy blond hair. Poutiest fucking lips I've ever seen on a woman. Full, perfect tits that strain against the fabric of her dress. Tan legs for goddamn miles. I'm not certain if she's his daughter, but they look similar enough to draw that conclusion. She's a spitting image of Phoenix. I want to know why Niles would willingly bring her here.

"Niles," my father booms, a wicked smile turning his lips up. "Please don't be rude. Introduce us to this beauty."

The beauty in question purses her full lips together and her cheeks blaze crimson.

"This, Ezio, is my darling daughter, Talia." Niles's features are tight, but he smiles anyway. "Talia, this is Ezio Demetriou. He owns this hotel."

We own everything, motherfucker.

"And," Niles continues, "these are Ezio's sons Aris and Kostas." He flicks his wrist at me like someone might swat at a fly trying to land on his fucking ice cream. It makes me want to break his goddamn hand.

It's then that her blue eyes lock with mine, flickering with emotion as though they glow. She's pissed. Confused. Upset. Hell, I would be too if Niles Nikolaides were my father. Last night, I'd been taken by the blond goddess who seemingly appeared out of nowhere, surprising me with her knowledge of the sculpture. Sassing me—Kostas Demetriou—over the meaning of the art. For a few short minutes, I'd enjoyed a rare moment of pleasure in my cold, hard life.

Clearly, the time for pleasure has come and gone.

Now, I'm staring back at the daughter of my father's mortal enemy.

And Niles has brought her here to bargain with.

When Aris leans in to say something to her, her stiff posture relaxes slightly. Irritation coils in the pit of my stomach like a snake. If it were up to Aris, he'd gladly sleep with the enemy, as long as it was fun. Everything's all about the fucking fun with him. Unfortunately for him, Father has his own agenda, and allowing Aris to bang the woman isn't a part of that plan.

"Please," Father says. "Sit."

My father takes a seat at one end of the table and I take the other. Niles sits to my father's left and Phoenix takes the seat beside him at my right. Aris escorts Talia with his hand on the small of her back to the seat beside me on my left. Once she's seated, he sits next to her. I can feel her staring at me, her anger at the situation projected my way, but I disregard her with my usual cool aloofness. I glower directly at my father, demanding an explanation.

It's what we do—speak without speaking. I've observed my father for so long that we can do it without even trying. We're an incredible team because of it too.

So why the fuck is he avoiding eye contact?

But I know that answer. He's got an ace up his sleeve for the hand he's holding. My father intends to win this game, and I'm stuck with a handful of cards in a game I didn't know I was playing. Last night, he bailed before I had a chance to corner him. He left me to pace around the hotel, lost in my brooding thoughts. After breakfast, we're going to have a good long conversation about whatever the fuck is happening right now.

I cut my eyes to the left when the servers start placing plates of breakfast down in front of everyone. Even the savory scent of bacon can't distract me from staring at her. Her cheeks are still pink and a strand of golden-blond hair hides her eyes from me as she focuses her attention on her plate. She reaches for a glass of ice water, a slight tremble in her hand. Poor thing is nervous as fuck.

With good reason, too.

Niles is a weak piece of shit who's brought her willingly into a den of wolves.

But why is she here?

As though clued into my thoughts, Father clears his throat, demanding everyone's attention. His eyes are hard as he stares straight at me. Eyes that usually communicate with me are closed off from any sort of negotiation. Whatever he says will be law in his eyes.

Don't kill her.

I don't know where the thought comes from, but it's there. She's too innocent to be in our world. I knew that last night when she breathlessly tried to hold her own in a conversation with me. I would destroy a woman like her in bed. For one moment, I considered pursuing her when she left. Fuck, how I wanted to. But even a monster has limits. Monsters aren't monsters all the time. Sometimes we're just hungry men who make decisions with our dicks. For her sake, I decided wisely. I let her walk away, much to my dick's disappointment, only for her father to bring her right back to me.

Foolish motherfucker.

"As you all can see, we're here for more than just pleasure," my father says slowly, taking his sweet ass time. "We also have some business to attend to." He stares pointedly at Talia before shooting Niles a smug grin. "Niles, I understand she's unaware of why she's here?"

Niles squirms, which makes my father's grin grow wider.

"Dad," Talia utters, a mixture of fury and hurt in her one word.

I clench my fist, wishing Father would have just let me kill the asshole last night. Could have avoided all this shit.

"Sunshine," Niles says, his voice weak and whiny. "I'm sorry. If there were any other way…"

Phoenix, from beside Niles, glowers at my father. Aris simply watches the entire ordeal with amusement. I want to know why the fuck my father would clue Niles in on business while leaving me in the dark. Whatever bullshit is going on will be the last. I won't sit idly while stuff is flung my way without any warning. My father is going to get the bitch-out of a lifetime once this breakfast is over.

"Talia, darling," my father croons. "Your father and I go way back." His jaw clenches and darkness shrouds his expression before he smiles it away. "And we've come to an agreement."

"What sort of agreement?" Talia breathes. Her hand trembles when she reaches for her water again.

"You are to marry my son," Father states with a devious glint in his eyes.

Her head turns sharply to regard Aris, who's frowning in confusion. Meanwhile, I'm about to explode with fucking rage. *If only it were that easy, Talia.*

"My eldest," Father corrects, searing his hard eyes into mine, daring me to argue.

Even as the volcano within me spills with fury, I don't speak a word against my father. Never. Not in front of weak, worthless pieces of shit like Niles Nikolaides.

Talia's head jerks my way so fast, I'm worried she'll give herself whiplash. Her blue eyes glow with accusation—as though I knew this all along. I meet her glare with one of my own. A glare filled with contempt for the Nikolaides name. She withers beneath my fierce stare.

"An arranged marriage," I state in a bored way. "Lovely. Can someone pass me the pepper before my eggs get cold?"

Phoenix grabs the pepper shaker and slams it on the table in front of me, making everyone's glasses slosh. "What the hell are you thinking, Dad?" he demands in a furious tone. "Talia? You negotiated Talia?"

My father's smile is victorious.

I want to ram my fist right into his face.

How dare he do this to me without warning?

"I fucked up," Niles admits. "I thought I could pay them back in time."

Father picks up his fork and begins stabbing at the eggs on his plate, clearly overjoyed at my emotionless response to the bomb he just dropped in my lap.

"Four point six million," Aris states, unusual anger tightening his voice. "Is that what your daughter is worth to you? A few million dollars?"

"She's worth everything to me." Niles shoots his daughter a pleading look. She won't look at him. She won't speak. She's taken to wringing her hands in her lap, her bottom lip slightly wobbling.

"I have a life," she utters so softly, I almost think it's meant just for me. "I can't just leave to marry some stranger because my father is a bad businessman."

"You have to," Niles says, hanging his head in shame. "They'll kill me if you don't."

Once again, she glowers at me. As though all of this is my fault. It pisses me off.

"You'd kill my father if I don't marry you?" she hisses, anger making her face turn red again.

"I'll kill your father if he doesn't pay," I bite out in a cold tone. "And since he put a four-point-six-million-dollar price tag around your pretty neck, it looks like I'm getting my payment in full."

She stands abruptly from the table. Furious tears well in her blue eyes, reminding me of the blue waters of the Aegean Sea. "Fuck you all," she snaps. "I'm not marrying anyone. I'm going home."

As soon as she rushes from the table, Phoenix bolts after her. I give a slight nod to Basil and Adrian. They follow after them. My *fiancée* isn't going anywhere. The sooner she realizes this, the better.

"Really, Dad?" Aris mutters, the muscle in his neck flexing. "A girl as payment? That's a new low."

Father's nostrils flare at his blatant disrespect. I flick my chin up at Aris, silently telling him to leave before he fucks things up. With a grumble, he loudly scrapes his chair back and storms off.

"Please don't hurt her," Niles pleads. "Promise me."

I have to refrain from rolling my eyes. Since when do worms negotiate with sharks? Fucking never.

"I'll promise nothing of the sort," I tell him sharply. "Say your goodbyes to her. I want you and your son off Crete and heading back to Thessaloniki by noon."

"Kostas," he croaks. "Please."

Ignoring his pleas, I grab the small bottle of jam and begin smearing some all over my toast with a knife that would go to better use cutting this motherfucker's throat.

"Kostas," he says once more.

"Noon, Niles. I suggest you not waste another moment with your *sunshine*. Your world is about to get really fucking dark."

I'm waiting inside my office that overlooks the bay when Father decides to grace me with his presence. He walks in, his features impassive. It's a much different look than from earlier where he was almost gleeful. Rather than sitting across from me, he walks over to the open door to the veranda.

"You know everything I do is for a reason, *agóri mou.*" *My boy.* Not anymore. I've long grown into a man—a business partner. Someone worthy of being told about a plan before it's enacted, not after. To say I feel betrayed is an understatement.

"Of course, *Patéras.*"

He turns to regard me, a wistful smile on his face. If he wants to play a game of calling me his boy like he did when I was six or seven, then I will take to calling him Father in the same way I would at that age.

"She is beautiful," he mutters. "At least you have that."

"At least."

He lets out a heavy sigh. "I didn't do this to anger you, Kostas."

No, this was all about his beef with Niles.

"Then what was it about?" I demand, my voice cracking, a clear indicator of how pissed I am.

"Niles owes me in ways you'll never understand," he practically growls. "Giving up his daughter to my son is—"

"Much more difficult than just killing him," I grit out. "Why not kill him and be done with it? Why drag his family into it?"

Father shrugs and steps out onto the veranda, silently indicating he wants me to continue the conversation out there. With a frustrated sigh, I rise from my leather desk chair and stalk after him. He leans over the railing, staring out onto the sparkly bay that's dotted with sailboats.

"It's too easy," he tells me with a shrug. "Niles deserves to pay in every way he can."

"But why?"

Rather than answering, he remains seemingly lost in thought. I'm growing bored of this nostalgic power games shit he seems to be playing.

"Do I really need to marry her?" I ask in an exasperated tone. "For how long? When will this be over and I can go back to the way things were?"

Father turns my way, his features dark with hate. "I don't mean for you to think of this as a punishment, Kostas. She'll be a wife in name only. Keep whores on the side if you wish."

My lip curls up at his words. He says that as though he truly believes that. If I've learned anything from my father, it's that loyalty is everything. His marriage to my mother is solid and unbreakable, bordering on obsession. If Ezio Demetriou can keep his dick in one woman for nearly four decades, then so can I.

"Until when?" I ask, ignoring his words.

"As long as it takes to satisfy me."

Selfish fucking bastard.

I'm used to him treating everyone, even Aris, this way, but not me. It's a brutal blow that I'm at a loss for how to get over.

"Don't look at me as though I've killed your puppy," Father snaps. "She's one woman. A beautiful woman you'll no doubt enjoy every second with once you break her in. Hell, give me some grandkids for all I care. But I need this transaction to take place. I want to destroy Niles."

"Why?" I bark out. "Why do you hate that weasel bastard so much? I get it, he's fucking weak. But why? You've always been straight with me."

Father shakes his head. "Every man has secrets he holds

38

onto. My hate for Niles is one of those. Just trust in my judgment. Do what you have to do when it comes to Talia, but make sure you dangle her in Niles's face whenever you can. Don't let her charm her way off this island. You'll marry her, and I'll continue to torment her father in every way I see fit. Are we clear?"

"Absolutely," I growl, fisting my hands, barely keeping my anger in check. "Perhaps you should go home, Father. I have important matters to deal with."

"You'll understand one day, Kostas."

Unlikely.

"Of course, Father."

He sighs and exits the veranda, slamming the office door closed on his way out. I look up and watch a plane jet across the bright, cloudless sky. After a few moments, I make my way back inside and place a call to a Greek jeweler. My beloved fiancée will need an engagement ring.

Jesus Christ, I could kill my father over this shit.

A sinister part of me, though, takes silent pleasure in the fact I'll soon own the gorgeous, innocent blond. She may be a Nikolaides, but soon she'll be a Demetriou. I have a feral need to chase this woman much like Pluto did with Proserpina, so I may pin her down, shove her pretty dress up her thighs, and sink my cock into her warm depths. I love when life imitates art.

A monster wouldn't be a true monster if he didn't hungrily sink his teeth into the offering he's been given by the lesser mortals. And, fuck, do I ever want to sink my teeth into her.

Talia.

Sweet Talia.

You'll learn to like it rough.

Proserpina sure did.

chapter
four

Talia

THIS HAS GOT TO BE A GODDAMN DREAM...NO, A nightmare. This can't be real. There's no way anything that was said during that bullshit breakfast can possibly hold any merit. We no longer live in the eighteenth century, for crying out loud! One cannot simply tell someone *who* she is to marry. We have rights!

A manic laugh escapes my lips as I remember my conversation with Kostas last night. Oh, the irony, that not even twelve hours ago we were debating over *The Rape of Proserpina*, and now here we are in a similar situation. My father giving his consent for me to marry a man who is apparently hell-bent on kidnapping me and forcing me into some underworld! I might not know everything that goes on in my father's business, but I've overheard enough over the years to know the men he does business with are part of some illegal crime organization. And my father is literally handing me over to them on a silver platter! As if I'm available for the taking. And to save his own ass. It's one thing for him to get himself into trouble, but now he's involving me in his mess.

Grabbing my phone off the nightstand, I consider calling Alex but stop myself. As much as I want to hear his voice and seek comfort in his words, how do I explain to him the ridiculousness of the situation I've found myself in? What would I even say? *Hey, Alex! I have a slight problem. My father screwed over some crime boss and has handed me over as payment.*

Ugh! No, there's only one person to call. I pull Mom's name up on my contact list, but just as I'm about to hit call, there's a knock on my door. Without even bothering to look, I swing the door open and find Dad and Phoenix standing on the other side. My father at least has the decency to look upset. Phoenix looks pissed, which tells me he didn't know any of this was going down.

"What do you want?" I hiss.

"Can I please come in, sunshine?" Dad begs. He takes a step forward, without waiting for me to answer, and I block the entrance.

"No, you can't," I tell him, clenching my fists at my sides. I am not a violent person, but right now, I'm desperately trying to keep from pummeling my father to the ground. And judging by the way Phoenix's jaw is clenching, I bet he'd hold him down for me.

"Please, I'm so sorry," Dad says. "If you would just let me in, I will explain."

"What the hell is there to explain?" I seethe, my tone dropping low as venom drips from it. "You sold your own flesh and blood to pay off a debt!"

Dad's back goes straight. "Don't you speak to me like that. I am sorry for what's happened, but I'm still your father. You will speak to me with respect."

"Respect?" I yell, fury bubbling up inside of me like a volcano preparing to erupt. "Fuck you and your respect!"

Before I see it coming, Dad raises his hand and slaps me across my cheek. My face whips to the side from the sheer force behind his slap. Instinctively, my hand comes up and rubs the sore spot.

"Dad! What the hell!" Phoenix roars. He shoves our dad up against the wall and gets in his face. "You did this shit! You lied about how much you owed and how bad it was. You don't get to demand respect, and you sure as fuck don't get to lay a goddamn hand on her." Phoenix cocks his fist back and punches Dad square in the jaw. Blood spurts from Dad's lip, and he folds himself over in pain.

"I'm sorry," he cries. "I'm sorry!" He glances up at me and wipes the blood off his chin. "Please forgive me, sunshine. You are everything to me."

Everything?

He thinks I'm *everything*?

Apparently so since he sold me.

Well, *Dad*, I hope it was worth it. I hope you can buy a new yacht or a bigger home or whatever it is you chose over your own daughter.

"I am nothing to you," I say, my tone flat, defeated. There's no denying his betrayal runs deep. "And you are nothing to me."

I turn to Phoenix, not giving *that man* another glance. "Is there any way of me getting out of this?"

Phoenix's eyes gloss over, and I already know my answer. He bridges the gap between us and pulls me into his arms. "I'm going to do everything I can to try to figure this out. I promise you. I won't stop until they let you come home."

I nod into his chest. "Thank you," I whisper, my voice overcome with emotion.

When he pulls back, he gives me a sad smile. "I love you. Be strong."

"Sunshine, please," Dad begs again.

"Take him away," I tell Phoenix. "I never want to see him again."

Phoenix nods in understanding, then grabbing Niles by his arm, pulls him down the pathway and out of my life.

Closing the door behind me, I press my back against the hard wood and take several deep breaths, needing to calm myself. My face falls into my hands, and my cheek throbs, reminding me I was just hit. I walk into the bathroom where the mirror is and check it out. My cheek is bright pink but doesn't show any signs of bruising.

With my heart thundering inside my chest like a war drum and my head pounding to the beat, I head back to the main room, needing to call the one person who's always had my back. My mom.

She answers on the first ring. "*Cara mia*! How are you? I've been waiting for your call."

The sound of her voice has me falling onto my bed in tears. "Mom," I sob uncontrollably, all of the built up adrenaline hitting me hard. "I need your help. I need you to come get me."

By the time I finish telling her all that's happened, and the little I know, she's crying as well. "I'm going to call your grandfather. He'll know what to do."

"Please hurry, Mom," I beg.

I hang up the phone and curl into a ball on the bed, hugging the soft pillows. I'm not sure how long I cry for, but when there's a knock on the door, my head is pounding, and my eyes are burning from the little bit of mascara I put on that's now running.

Thinking it's Phoenix coming back to check on me, I swing the door open, only to find it's Aris, Kostas's brother, the playful flirt I met at the bar last night. I shoot him a glare, and he flinches. Good!

"What the hell do you want?"

Aris raises his hands in mock surrender. "I didn't know."

"So, you're telling me when we were talking, you had no idea who I was?" I tilt my head to the side and throw a hand on my hip. "You didn't know I was my father's daughter?"

"At first, no, but once we started talking, I put two and two together…"

I grab the edge of the door, about to slam it in his face, when he slides his foot in the doorway to prevent it from closing. His eyes land on my cheek, and he steps closer, widening the door.

"Who did this to you?" His fingers come up to touch my face, but I take a step back. "Who did this to you?" he repeats.

"My—Niles," I say, refusing to ever refer to him as my dad again.

Aris's jaw ticks. "He's lucky he already got on that plane."

"He may have physically hurt me, but what you guys are doing is even worse."

Aris flinches at my words, as though I've slapped him like my father slapped me. His eyes plead with me to understand. Understand what? That he's not the same monster as they are? But when his gaze softens, I find my heart does too.

"I didn't know what my father and Kostas were

planning," he utters in a tone that begs for me to understand. "I swear. I only came by to see if you're okay."

I assess his features in an attempt to get a read on him, and for some reason, I believe him. His brows are furrowed in worry, and his lips are pursed in a concerned frown. I think back to earlier, during breakfast. When Ezio announced I was to marry his son, I had assumed he meant Aris. When I looked over at him, he genuinely looked as confused and shocked as I did. And then when his father clarified it would be his eldest son I would be marrying, Aris looked almost…angry.

"I'm not marrying your brother," I state. "So, if you're here to try to talk me into going along with this craziness, you can leave now."

"That's not why I'm here. I told you…I came by to see if you're okay. Why don't we walk down to the bar and get a drink?"

Figuring it's probably better to have Aris as an ally than an enemy, I nod once. "Let me grab my phone." I need to make sure I'm available when my mom calls back.

After grabbing my phone, I take a quick detour back into the bathroom to clean up my face and hair, so I don't look like a hot mess. Then I slip on my wedges and grab my purse. It's probably best if I bring it everywhere with me in case I need to run at any moment. It's all I came with, and it holds everything I have. A little bit of cash, my credit cards, my license, and my passport. *My passport!* Why didn't I think about that before? It won't be easy, but at least I know I have a backup plan.

"You ready?" Aris asks.

"Yep."

In the light of the day, the hotel is even more gorgeous.

It was exquisite last night, but with the sun shining, I'm able to see every detail of the place. The pool is kidney-shaped, with a bar on one end and a beautiful rock waterfall on the other. Several people are already swimming in the pool and lying out in the loungers with drinks in their hands.

"Wine?" Aris asks, lifting the bottle from last night.

I shake my head. I need to keep a clear head.

"Just a lemonade if you have it. If not, water."

He pours my drink then pops a top on a beer for himself. We take our drinks over to two empty loungers that are under an umbrella and have a seat.

"You're from Italy, right?" he asks after a few minutes of silence.

"Yes, Rome, but I go to school in Florence at the Florence Art Institute." And then it hits me. If somehow Kostas and his dad get their way, will I be allowed to go back to school in the fall? Or will he force me to stay here with him? Away from my mom, my family, my life.

"What's wrong?" Aris asks.

"I was just thinking about school. I'm supposed to be starting my senior year. I hope this all gets sorted out before then."

"Talia, I don't think you understand—"

His words are cut off by the sound of my phone ringing. "I need to take this," I say before I answer the call. "Mom."

"No, Talia, it's your grandfather."

"Nonno!" A sob escapes my lips. "Please tell me I can go home." There's a deafening silence on the other line that causes my body to grow cold with fear. "Nonno," I repeat.

"Talia, you need to listen to me," he says, his tone unlike anything I've ever heard. It's flat and cold, devoid of all emotion. "Your father made some terrible choices, and because of that, the Demetrious have decided the way for him to pay is through you. I've spoken to Ezio, and the decision has been made. You will marry his eldest son, Kostas, and become his wife."

"No!" With a shaky hand, I set my drink on the table next to me. "Please, Nonno, I can't marry him. I have a life. A boyfriend. I have my senior year! I didn't agree to this." Another wave of fury spreads through my veins like wildfire. How dare my father—No! Niles! How dare Niles use me to pay his debt! He's a selfish bastard! "I'm not marrying him," I tell my grandfather. "I don't care if they kill Niles." My eyes swing over to Aris, who is staring at me with pity in his eyes.

"You don't have a choice," my grandfather says so nonchalantly one would think he was discussing the weather and not the fate of my future. "The decision is final."

At his words, I nearly drop my phone. My hands are trembling with fury, and I have to clasp the device tightly. "Ezio told me if I don't marry Kostas, Niles will die. Well, fuck him! He did this to himself. Let. Him. Rot." Without thinking about where I am or what I'm doing, I lean forward and swipe the glass off the table. It smashes against the ground, shards of glass flying in every direction. It's not enough to tame the rage rolling through me, but it helps tamper it down a notch.

"Talia," Nonno snaps. "Do not take up that language with me. I understand you are upset, and you have every right to be. But you will not speak to me with such disrespect."

Seriously? All of these men want to jerk me around and dictate my life, then demand respect? Respect is earned. And as far as I'm concerned, they've all lost mine.

"Now, you will listen to me," my grandfather continues. "The Demetrious family is not one you go against. The only

47

way to get out of this would be death…for you. They've already decided, and once they make a decision, it's law."

My body falls back onto the lounge chair. My shoulders sag, and my head lulls forward in defeat. "So, that's it then? My life is being taken from me? I'm being kidnapped against my will and being forced to marry that…that man." I can't think of anything to call him at the moment that would be fitting. "I would rather die," I cry out.

"Oh, Talia, don't be dramatic."

"Dramatic?" I pop my head back up. "Dramatic? You aren't the one stuck on this island with complete strangers. What about my school? And my friends? What about Alex? My apartment?"

"Your life will be wherever Kostas decides. I'm sorry, Talia. I tried to speak to them, but they made it clear this marriage will happen."

A gut-wrenching sob tears through my chest. Complete hopelessness converts into tears that rain down my cheeks at lightning speed. If I don't find a way out, I'm going to be sentenced to a life underground, just like Proserpina. But unlike her—who at least was stuck with Pluto, who in some versions of the story appeared to be a decent husband, despite beginning their marriage in such a horrible way—I'm being taken by Kostas. The man who found dark humor in Proserpina's rape. The man who tried to argue that she enjoyed it. That the statue screamed passion.

I'm once again overcome with rage as the realization strikes that I have no one I can count on but myself. My own father was the one to hand me over. The rest of my family has their hands tied behind their backs. The only chance I have at getting out of this is me. I need to formulate a plan. And to do that I need to be alone.

When I stand, ready to flee back to my room, Aris says my name.

"Are you okay?" he asks, worry dripping in his words.

"No," I tell him honestly, "but I will be."

"I'm really sorry your grandfather wasn't able to get you out of this mess." Even though it's his family who is causing all of this to happen, I feel like, to an extent, he might genuinely mean that.

"It's not your fault. Thank you for being so kind to me." I kneel to pick up the pieces of glass, but Aris stops me.

"Someone will clean that up. Would you like to go for a walk? The bay is beautiful at this time."

"Raincheck?" I ask, even though I don't plan to be here for him to collect. I don't care how I have to do it, I will be getting the hell off this island. "I think I need some time to myself."

"Sure." His lips curl into a soft smile. "Let me see your phone."

I hold it closer to my chest. If he takes my phone from me, it will mess up my plan.

"I'm just going to input my number into your contacts in case you need something or someone to talk to."

Reluctantly, I type in my code then hand my phone over to him. After a few seconds, he hands it back.

"The restaurants serve all day. Just let them know your name and they'll serve you anything you want."

"Okay, thank you."

On my way back to my room, my phone pings with a text, reminding me I don't want to just change his contact from Dad to Niles, but to block his number altogether.

Dad: I'm so sorry, sunshine. I hope one day you can forgive me. There was just no other way.

And with that text, my anger is back with a vengeance. The second I step into my room, I allow myself to lose it. Picking up the crystal vase from the end table, I imagine it's my dad's head as I cock my arm back and throw it as hard as I can. It bounces off the wall and shatters when it hits the wood floor.

Damn, that felt good.

I grab something else—this time, a lamp—and chuck it across the room. It smashes against the wall, fragments raining down and landing on top of the broken crystal.

I take a deep breath. And then I grab the other lamp and throw it.

Item after item, I throw everything I can get my hands on until my arm is dead and there's nothing left to throw. Until my anger has dissipated enough that I can form a coherent thought.

And then I formulate my plan.

I pull up my airline ticket and call the airline. After my flight is booked, I call Alex.

"Talia, how are you?" Alex asks when he answers the phone. His voice is groggy, and it's then I remember there's an eight-hour time difference between Chicago and Greece.

"I'm good. I'm sorry to wake you, but I have great news. My father is letting me come visit you after all. My flight leaves in a few hours."

"That's fabulous!" he exclaims, his voice brighter and more awake. "I'll pick you up at the airport. What time will your flight arrive?"

"It's a twelve-hour flight, so I should be there at six o'clock your time."

"Once you find out your gate number, call me so I know where to meet you."

"I will. I can't wait to see you."

After we hang up, I make sure I have everything I need in my purse, and then, leaving my room key on the nightstand, I slip out. I head up the path and find a side exit. I thought about snagging a cab from here, but then they could track me. So instead, my plan is to walk as far as I can go and then hail a cab outside of the hotel.

My plan works. After walking the mile down the long roadway, I sneak behind a guard gate and exit along the back. When I step out of the trees, I'm standing on the sidewalk facing a busy street. Several cabs drive up and down the road, and not even a second after I've waved my hand, one pulls to the side.

"Heraklion airport."

The driver nods once and takes off. Fifty minutes later, I swipe my credit card and exit the cab. I find the airline I'm flying with and check in. Because I don't have any bags to check, I'm pushed through the line quickly. As I watch the line to go through security move forward, my heart pounds against my ribcage. I'm almost in the clear. Just a few more people and then I'll be on the other side.

Three more people.

Two.

One.

"Put your belongings in the bin, then step through," the guard instructs.

"That won't be necessary," a cold, menacing voice says. "She won't be going anywhere."

Like ice straight to my veins, my body freezes in its place. I don't have to turn around to know who is standing behind me.

Pluto…and he's here to drag me back into the Underworld against my will.

chapter
five

Kostas

S HE LEFT. JUST LIKE I KNEW SHE FUCKING WOULD. Grabbed her purse and waltzed right out the door. I have to give her credit. Sneaking away rather than taking a cab from the front entrance of the hotel was clever. Not clever enough, though. I anticipated her move. She's a Nikolaides after all.

Not for long.

Every person we pass ignores her fuming. Around these parts, they see me and they move the fuck on. Nobody messes with my family. Not locals, not airport workers, not cab drivers, not even goddamn tourists. Everyone sees the blinking neon sign above my head that says: Don't fuck with me.

Or else.

Those who fuck with me and my family—like Niles Nikolaides—learn what else we have in store for them. In his case, he forfeited over his blond vixen of a daughter. Others pay with their blood. I prefer blood, but in this instance, I'm not unhappy about getting this furious woman into my bed.

Forever.

The thought is equal parts disturbing and thrilling. I'd never admit to my father I'm a lonely bastard who wishes he had someone to come home to every night. He's happy with Mamá, and has been for my entire life, so it's only natural I crave the same for myself.

We exit the airport without incident. My charcoal-gray Maserati GranTurismo sits parked in the fire lane. No one writes a ticket. They just ignore me as it should be.

"Get in," I bite out, my voice cold and commanding as I open the passenger side door.

Her plump lips press together as though she's thinking desperately of arguing, but in the end, she lets out an exaggerated huff before throwing herself into the car. I close the door and catch the eye of a security guard.

"Women," he mutters, chuckling at me.

"Women," I agree. I smirk at him before climbing in my car.

She's quiet as I drive away from the airport and onto the main road. Her thoughts are loud, though. A cacophony of accusations and hate bouncing around inside the vehicle as though they can physically harm me.

I'm untouchable, moró mou.

I shift through the gears and fly down the road, passing cars along the way. She clutches the side of the door and the console as though that will help her if we were to crash. It won't. Lucky for her, we won't crash either. Next to crushing the bones of motherfuckers who cross me, I love to drive and I'm good at it. My father and brother prefer drivers, but not me. I'll take one of my many cars for a ride any day to escape the stifling responsibilities that weigh on me continuously.

"Am I in trouble?" she finally asks after a few minutes, darting her worried gaze my way.

"For trying to flee the country and hide from me?"

She nods, fear gleaming in her blue eyes.

"I didn't make the rules clear, so I suppose not," I tell her, catching her gaze briefly before I turn my attention back on the road. "However, if you run from me again, you'll be punished. Severely."

"You'll kill me?"

"My punishments are never so simple."

She doesn't try for more conversation, and I offer none. The drive takes less time than it should because I drive like a bat out of hell. When I finally pull into the hotel, I drive around to the back and down a long road that's far from tourists' eyes.

"Where are we going?" she demands, as though she has every right to make demands of me. "I thought you were bringing me back."

Ignoring her, I climb out of my car and make my way over to her side. I open the door and gesture for her to get out.

"Are you going to hurt me?" she asks, the bravado in her tone gone without a trace.

"Not at the moment."

Her lips press together, but she exits the vehicle. I grip her bicep and guide her to the groundskeeper's house on the corner of the property. The groundskeeper nods when we enter his small home unannounced. My barging in with someone in tow is nothing new. I haul her through the living room and into the kitchen. Pushing through the cellar door, I walk her down the narrow, steep stairs into the *kelári*.

But there is no wine in this cellar.

Only sad attempts for mercy.

There's no mercy here either.

Adrian sits on the sofa in the corner with his feet perched on the coffee table. In the center of the room, tied to a chair, is a man. Not just any man, but a man who thought he could lie to me.

"Cy," I greet. "Did you miss me?"

His brown eyes are wild and he whimpers from behind the red scarf that's stuffed inside his mouth. Sweat pours down his forehead and his T-shirt is soaked through. His feet are a mess, just like I left him.

When Adrian sees Talia, he sits upright and pats the sofa, understanding washing over him. She is to watch. She needs to see. "Come sit, miss," he urges.

As though he is the villain in this dank cellar, she takes a step nearer to me. Rather than allowing her any comfort, I release her arm and swat her ass. "Go, Talia."

She shoots me a venomous look over her shoulder. I bite back a chuckle. Fiery, even when fearful. Impressive. Once she sits as far away from Adrian as she can get, I remove my jacket and drape it over a chair.

"Talia, *moró mou*," I rumble. "Meet Cy. Cy, meet my fiancée."

Cy cries, but no one cares.

"Cy is a bad man," I tell her. "A bad man who must be punished. Do you want to know what he did that was so heinous to be tied to that chair?"

She shakes her head furiously, tears welling in her blue eyes. "No."

So brave this woman. Challenges me continuously.

"Allow me to regale you anyway," I say with a smile. "Cy here was asked where his brother Bakken was. Bakken is a thief and a killer. A pirate of sorts. An Aegean Sea asshole who boards ships that do not belong to him and cuts throats of innocent people. Bakken thinks if he kills people in my territory, that the Hellenic police will come after me and my family."

Her brows furrow as she waits for me to continue, her eyes glued to Cy's bloody feet.

I roll my sleeves up before whistling at Adrian. "Give me your sock."

He groans but kicks off his shoe. The big brute pulls off his black sock and tosses it to me. I set the sock down on the table and place my hands on my hips.

"Talia, Cy was wrong. The Hellenic police are my father's friends. They'll be at our wedding. There's a blurred line between good and bad. You'll soon learn to straddle it with me." I turn my head to regard Cy. "We burned your brother alive on his own ship. We found him no thanks to you."

Cy whimpers and shakes his head. He isn't allowed to speak anymore. There was a time when I allowed him to, and he lied. Told me his brother had fled to Istanbul. In reality, his brother was floating around in my territory, fucking with what's mine.

"Know what happens to liars, Talia?" I demand, my attention once again on her.

She flinches and shakes her head.

"Use that pretty head of yours," I growl. "Amuse me and guess."

"T-They lose their tongue?" she asks, her bottom lip trembling.

Adrian snorts out a laugh.

"I suppose that'd make sense," I say as I squat in front of Cy. "But a madman doesn't make sense. Therefore, liars get a different treatment around here."

I pick up the knife from the floor. Earlier, when my

father left my office, I came straight down to the cellar to work on Cy. I'd barely started when Basil told me that my fiancée had fled. Cy's been waiting all this time.

The stench of piss permeates the air, but it's to be expected. I inspect my blood-crusted blade and flash Talia a wide smile. When I continue my sawing through his leg, just above his ankle, he screams through his scarf. I can hear Talia gagging from nearby. The knife is sharp, but it still takes me a good half hour to saw through the bone. Blood gushes everywhere, and I'll have to throw out these shoes, unfortunately. Eventually, I break through the bone and finish sawing through the muscle until I've completely removed his foot. Cy's head lolls to the side, but he's still awake. Good.

Adrian leans forward and picks up the sock from the table before tossing it to me. I stuff the hacked off foot into the sock. As I stand, I seek out Talia's face. She's buried her face in her hands as she sobs.

"Make her watch," I command in a cold tone. "Make her see."

She cries out when Adrian grips her wrists and pulls them away.

I tie a knot in the sock close to the severed foot and then hold the tube end in my grip. With a hard pop, I whack Cy in the head.

"You're s-sick," she croaks out. "A fucking sick monster!"

Whack! Whack! Whack!

I ignore her as I beat the shit out of Cy with his own goddamn foot. He groans and gurgles.

Whack! Whack! Whack!

When I hit him just right across his nose, it pops as it breaks. Blood gushes down his front like a river of crimson. I whack him in the face again, his blood splattering everywhere.

Whack! Whack! Whack!

I nail him hard in the throat, making him gag. Enough whacks to his throat and I'll crush his windpipe. Yanking on his hair with one hand to tilt his head back, I swing with the other over and over against his Adam's apple with his severed foot. A nasty crunching sound can be heard and then raspy wheezing. I continue nailing him with the foot until the sock rips and the foot flings out. Blood covers my front and I'm breathing heavily with exertion.

"I hate liars," I snarl, my eyes locking with Talia's blue, terror-filled ones. "People loyal to me don't lie. I expect you'll learn to be quite loyal."

I move to stand behind Cy, staring at the Nikolaides woman, who seems to want to learn lessons the hard way. Gripping Cy's head, I twist hard to the right, snapping his neck and ending his miserable existence.

"Call Franco to clean this up," I bark out to Adrian as I head over to the sink. "And give me your shoes." I unbutton my shirt and peel it off before tossing it over to where Cy's body sits. I kick off my shoes and step into the clean ones Adrian offers to me. Then, I start washing what I can of the blood off me. "Tell Phynn I'll want my car detailed by tomorrow. This shit will stain."

Adrian is already on the phone to Franco. Franco owns a funeral home and crematory. For his aid in disposing of bodies, he receives preferential treatment from our family and handsome payments.

"Be a doll, will you, and grab my jacket," I instruct to Talia.

When she makes no moves to get up, her body trembling violently, I whistle sharply.

"Now, *moró mou*."

She rises and stumbles over to the chair with my jacket before snagging it up. It gets tossed to me as she storms up the stairs. I pull it on along the way up and grab her before she's made it out of the door. Pinning her to the wall, I glower down at her.

So small.

Breakable.

Mine now.

"Your attitude fucking sucks," I growl. "Learn to keep it in check."

"Or what?" she hisses. "You'll beat me with my own foot?"

Smirking, I release her. "I'm sure I'll come up with something clever to teach you a lesson should you disobey."

Her blue eyes flare as she pulls away from me. "I hate you."

"You wouldn't be the first." I give her ass a swat. "Pick up the pace. We have dinner reservations at six. I imagine you'd like a shower and a nap before then."

"I'm not going to dinner with you," she chokes out, turning on her heel in the kitchen to glower at me. "I can't stand to look at you."

Reaching forward, I delicately twirl a strand of her blond hair around my finger and tug. "This is where you seem to be confused. You think you have a say…" I lean forward and rest my forehead to hers. "You. Have. No. Say."

She pulls away from me and rushes out. I stalk after her, pleased to find her getting back inside my car. *Good girl. May as well learn your place in the Demetriou world right away.*

Once inside my vehicle, I reach over and take her trembling hand. She attempts to pull it away, but I'm stronger.

"What size ring do you wear?"

"Fuck you," she breathes, hate dripping from her words.

"Soon, *moró mou*. Don't worry." I chuckle when she hisses at me. "Size six?"

She stubbornly refuses to speak. I pull her hand toward me and inhale her skin before nipping at the back of it.

"Tell me," I warn. "You don't want to learn how persuasive my teeth are when I am needing information." I catch her flesh between my teeth and bite hard enough to make her squirm, but not hard enough to leave a bruise.

"Seven," she chokes out. "I'm a seven."

I release her skin and kiss the back of her hand. "Thank you. You'll learn," I explain with a smile. "Do as I say and I'll reward you. Refuse me and I'll punish you. Understand?"

She nods rapidly, tears streaking down her cheeks.

"Good girl."

chapter
six

Talia

"**W**HERE ARE WE?" I ASK AS KOSTAS PARKS his car in what looks like a private underground carport. "I think my room is on the other side."

The hotel is huge, but I've explored enough of it to know my room is on the south side of the property, and we're currently on the north side.

"We're at my place," Kostas states coldly. "Your stuff has been moved here."

He exits his vehicle, and without waiting for me, stalks down the walkway. I consider, for a brief second, running in the opposite direction, but then flashbacks to only a few minutes ago surface: of the bloodied man. Kostas sawing off his foot and then beating him with it. Kostas snapping his neck like it was a chicken bone. And I follow behind Kostas.

It's not that I'm giving up on escaping, but I'm not stupid enough to be careless about it anymore. I underestimated him. I lumped him into the same category as my father and the men I've met over the years who work for him. Kostas is *not* my father. He's on an entirely different level. Leaving is going to require extensive planning because if he catches me the next time, I have no doubt he will make me suffer the way he made that man suffer in the cellar.

I shiver at the thought of what he would do to me if he caught me trying to leave again. No, the next time I leave, I have to make sure I completely disappear.

When we step through the threshold of Kostas's place, I realize that while the outside looks similar to the hotel rooms, inside is vastly different. For one, it's massive. Just the foyer and living room are at least twice the size of the entire room I was staying in. I thought my room was exquisite, but his puts my room to shame.

Brown and white marble flooring expands across the entire area. Plush coffee-colored leather couches, a mahogany wood coffee table, and a beautiful fireplace make up the living room. The walls are different shades of brown with a few strategically placed pieces of art hanging up. It's clearly a typical bachelor pad, but upgraded to fit Kostas's level of wealth.

I follow him past the expansive kitchen that matches the living room perfectly, with its mahogany wood cabinets and marble countertops. Complete with stainless steel appliances. As I walk through Kostas's home, I quickly come to the realization that my family's money couldn't even afford to have a conversation with Kostas's family's money. This is why Nonno said their decision is law. They can afford to make things go their way.

Kostas stops when he enters what appears to be the master bedroom. The same color scheme has continued into his room, but to soften it a bit, cream has been added to the mix. In the center of the room is a king-sized four-poster bed. If in any other standard master bedroom it would appear overwhelming, in this room it fits perfectly. The bed is solid wood and has intricate designs running up each of the poles. When my eyes land on the cream-colored sheets, it hits me. I'm expected to sleep in this bed with Kostas. The man who just singlehandedly took the life of another man.

"We're not married yet," I blurt out, terrified all over again. "Shouldn't I sleep somewhere else until we are?"

Kostas, who has already stripped down to his boxers, raises a single brow. "If you're afraid of me stealing your virtue, don't worry. I have no intention of touching you until we're married. My mother raised me to be a gentleman." He smirks. "But later tonight, you *will* be sleeping in this bed with me."

My eyes rake over Kostas's body. Various tattoos cover his chiseled chest, rock-hard abs, and corded biceps and forearms. He's not overly muscular, but it's apparent he works out and keeps in shape. *It's probably all from sawing off body parts and then beating people with them...*

The only man's body I've ever paid any attention to was Alex's, and the vast difference between the two men is evident. Where Alex is toned and lean, his body is clearly that of a boy, while Kostas's body...it's all man...and scary.

"You like what you see, *moró mou*?" Kostas asks when he catches me checking him out. My eyes swing back up to meet his hazel ones. They're no longer dark like they were in the cellar. No longer angry. Now, they're softer, taking on a beautiful honey color. For a moment, I'm mesmerized by the way his eyes change according to his mood. Earlier, it's clear he was angry, but right now, I can't quite figure out what his mood is.

"I asked you a question," he utters, his eyes brightening just a tad.

"No," I say, answering his question, "and stop calling me *moró mou*. I'm *not* your baby. I'm not your anything." I flinch as soon as the words are out, afraid of what his reaction will be. I've never been good at simply obeying. My mother always told me I'm stubborn and strong-willed, and I can do anything I put my mind to because I'm not the kind of person to give up. I always considered those traits a good thing, but now, those same traits may be what gets me killed…or worse.

Kostas cuts across the room and is in my face before I can apologize. He pushes me against the dresser, the carved wood digging into my back. His hands come down on either side of my body, caging me in, his face only a hairbreadth away from mine. His gaze locks with mine.

"You. Are. Mine," he growls. "And the sooner you accept that, the better off you'll be. This time next week you will be my wife. The type of life you want is up to you. You can play nice, and I will give you the world. The sun, the stars, and the motherfucking sky. Or you can make shit difficult, and I will take it all away, leaving you with nothing but darkness."

His eyes drop to my mouth, and his tongue darts out, wetting his lips. And suddenly the look in his eyes makes sense. Lust. He's turned on. And he's going to kiss me. He's testing me. Wanting to see if I'll play nice.

I haven't made my decision yet when his tongue traces my top lip, then my bottom one. My eyes close of their own accord, clearly making the choice for me, when a jolt of pain sears through me. My eyes pop open, shocked. It takes me a second to figure out what just happened.

The asshole bit me! I suck in my bottom lip and can taste the metallic liquid. He fucking bit me and drew blood! Kostas's lips curl into a devious smile that pisses me off because I was actually going to let him kiss me.

"Real nice," I hiss, trying to hide my embarrassment.

I attempt to push his arm out of my way so I can escape—to where, I have no idea—but he doesn't budge. Instead, his chin dips down and he captures my bleeding lip with his mouth. My hands push against his chest, but it's futile. He's stronger. His sturdy yet surprisingly soft lips suck in my own, and he licks across my flesh. I stop pushing against him, frozen in place. Unsure of what to do. And then his lips descend on mine. His tongue pushes through my parted lips, and I can taste my blood mixed with something else... something minty.

And it's as if my body has a mind of its own, because before I can give it any more thought, my lips are moving in sync with his. Every swipe of his tongue is controlled, deliberate. I've never felt so exposed. I'm fully clothed, and the only part of my body he's touching is my mouth, yet I feel like he's able to see all of me. Every hidden and private part of me.

Suddenly, it's all too much. This isn't right. I shouldn't be kissing him. He's still wearing the blood of the man he just tortured and killed. But I can't stop it. His mouth dominates mine, and I'm defenseless to end it. So, instead, I just let it happen.

When Kostas pulls back, and his eyes meet mine, they're blazing with an emotion I can't quite pinpoint. He doesn't quite look mad. Maybe confused. *That makes two of us...*

He steps back and draws his bottom lip into his mouth as if he's still tasting me. "I need to shower. Be ready at five thirty." And with that, he turns on his heel and stalks into the bathroom, slamming the door behind him—leaving me to wonder what the hell just happened, and if maybe Kostas was right. Maybe there was more to Proserpina's feelings.

Maybe she was scared of wanting him. Scared of what she felt for him. It would make sense. Because right now, even though I don't want to admit it, I can completely relate to how Kostas described Proserpina. And I've never been more scared.

Ring…Ring…Ring…

My eyes pop open, and I glance around the room, taking in my surroundings. I'm in Kostas's master bedroom, in his bed. He kissed me. And I *might've* enjoyed it. But then he walked away. Despite not wanting to do as he instructed, I was exhausted, and after fighting sleep for a few minutes, I ended up passing out.

"An *Alex* is calling you," a deep voice says. I whip my head around to see Kostas standing next to the bed with my cell phone in his hand. I reach out to take it from him, remembering I never called Alex to let him know what my gate number would be, but Kostas pulls it back before I can grab it. "Who's Alex?"

"Nobody," I say before I can think about it.

Kostas kneels so he's eye level with me, his features darkening and confirming what I noticed earlier: his eyes change according to his mood. "Did you already forget what happens when people lie to me?" he asks. "Let's try this again. Who. Is. Alex?"

Sitting up, so I don't feel at such a disadvantage, I tell him the truth. "He's my boyfriend."

I gauge Kostas's features to see how he's going to react to my truth. Outwardly, he gives nothing away. But his eyes—they're all too telling in the way they blaze with anger, so hot, that with one strike, they could catch the room we're in on fire.

The phone rings in his hand again, and he silences it. "I will not have my wife spreading her legs for anyone but me. I suggest you handle this problem. Otherwise, I will handle it for you."

I don't need to ask to know his way of handling it, will end with someone—Alex—dying.

The phone rings once again, and this time he lets me take it. "I have work to do. I'll be back at five thirty to get you. Be ready."

I wait until he's out of the room before I call Alex back.

"Talia, are you okay?" Alex asks, worry in his voice. "You told me you would call me with the gate number and you never did. You should have already been on your way, so I was worried."

I close my eyes, refusing to let the tears fall. I can't do this to him. I can't have him worrying about me. Who knows when or if I'll be able to get away. And if I do, going to Alex will mean putting a huge target on his chest. Kostas killed that guy earlier without a second thought, and I don't doubt he will do the same to Alex if he views him as a problem.

"Alex, I'm not coming."

"Why? What's wrong?" His concern solidifies my decision. If I leave him hanging, he's going to continue to worry, and I can't have him involved in any of this.

"I can't be with you anymore. I'm sorry, but I'm with someone else now."

The line is silent for a long beat before Alex finally responds. "I don't understand." Of course he doesn't. We were just making plans to spend the summer together and now

I'm breaking up with him. I have to cut ties completely, though. I have to make it clear it's over so he doesn't try to contact me.

"I'm back together with my ex. I'm sorry, but you were nothing more than a rebound. I thought I was over him, but then I saw him again and realized I still loved him." I swallow the large lump in my throat and then add, "We're engaged to be married."

"This doesn't make any sense!" Alex shouts through the phone. "You were just coming here."

"You don't have to understand," I tell him. "You just need to know it's over and that I don't want you to ever contact me again. Goodbye." I hang up before he can argue and then block his number from being able to call or text me.

For a moment, I sit and stare at the wall, trying to figure out how my life has come to this. Not even twenty-four hours ago, I was on top of the world. I was excelling in school, had a loving boyfriend. I had my entire future planned out. Now, I've lost my father…no, I take that back. I didn't lose him. He lost me. He handed me over. And by consequence, I've lost my entire life. Will Kostas even let me see my mother? In the blink of an eye, I've lost *everything* that means anything to me, and there's a good chance I'm never going to get any of it back.

A sudden wave of anxiety hits me, and I reach up to my throat, struggling to breathe. It's all just too much. This can't be real. I keep hoping that I'm going to wake up and it will all be a horrible dream. But deep down, I know…this isn't a dream at all. This is my reality.

I close my eyes and count to ten, trying to even out my breathing. When that doesn't work, I get up and head into the bathroom to splash some water on my face. Checking myself out in the mirror, I see the pink is gone from the cheek where I was slapped. I also notice I'm all wrinkled. I'm going to need to change for dinner. Change…Kostas said all of my stuff was brought here.

Stepping back into the bedroom, I spot an armoire similar to the one in the room I was staying in. Opening it up, I find the outfits that were in my room are now in this one. I move to the dresser and open each of the drawers: bras, panties, silk pajamas. Oh my God, he really did have all my stuff moved. When the hell did he find the time?

It's as though he planned this all along.

Predicted my moves before I made them.

He's a genuine nut job.

Curious, I open the closet door to see if there's anything of mine in there as well. It's a huge walk-in closet. When I step inside, I notice the back wall first. It has floor-to-ceiling shelves filled with various styles of shoes. The top half are all men's, but the bottom half are women's. I pick one up and see it's a size eight. My size. As if it's burned me, I drop it back down where I got it from.

He's a psychopath.

What kind of person does this?!

Turning around, I take in the two side walls. Each are filled wall-to-wall with clothes. On one side are men's clothes. From suits, to collared shirts, to a couple hoodies, with a few pairs of jeans hanging up at the end. On the other side are all women's clothes. There must be thousands of dollars' worth of clothes in here. Needing to confirm they're for me, I check out a few of the tags. All my size.

Psycho. Creep. Stalker.

Oh my God. I have got to get away from this man.

Backing up slightly, I bump into a dresser island in the

middle of the room—yes, his closet is the size of a freaking room. It has several drawers, and on the end there's a bench where you can sit to put on your shoes.

With a deep breath, I try to steady my nerves and calm myself. I grab an off the shoulder sweater and a pair of shorts and quickly change into them, needing to get out of here. Out of this closet. Out of this room. Out of this fucking house.

Since I have some time before dinner, I leave the villa, desperate for fresh air and to clear my head, but as the door closes behind me, I realize I don't have a key. "Shit!" I try to turn the handle, but it's locked. Unlike the room I stayed in last night, Kostas's door has a number pad on it, and I don't know the code. Nor do I know his phone number. "Just great." I groan.

"Locked out?" a masculine voice asks. Unlike Kostas's dark, cold tone, this voice is melodic and playful. Aris. I turn around and find him leaning against the wall, in a pair of board shorts and boat shoes, with his leg propped up, and his arms crossed over his shirtless chest.

"Do you know the code?" I ask, nodding toward the offending panel.

Aris laughs, light and throaty. I haven't heard Kostas laugh yet, but I imagine it would sound the complete opposite. I don't really know either of them, but from what I've seen, they seem to be polar opposites.

"It's not funny," I snap. "Your brother told me to be ready at five thirty. The last thing I need is him…punishing me." I mumble the last two words.

"Ahh…" Aris grins. "So, you've already had a chance to get to know my brother."

"If you call watching him torture a man with his own limb that he cut off using a knife, getting to know him, then sure, I know him *real* well," I smart. My words come out harsh and sarcastic, but my voice cracks at the end, giving away how overwhelmed and scared I am.

Aris steps off the wall and stalks toward me. "Come here." His voice, so sweet and soft, is my breaking point. A single tear squeezes past my flimsy barrier and rolls down my cheek. Aris, not missing a beat, swipes his thumb across my flesh and catches it. And then another falls, and another. And the next thing I know, I'm in Aris's arms, crying onto his shoulder.

"Shh," he coos. "It's okay. It's going to be okay."

I don't know how, but without even asking him, I know Aris is nothing like his brother. They both might work for their father, but Aris isn't stone cold like Kostas. He's different. Softer.

"How can you say that?" I murmur. "I'm being forced to marry a man who made me watch him take another man's life to show me what he's capable of. How can anything ever be all right?"

It can't.

It won't.

"What can I do?" he asks, but before I can answer, someone else answers for me.

"You can get your fucking hands off my fiancée for starters."

chapter
seven

Kostas

ARIS MEETS MY GLARE OVER TALIA'S BLOND HEAD with a maddening smirk that used to get his ass beat when we were kids. I swear he lives to taunt me. Wisely, he drops his arms.

Talia jerks away from him and crosses her arms over her chest. My gaze flits to her smooth, sexy shoulder that's exposed. Golden like honey. I bet it tastes sweet too.

"I don't know the code to get back in," she mutters, not meeting my gaze.

"You were supposed to stay put," I say, stepping closer.

"What *is* the code?" Aris implores just to fuck with me. He sure as hell isn't welcome in my villa.

Shaking my head at him, I bite out my words. "Don't you have some errands to run for Daddy?"

All humor is wiped off his fucking face. If anyone has daddy issues, it's my brother. It boils his blood that he's a glorified errand boy and I'm the heir to the Demetriou kingdom. Instead of losing his cool like I wish he would, he straightens his spine and shoots me a nasty glare.

"Excuse me, Talia," he mutters. "I have work to do. See you at dinner."

As soon as he's gone, she frowns at me. "He'll be at dinner with us?"

I walk over to her and grip her wrist. She smells like lavender, a pleasing scent that simmers some of my rage at seeing Aris swooping in on her like a fucking hawk. "It's a family dinner," I explain, studying her plump lips. "My father and mother will be there as well."

Her blue eyes widen. "I'm going to meet your mother?"

"You're my fiancée," I remind her with a smirk. "Of course you'll meet her. She's been told about you and will be helping to plan our wedding." My voice drops to a low octave as I reach up to brush a blond strand of hair from her eyes. "You'll respect my mother, yes?"

The unspoken threat lingers in the air between us.

Ignoring my words, she narrows her eyes at me and huffs out, "You're sure taking this marriage debt seriously."

Sliding my hand to her throat, I gently caress her soft skin. My thumb lingers on her fat vein that throbs wildly. I make her nervous. Good. "I'm a successful businessman. I take *all* business seriously," I utter, my eyes locked with her flaring blue ones. "And, like my father, I take marriage even more seriously."

She swallows and her throat moves against my palm. This woman is so delicate. A butterfly caught in a spider's web—her wings about to be tied down indefinitely.

"Come now, *moró mou*. We have important matters to see to."

I release her neck but not her wrist. She hesitates for a fraction of a second when I pull her with me, but I'm stronger and she's forced to follow along. Soon, she falls into step beside me and I release my grip on her. We walk down the stone pathway between other private villas until we come to the side entrance of the hotel. Her curiosity and apparent appreciation of our hotel gets the better of her once we step inside. When we pass a painting I had flown in from Portugal recently, I sense her hesitation. She wants to look at it but is afraid to ask.

If she is to be my wife, she'll have to tap into that bravery sooner rather than later.

Animals can sense fear. They thirst for it. Can scent it in the air. Hunt it down. Humans are no different. She wants to be hunted? I'll fucking hunt her.

"This way, *mikró kounéli.*" *Little rabbit.*

She shoots me a venomous glare—one that's better suited for a reptile that eats little rabbits. Her sudden flare of animosity has heat coursing through me straight to my dick. I let out a dark chuckle before guiding her to my office where Faustus and his team await.

Once inside my office, she stumbles slightly. I place my palm on the small of her back to steady her. Faustus—a world-renowned jeweler from Athens—has set up my office with his best pieces. Several men stand in corners, their black suits and impassive features meant to blend in. In reality, they're there to keep anyone from robbing Faustus blind of his precious treasures.

"Faustus," I greet, reaching to shake hands with the short, white-haired man.

"Mr. Demetriou." He shakes my hand and then offers his to Talia. She's been brought up to be a lady, apparently, because she smiles and takes his hand. "Lovely woman."

"Thank you," she utters. "What's all this?" She shoots me a questioning look.

"This," Faustus answers for me, "is the finest gold, platinum, silver, and stones in the entire world." He grins wide at her, his white mustache stretching across his face. "Only the finest for a Demetriou."

I can tell it's on the tip of her tongue to argue that she's still a Nikolaides, but she wisely keeps her mouth shut.

"Come," Faustus tells her. "Sit."

I sit in my desk chair while he sits in the chair next to her, opposite my desk. Faustus pulls one of the jewel-covered black trays over to her lap. As he explains the quality of each piece, I study my fiancée. Her brows are furled and her nostrils flare. She'd love to be anywhere but here, no doubt, but that's too fucking bad. After seeing Aris with his arms wrapped around her, I'd nearly exploded with fury. She needs a heavy, priceless ring on her finger so the whole fucking world knows who she belongs to.

Touching my woman will have consequences.

Aris knows this and yet he tests my patience.

Because he's my brother, he's allowed a small sliver of leniency. But my graciousness toward my flesh and blood has been eliminated. I won't cut him with words next time. No, I'll cut him with something much sharper.

"You prefer pink?" Faustus asks her, offering her a rather large pink diamond to inspect.

Her face sours and she shakes her head. "These are all too big."

Faustus snorts. "Nonsense. No diamond is too big for a beautiful woman."

"Pick the one you like," I instruct. "You're not leaving here until you do. Choose wisely."

She rolls her eyes, making her seem younger and less overwhelmed. That, too, gets my dick hard. I smirk as she takes the pink diamond. I can tell she doesn't like it.

"No pink," I tell Faustus. "Perhaps something to match her eyes."

I nod to the small tray that's covered by a black cloth. Jewelers like him are all the same. They tease and tease until they get to the truly priceless gems. I don't have all day. I want a ring on her finger by the time we leave this room. Preferably the most valuable one.

Faustus, clearly peeved that I've cut short his show, frowns at me before reaching for the tray. He swaps out the one on her lap for the new one.

"This is as rare as they come," he explains, his voice turning to a whisper as he foreshadows what must be the best diamond here. "Priceless."

He pulls away the cloth to reveal a square light blue diamond already set in a platinum band. It sparkles from the sun streaming in the window, nearly blinding me. This will do. This will do nicely. Her eyes have locked onto the ring and she can't hide her appreciation for it. The blues in her eyes sparkle exactly like that of the diamond.

"This is a 24.18 carat emerald-cut vivid blue diamond called the Aster Blue. It comes from a South African mine and is the largest of five gems cut from a 122.52 carat rough blue diamond unearthed in 2001." He smiles at her. "Blue diamonds are among the rarest this world has ever seen. This diamond even rarer due to the size and cut. The jeweler who first owned it selfishly kept it for his wife, but eventually sold it in an auction seven years ago."

She looks up at Faustus. "Why did he sell it?"

Faustus's smile falters and he shoots me a panicked look. I, too, am curious about how a man would give his wife a priceless stone and then sell it.

"Is it important? Look at the way it catches the light," Faustus tells her.

Her head bows to inspect it, but irritation churns in my gut at his blatant refusal to answer her question. All it takes is for me to lean forward in my chair, my gaze burning into him, for him to give up the goods.

"He sold it because his wife left him. Ran away with his brother." He cringes, shooting me an apologetic look. "She left the ring and a note. His broken heart could only be soothed by the hefty amount the diamond brought in."

"Do you ever plan to leave me, *moró mou*?" I taunt, my voice dropping to a deadly low level.

Her blue eyes snap to mine, fear gleaming in them. With one hard stare, I challenge her to lie to me. We both know this morning, she'd done just that.

"I would like to try it on," she says, ignoring my question and holding out her dainty hand to Faustus.

Beads of perspiration dot his forehead as he eagerly takes her hand, clearly desperate to change the line of con-versation. He slides the massive light blue diamond on her slender finger. Possessiveness claws its way around my heart at seeing it on her hand. She'd be a fool to not choose it. It's perfect on her.

"How much is it?" she asks, her nose scrunching as she regards him.

"Priceless." He grins at her, before glancing my way. "Nothing a Demetriou can't afford."

"I guess I'll take this one then," she says in a breathy voice.

"You guess?" Faustus chokes out. "My lovely lady, this blue diamond is worth fifty-seven point seven million dollars."

Talia jerks her hand back, snapping her gaze my way, horror in her blue eyes. "That's insane!"

"It is the one," I tell Faustus blandly as I pick up my desk phone and dial Aris's secretary, Carlene. When she answers, I bark out my request for her to wire the money to Faustus. By the time I hang up, Faustus is beaming and Talia looks as though she swallowed something poisonous. "I thank you for your time, Faustus." With a nod, I dismiss them.

Talia remains still, the shiny diamond ring sparkling, as the men pack up the jewelry. They work quickly and quietly. After a brief handshake with Faustus, I rise and see them to the door.

"Talia, come," I bark out.

She jolts at my words and stands. Crimson paints her neck red, making me wonder what it is she's embarrassed about.

"Bring me the ring," I order, holding out my palm.

Her nostrils flare, but she obeys, stalking over to me. She plucks the ring from her finger and hands it over. Once it's safely encased in my fist, I grip her wrist and walk her out to my veranda.

"Talia Nikolaides," I say, pulling her hand up and kissing her knuckle. "You are to be my wife." I'm not asking for her hand in marriage, I'm taking it. I slide on the impressive ring, enjoying the way it shimmers in the sun. "And if you leave me like the poor man who first owned this ring, I will extract all fifty-seven point seven million from you. Blood, sweat, tears. However I can get my payment." I thread our fingers together. Her eyes flare with worry. "You know this, yes?"

"Yes," she breathes, her bottom lip wobbling wildly.

"Good." I kiss the back of her hand. "Four. Seven. Seven. One. That's the code to our villa. Don't share it with anyone."

She nods emphatically. "Of course not."

I lean in and kiss her cheek. "Run along and get ready for dinner. Dress nicely."

As soon as she plucks her hand from my grip, she high-tails it out of my presence. I'm staring out at the bay when a little while later someone approaches me from behind. Familiar fingernails scratch down my spine, making me smile.

"Look how handsome you are."

I turn to take in a pair of brown eyes that shine with love for me. Her face is youthful despite her age. Red-painted lips curl into a smile.

Pulling her into my arms, I hug her tight and inhale her hair that smells of oranges.

"Is it true?" she asks, pulling away to search my face, tears shining in her eyes. "You've found someone?"

I found her at the bottom of a Nikolaides hole. Like the priceless diamond, I unearthed her and made her mine. Unlike the jeweler, I'll make sure she wears that ring until her very last breath.

"It is," I grunt. Guilt niggles at me when her brown eyes flood and then spill over with her emotion.

"Oh, Kos," she chokes out. "Is it love?"

"It's something." I smile at her. "You look beautiful. Did you come alone?"

Her face pinches. "No, he's here, too." Worry flickers in her eyes. "Are you happy?"

I'm as happy as a man like me can get.

"Of course, Mamá."

I'm marrying the most beautiful woman in Greece and she's the daughter of an enemy. Of course I'm fucking happy.

The woman who raised us to be kind, honorable men hugs me once more.

Sometimes I almost feel sorry for her. Because for every good thing she taught us, my father taught us three more bad ones.

I'm not a good man.

Good men don't turn good women into Demetrious.

Only bad men do.

Mamá, of all women, should know that.

chapter
eight

Talia

"Hēdonē?" My eyes flicker from the seductively lit sign above the restaurant we're about to enter, to Kostas.

His expression is cold and emotionless, but I'm learning his eyes don't lie. The hazel seems to flicker with amusement. I imagine he's thinking the same thing I am. *Another goddess. Another story.* He arches a brow as though to say, "And your point?"

"Your restaurant is seriously named after the Goddess of Pleasure?" It'd be romantic coming from anyone but the man who is taking me as his wife in exchange for a debt. Speaking of which…

Don't look at it.

Don't look at it.

I have no choice. I sneak a peek at the massive diamond on my finger. It's heavy and sparkling. It's a beautiful ring, but it's ridiculous and over the top, especially for a marriage that's not even real.

This is forced imprisonment, where he's the warden and

I'm in unseen shackles with the walls around me rising higher by the minute.

I'll never get away from him.

Kostas doesn't give me a response, just tugs on my arm to keep me moving. We're halted by a familiar voice.

"Don't let the name fool you," Aris says as he approaches. "My brother prefers pain over pleasure. Isn't that right, Kostas?" Aris pats his brother on the shoulder, and Kostas's entire body visibly stiffens. Darkness gleams in his eyes, not much different from the violent look on his face when he tortured that man. "It was our mother who named the restaurant. She's the romantic in the family."

Aris shoots a playful wink my way. Taunting his brother on purpose. I may not like Kostas, but Aris is practically signing my death warrant. In an effort to show I'm not encouraging things, I lean into Kostas.

"Unless you want to learn firsthand about the pain I prefer, I suggest you shut your fucking mouth," Kostas snarls, stepping away from me and toward Aris.

The air crackles with electricity—two storms about to collide. Unfortunately, from experience, I know one storm is more violent than the other.

Aris laughs as if Kostas is joking, but I can see it in his posture, he's preparing for the possibility of a fight. And with Kostas, it could end deadly.

"Oh, boys," a female voice says. "No fighting tonight. We have much to celebrate." A beautiful, smiling woman steps into view, and both Aris and Kostas immediately stand down, giving her a sincere smile. The animosity still lingers in the air, but for this woman, they've put a lid on it for now.

Her brown hair is down in waves, and her lips are painted a bright red. She's dressed in a gorgeous black cocktail gown with a matching pair of stilettos. She looks like the female version of Aris, and I know right away, she's their mother. She gives each of them a kiss on their cheek, and then she places her attention on me.

"I'm Nora," she says, giving me a kiss on each cheek before she steps back. "And you must be Kostas's fiancée." She beams. "I'm ashamed to admit that while I've heard about you, Kostas and his father neglected to tell me your name."

"Oh, my dear wife," Ezio purrs in a somewhat condescending tone. "I was going to wait until we were all seated to make introductions."

He's dressed in a black suit similar to the one he wore this morning. He wraps his arm around her waist and grins wide. Unlike Kostas's smile, which comes across dangerous with a hint of seductiveness, or Aris's, which gives off a playful vibe, Ezio's smile screams barely hidden malice. It's the kind of smile that sends chills up your spine and leaves you afraid of what's to come.

"This is Talia…Talia Nikolaides." He draws out my last name slowly, and his grin grows wider, making the tiny hairs on the back of my neck stand at attention.

Nora's bright smile falters for a split second before it's back and even brighter than before. "It's nice to meet you, Talia," she says. "Shall we go in?" She nods toward the restaurant. "We can get to know each other over dinner."

What's there to know?

I'm a captive on this island, forced to marry a monster.

The end.

Happily fucking ever after, lady.

Rather than going off on this poor woman who doesn't fit in with these malevolent men, I plaster on a fake, polite smile that would make my grandfather proud.

"Come," Kostas instructs, his voice low and commanding.

Placing his palm against my lower back, Kostas guides us through the door and past the hostess stand. Like everything else at this hotel, the restaurant is over the top gorgeous. The walls are an off white with wrought iron lamps hanging every few feet apart, casting yellow and orange hues onto the walls, making it appear as if the walls are on fire. There's a large stone fireplace that takes up the entire back wall. The tables are a soft white, and the chairs are all black leather and wood wingback with orange cushions. The floor is made up of red and orange swirls.

Like fire licking up from Hell.

Who knew Hell could look so pretty?

The Devil sure is…

I know without asking he had something to do with designing this restaurant.

When we arrive at our table, Kostas pulls my chair out for me. "Thank you," I whisper, still in awe of my surroundings.

"I thought you might like this restaurant," Kostas says, sitting next to me.

For one moment, he seems as though he might be genuine. As though he's a dutiful boyfriend who knows what his girlfriend likes. But he doesn't know. He's an actor. Not unlike Alex. Difference is, Alex really was the dutiful boyfriend who cared.

Was.

Sickness roils in my belly, and tears threaten, but I push them back.

"It's beautiful," I murmur, plastering on a fake smile, because apparently, I too am supposed to play a part. And I'm fearful of the consequences if I don't. "Did you help design it?"

His mother seems unaware of the awkward vibe hissing in the air. Pride shines on her pretty face.

"It was both of us," Nora admits as her husband pushes her chair in and sits next to her, on the other side of Kostas. We're at a round table that seats five people, so Aris sits in the empty seat to my right, which happens to be between his mom and me. "Do you enjoy Greek mythology?" she asks.

One quick glance at Kostas and I try not to shudder. His intense, calculating glare is on me, daring me to bark out what I want to say.

What does it matter anymore what I enjoy?

"I do." I place my napkin on my lap, forcing another smile for her. "I'm studying art at the Florence Art Institute. I prefer the performing arts, but I've taken several art classes and have taken a liking to classic mythology." Too bad I'll never get to go back and finish.

The waiter comes over and pours us each a glass of water, and Kostas orders a bottle of wine for the table.

"Florence?" Nora questions. "How was it you met my son from all the way over in Italy?" She tilts her head to the side slightly, and it hits me that she really has no clue as to why I'm here and engaged to her son.

I shift in my seat, shooting Kostas a questioning look. I may have studied theater, but I'm not a liar. Am I supposed to just make up some romantic story of how we met?

Kostas's hand lands on my thigh under the table and squeezes as he saves me from her line of questioning. "Talia was visiting with her father on vacation. We ran into each other in front of Bernini's sculpture and debated the story of Proserpina."

Nora's face pales at his answer, making me wonder if she knows more about her dark little prince and her wicked king of a husband than she lets on. She nods, as though she believes her son is a romantic. But she's half present and half lost in thought. Though her smile is steady on her face, it's not as bright as it was initially.

"How romantic," she finally says, regarding Kostas as though she truly believes that.

"Yes," I grit out. "So romantic."

I want to ask her if she thinks it's romantic the way her son defends Pluto in the sculpture. The captor. The rapist. It's on the tip of my tongue, my inner Nikolaides fire brimming to the surface.

Kostas's grip on my thigh tightens to the point of pain, reminding me of my place. He leans over, his lips grazing my earlobe, and whispers, "We can discuss it more when we get home tonight, *moró mou*. I just might be inclined to show you what else I find *romantic*."

A threat.

It coils around me and suffocates me.

Thankfully, the waiter comes over and saves us from this conversation. Kostas orders for me, which might normally grate on me, but I'm too flustered to care.

The rest of the dinner goes fairly smoothly considering I'm dining with a demon, a poor, unsuspecting woman, and Aris, who appears to be *almost* as much out of place as I am. The men discuss a new hotel they're opening up on Crete island, and Nora gives her input when asked. I remain silent, lost in my head.

While this family chatters happily with one another, all it makes me do is long for the loss of my own. If I were at dinner with Mom and Stefano, he'd be proudly talking about some new securities he's invested in while Mom gushes about a pair of shoes she recently bought. I'd order my own damn food and I'd join the conversation without fear of saying the wrong thing.

And what happens when I do step out of line?

I chance a quick glance at Kostas. His hazel eyes are sharpened as his dad speaks, but I have no doubts he's got me locked in his side eye. I'd like to convince myself he's civilized as he sips his wine and discusses potential property locations with his father.

But he's not civilized.

He cut off a man's foot and beat him to death with it, for fuck's sake.

As though clued into my thoughts, his eyes slide my way, cutting me to the bone. I've never met a man who can say so little with his mouth, but scream everything with his eyes.

Behave.

You're mine.

Buckle up, sweetheart, because this is your life now.

I tear my gaze from his and gulp down my wine, hating the way heat creeps up my neck. I'm embarrassed. A ridiculous sensation, but it's the truth. Embarrassed I was born into a family who would sell me like a head of cattle. Sold to a slaughterhouse, no less. It can't get any more embarrassing than that.

When dessert is finally brought out, Nora turns her attention to me. "I was thinking since we only have a week to plan your wedding, we could get started tomorrow."

The spoon that was almost to my mouth, filled with custard, falls from my fingers and clangs against the ceramic plate. Holy shit.

One week.

One week and I'll officially have been sold to the Devil. Lovely.

Kostas mentioned the timeframe before, but it didn't hit me until right at this moment. I'm about to become his wife in less than a week.

I think I'm going to be sick.

As if he can sense my freaking out, Kostas makes it a point to glide his hand up my thigh and under my dress. My hand flies under the table to stop him, and he glares my way.

Mine.

He doesn't have to say it, because those beautifully horrible eyes do it for him.

I try to remove his hand, and he releases me, only to thread our fingers together. Like we're a real couple. This is the same hand he used to kill a man.

"Have you seen the ring your son bought me?" I ask Nora, using my question as an excuse to take my hand back. Reaching over Aris, I extend my arm to show her the ridiculous rock that sits on my ring finger.

As soon as I realize what I've done, a cold dread settles over me. I'm practically leaned across Aris's lap—a place I know for a fact Kostas doesn't want me to be.

"Oh, it's gorgeous!" Nora coos. "See, Aris, your brother *can* be romantic."

Aris snorts but doesn't argue with his mother.

I quickly shrink back after she's inspected the diamond and glance over at Kostas. His expression is hard and unreadable. His eyes, though, are blazing with fury.

Oh God.

My hand trembles, and he takes it again. This time, I don't pull it away. I let his thumb sweep over the back of my hand and truly pretend he's trying to comfort me.

But silly me…

The perpetrator doesn't comfort the victim.

Hot tears well in my eyes, but I quickly blink them away. My mother didn't raise a victim. She raised me to be strong and feisty and assertive.

I miss my mom.

I miss home.

"I was thinking we could go in search of the venue tomorrow," Nora says, pulling me from my near meltdown. "I've made a list of the best locations. Kostas mentioned hiring a wedding planner, but I thought it would be fun for us to do it ourselves. There are some gorgeous churches in the area. What do you think?"

I always envisioned a beautiful church wedding where my soul mate and I would exchange heartfelt vows, and afterward attend the reception filled with our closest family and friends. My husband and I would spend the evening in each other's arms until it was time to say our goodbyes and leave for our honeymoon. Now, all of my dreams have been shattered.

I'm living in a nightmare.

It doesn't matter if it's the most beautiful wedding ever put on, it'll be a hateful shame. A vengeful way to get back at my father. A lifelong sentence for a crime I didn't commit.

"Talia," Kostas rumbles from beside me, a low warning in his tone.

I don't know why her sons and husband haven't told her that this wedding isn't a romantic union of two people in love, but of a debt being paid, but I'm not going to be the one to tell her. I can guarantee, based on Kostas's behavior, that the devilish momma's boy at my side would not like that at all. So, even though I have no desire to plan any aspect of this sham of a wedding, I nod politely.

"Uh, sure," I stammer out. "That sounds like fun."

"Perfect!" She beams. "I'll be by at ten to pick you up."

She seems nice. Really nice. I wonder if she's nice enough to betray her own family and help me escape this hellish island.

"Do you live here as well?" I ask.

"No, Ezio and I live about twenty minutes just outside of town, in the home Kostas and Aris grew up in. You will have to bring her to visit soon," she says to Kostas.

"Of course, Mamá," he assures her in a gentle voice that's as fake as my smile.

We wrap up dessert and I'm spared from any more probing questions. For the most part, this family leaves me out of their seemingly common dinner conversation. All too soon, I'm broken from the most normal situation I've been in since I got here, to leave.

Off to be alone with my *fiancé*.

Wonderful.

Cue panic attack.

After we say our goodbyes, Aris heads toward the bar. Kostas places a palm on my lower back, guiding me down the hallway and out of the hotel. The night is warm with a slight breeze. I wish it'd strengthen and carry me far away from here. Unfortunately, though, my luck doesn't hold out, because before I know it, we're standing in front of Kostas's impressive villa.

The Devil's den.

And I live here now.

Terror claws its way up my throat. We'll be alone. Together. Sharing a bed. Images of what might happen in that bed claw at my mind, causing a hemorrhaging of fear to drown my every thought. One gentle push once the door is open and I'm thrust right into my living nightmare.

The door closes with a click behind us. He's quiet. Too

quiet. The hairs on my arms stand on end as I anticipate his next move.

"Relax," he rumbles. "I'm not going to eat you. *Yet.*"

Anger surges up inside of me and fuels me out of my state of terror. I shoot him a scathing glare that earns me a smirk instead. This, I can do. Sparring with an asshole. I did it all the time with my father. As long as he doesn't pull out his knives or tie me to a chair, I think I can handle this.

Rather than attack me like I conjured up in my mind, Kostas heads straight for the bedroom. I follow behind, watching as he removes his jacket and unbuttons his shirt, hanging both over the back of the chair. I'm frozen in place as he toes off his shoes and slides his dress pants down each muscular thigh, leaving him in only his briefs.

I let my guard down too soon.

Is this where we role play, our own little parts in this fucked-up play?

Pluto and Proserpina.

The rapist and his victim.

"Keep eyeing me like that and I'll fulfill those dark fantasies rolling through your mind," he bites out, his intense hazel eyes searing into me. "Every last one of them. All night long."

Averting my eyes, I stare down at the floor, frozen on what to do next. He stalks over to me until his black socks come into view.

Socks.

So simple and normal.

That is, unless you're using said sock to contain a murder weapon.

His fingers grip my jaw and he lifts my chin until I'm forced to look at him. He runs his thumb along my bottom lip, dragging the flesh roughly to the side.

"This is the part where you get ready for bed also," he explains, his voice dry and condescending. "Understand?"

I swallow down the mixture of hatred and fear that have tangled inside my throat. Furious tears burn at my eyes. One escapes and slides down my cheek. He leans forward, kissing the wetness.

"You have an early morning. I suggest you move." With those words, he releases me and motions at the dresser before turning his back to me.

I focus on grabbing my own change of clothes from the drawer, but unlike Kostas, who's clearly okay with being on display, I close the bathroom door and get changed in there. When I come out, dressed in the silkiest pair of pajamas I've ever felt, Kostas is already in bed and the room is darkened. He's staring down at his phone and it illuminates his face, making him seem darker and scarier than he already is, which is quite a feat if you ask me.

When he tilts his head up, I snap my eyes down and walk around to the other side of the bed.

I've never slept in a bed with a man before, and I have no clue what I'm supposed to do. He said we're waiting until our wedding night to have sex, but does that mean we're waiting until that night to do everything? Suddenly feeling inexperienced and sheltered and terrified out of my mind, I tug my blankets up to my neck and lie on my side, facing away from Kostas, in hope that he'll let me go to sleep without asking anything of me.

But sleeping beside a monster is easier said than done.

No matter how tightly I squeeze my eyes shut, I know he's there, lying in wait. Just waiting to sink his teeth in and take a bite.

Just as I begin to relax, I hear him set his phone on

the nightstand. The bed moves slightly as he adjusts to get comfortable.

"You're shaking the bed," he rumbles, pulling me slightly into his chest. "Are you crying?"

"No," I rasp out.

He wraps his arm around my front and nuzzles his face into the crook of my neck. "Are you afraid of me?"

"Y-Yes," I admit, knowing lying to him is futile and stupid.

"Mmm," is all he says. As though my being afraid is hardly an interesting thought to him. Then, his grip around me tightens as he draws me closer, his hips slightly flexing as he rubs his very obvious erection against my butt. "Fear can be healthy. Keeps the heart pumping like it should."

I hate this man.

I hate him with everything I am.

His palm spreads out over the front of my pajama top above my breasts. He caresses me gently with his thumb.

"Your heart is certainly beating like a champ." He slides his thumb lower, grazing my nipple and causing it to harden. "This works too."

I'd burst into tears if I weren't so pissed at his arrogance.

"Fuck you," I whisper, the hate vibrating through me.

"Don't worry, *moró mou*. I will. And soon."

chapter
nine

Kostas

I'M AN ASSHOLE.

The poor girl thought I'd rape her.

I am a lot of things, but I don't have to force women. My sweet little fiancée will one day beg, whether she likes it or not. I'll spread her out on the bed and bury my face in her cunt until she doesn't push me away, but instead tugs me to her.

My phone buzzes and I groan. Fucking Aris. If he knows what's good for him, he'd leave me the hell alone.

Aris: We need to talk.

Me: I'm busy.

Aris: Too bad.

I toss my phone on my desk, swallowing down my irritation. It's not like I can avoid my brother forever. He's a part of the family business. Without his incredible ability to manipulate numbers in our favor, we wouldn't have half the fortune we do. Unfortunately, Aris is a necessary part of my world.

While I wait on the smug bastard, I think about this

morning. I'd left Talia sleeping. At some point in the middle of the night, she'd softened toward me. In her dreams, I'm not a total monster. Her hand had snaked up my chest and she'd held on to me. Selfishly, I'd inhaled her hair while I wondered about my future with her.

It's not real.

I ignore the words inside my head. Maybe Talia and I are forced into this arranged marriage because her father is a stupid, spineless bitch, but there's no reason I can't make this work in my favor. Talia is a fucking knockout. Exactly my type with her curvaceous body, plump dick sucking lips, and tight ass. Her mouth that she tries desperately to keep in check is more than attractive. It gets my cock achingly hard.

"Ahh," Aris chirps from the doorway. "Up bright and early this morning, dear brother."

Leaning back in my chair and crossing my arms over my chest, I watch my brother with disinterest. With one look, I convey to him that I'm more superior than he will ever be. Father chooses me as his second-in-command. I'm the one who deals with the dark, nefarious deeds that cloud around the Demetriou name. It's me who takes a wife for a business debt, because soft men like Aris would cave at a few tears.

Aris is too soft, too sweet, too passive.

But he looks at my fiancée like he might try to assert a little power over me.

Over my fucking dead body.

"Get to the point," I bite out, darting my eyes to the clock. "I need to ravish my bride-to-be before our mother whisks her away to do wedding things."

His jaw clenches and his eyes flare with anger.

One point for me, little brother.

"I didn't know rape was in your repertoire of evil deeds," he hisses, losing some of his good boy cool.

I laugh, but it's cold and heartless. "There's a lot you don't know about me."

"You're a cruel motherfucker." He drops into the seat across from me. "But she'll be your wife. You sure you want to start out a marriage with hate?"

"She didn't hate me last night when she was snuggled up against me," I taunt, loving the way his eyes flicker with rage. That's right, asshole, she's mine. Little baby brothers don't get gifts from Daddy.

His nostrils flare, and he casts his gaze out the window. Finally, he takes a calming breath, huffing out his words. "Cy and Bakken Galani's family are retaliating."

I lift a brow. "The Galanis are roaches, brother. Plentiful and difficult to kill with usual methods. That is why we drive them out of their hiding place and stomp on them."

"Your arrogance is a weakness," Aris sneers. "It'll get you killed by our enemies one day. Who knows, maybe it'll be one of the Nikolaides. Phoenix seems like he'd be quite a match for you."

"Phoenix is on his daddy's leash. And Niles is on ours," I remind him. "As long as Talia warms my bed, those rats won't try a goddamn thing."

"Perhaps not the Nikolaides," Aris concedes. "But the Galanis are fired up. My contacts state that their other brother Estevan is pissed. He's the reckless one. I wouldn't put it past that fucker to blow up the damn hotel."

"I'll send out some men to hunt him down. Get me names of anyone in Estevan's circle. We'll drive them out and stomp on them. Surely this we can agree on, brother."

Aris grimaces. "Surely."

"Now," I state as I rise, "you'll have to excuse me. I need to wake my future wife up."

His eyes narrow on me. "That ring wiped out your account."

"So move money from my offshores. By the end of third quarter, I'll have made it back. Taxes are due soon." I raise my eyebrows to dare him to challenge me more.

"Whatever, man. Just don't be a total dick to her. She's been through enough."

"But being a dick is so entertaining," I say with a smirk.

Once I'm out of my office, I stride out of the hotel to my villa. I slip in quietly and find Talia sitting at the bar eating a bowl of cereal. Her blond hair is messy and dark circles ring her eyes from stress or lack of sleep. She picks up the bowl and gulps down the milk. It's cute and shows her age. As soon as she realizes I'm looking at her, she stiffens, shooting me a hateful glare.

"My mother will be here within the hour."

She pushes away the bowl, a feral gleam in her blue eyes. "I'm not going."

"Excuse me?"

The brave woman slides off the barstool and shrugs. "I can't pretend, Kostas. I can't and I won't. You want to treat me as your prisoner, then do it. I can't go on acting like this is something I want."

"Don't be dramatic, *moró mou*. You'll shower and dress. Quickly now." I stalk past her and into my bedroom. Once in the bathroom, I turn on the shower before walking back into the living room.

She crosses her arms over her chest in defiance.

"Go," I bark out.

Her head shakes stubbornly. "No."

Now she's really starting to piss me off.

"Do I need to remind you who I am?" I rumble, locking eyes with her.

"Haven't forgotten," she hisses. "If you're going to kill me, just do it already."

I roll my eyes and storm over to her. "If I wanted to kill you, I would've done it already. We'll have far more fun playing together. Don't quit the game now, ómorfo korítsi."

Her nostrils flare at the words *beautiful girl.* "I hate you."

"Too bad," I growl, rushing her. She shrieks when I toss her over my shoulder and stride out of the room. Her useless hands pound against my lower back. Once in the bathroom, I drop her to her feet. "Take them off or I take them off for you."

She shakes her head, backing away from me.

"Suit yourself," I snap, irritated that she's acting like a spoiled brat. I grab the front of her pajamas and yank her forward. Her hands grip my suit jacket to keep herself from falling.

"Stop!" she yells, attempting to claw at me.

I wrangle her out of her shirt easily enough, but she's wiggling too much for me to get her pants off. Flipping her around, I push her against the wall and grip her wrists behind her with one hand. She cries out when I yank her pants and underwear down in one pass. When she's naked, I swivel her around and pin her against the wall by gripping her biceps. Her tits jiggle with every breath she takes and her skin burns crimson.

"Are you going to bathe yourself?"

Her blue eyes burn into mine with challenge. "And if I don't?"

I nudge her knees apart with my knee and slide up to her

cunt. "I would be more than thrilled with the husbandly duty of washing my future wife." I lean in and nuzzle the side of her neck with my nose before nipping at the side of her throat. "Just be warned. I'm very thorough."

Pulling away, I regard her with a lifted brow. Her lips press together, barely containing words she desperately wants to say. Words that will get her in trouble. I slide my palms down her arms and then take her hands in mine. She jerks them from my grip, so I clutch onto her naked hips instead. When I rub circles on her soft flesh with my thumbs, her breath hitches and her nipples harden. I'm painfully hard in my slacks, and if my mother wasn't on her way, I'd throw out my stupid waiting until marriage for sex shit and take her right now.

The eyes don't lie.

Behind her thinly veiled hate is lust. Desire. Need.

"Make the decision now, Talia."

Her eyes flutter closed when I slide my fingers along her lower stomach in a teasing way. As my knuckle runs along her slit, she sucks in a sharp breath.

"I, uh, I can do it myself," she whispers. "Please."

"Pity," I say with a faux pout. "I was looking forward to washing your dirty little body." I slide my hand back to her hip before turning her to face the shower. I smack her ass hard enough to earn me a hateful scowl over her shoulder. "Quickly now. My mother doesn't like tardiness."

She climbs into the shower and glowers at me through the glass. "You can leave now."

"Quality control," I say, holding my palms up. "It's a dirty job, but someone has to do it."

Her middle finger goes up and she spends her entire shower washing herself one-handed so that she can flip me off the whole time. I've killed men for lesser offenses.

Not her.

With her, it's fucking cute.

Keep testing me, *moró mou*. It gets my dick really goddamn hard.

The water finally shuts off and I'm waiting with a towel. She must have cooled in her shower because she won't meet my gaze. I wrap the towel around her and hug her to my chest. Her body grows stiff when my mouth brushes along her ear.

"Adrian will accompany you and my mother today. Don't try anything funny like running away. You won't get far."

She turns her head slightly toward me. My lips hover above her cheek.

"What if I tell your mother about what an awful monster you are?" she challenges, her voice breathy despite the brave words she speaks.

"She'll laugh it off because she's sweet and polite," I tell her, pressing my lips to her cheek. "And then you'll have to come back home and deal with me."

"What will you do?"

"What won't I do is a better question."

Her body trembles. "You scare me."

"You'll soon grow to love it."

"I'll never love *you*."

I slide my palms to her stomach and then up to her breasts. "You will if I *make* you." I tug away her towel, once again leaving her naked. Stepping back, I admire her perfect ass. "My mother will want to take you somewhere nice for lunch. A dress will do."

"You're an asshole."

I slap her ass hard before leaving her to get ready.

Because that's what assholes do.

chapter
ten

Talia

NORA AND I HAVE SPENT THE DAY DOING ALL things wedding related. We've found the most gorgeous wedding gown—one I would die to wear if it wasn't Kostas I'm marrying. Ordered the bridesmaids' dresses—for bridesmaids I don't even know and won't meet until the wedding rehearsal dinner on Friday. Apparently, Kostas's parents both have extended family, who will all be a part of the wedding, and Nora confirmed all of their measurements. We confirmed the church we'll be getting married in, and the beautiful garden venue for the reception. We scheduled the catering company and designed the wedding cake—an exquisite five-tier wilted magnolia petal design. It will match the color scheme we decided on—soft pink and cream. We only stopped once for a quick lunch.

In one long, exhausting day, Nora and I have planned the wedding of my dreams. If I could wave a magic wand, this is exactly what it would all look like, except for one detail. The groom. And that one detail is what ruined every moment of the day. I tried to picture walking down the decorated aisle in my wedding dress, but only imagined Kostas scowling at me. I imagined us cutting the beautiful cake and partaking in the tradition of *feeding each other*, but all I could envision is Kostas glaring at me.

I saw several of the receipts from today, so I know this wedding is costing the Demetriou family a small fortune—not that they can't afford it—and it's all a waste. An unnecessary show. The church and reception and decorations and wedding attire might all be perfect, but none of it matters because the wedding is a sham. The vows we'll recite will be fake. The exchanging of rings will have zero meaning. And all for what? So Kostas's mom can enjoy her eldest son getting married? So my da—Niles, can have it rubbed in his face that his daughter has been bought in exchange for his debt? It doesn't make any sense. He doesn't even live anywhere near Kostas and his dad. How is it fair that he's now debt free and I have to spend the rest of my life married to a man who is hell-bent on making my life miserable?

"I was thinking we could go to dinner," Nora suggests from the back of the town car. We've just left the bakery and are heading back home. *Home.* The word leaves a sour taste in my mouth. This place will never really be home. "Aris mentioned he's just finished up a meeting and is available to join us." Nora smiles sweetly. If the circumstances were different, and I was marrying Kostas out of love and not to fulfill an obligation, I would feel lucky to have Nora as my mother-in-law. In all of the movies I've seen, the mother-in-law is always a bitch, trying to create a wedding the bride hates. But not Nora.

The entire day she has been nothing but sweet to me. When I was standing on the alteration pedestal in my wedding grown and began to cry—she assumed they were happy tears—she pulled me into a hug and whispered, "I am so happy my son has found love. It takes a strong woman to love a Demetriou man. Thank you for loving my boy."

I wanted so badly to tell her that it's impossible to love a Demetriou man, and that it would never happen, but then I remembered that she does in fact love one. How? I have no idea. But she does. So I kept my mouth shut and nodded and told her the only honest thing I could think to say. "I'm so glad you're going to be my mother-in-law."

"Talia," Nora says, bringing me back into the now. "How do you feel about dinner?"

"That sounds wonderful," I tell her truthfully. For one, I really do love her company, and it will mean less time I'm stuck at home with Kostas taunting and torturing me. Sick, sadistic asshole. It's like he gets off on messing with me. Not that it should surprise me. The guy also gets off on beating men with their own limbs. God knows what else turns him on.

My mind goes to earlier this morning, Kostas provoking me in the shower. I thought for sure he was going to force himself on me, and shockingly, while my brain screamed no, my body...my damn traitorous body reacted oppositely. My nipples hardened in want, and the area between my legs tightened in need. For a split second when I thought maybe Kostas was going to take me right then and there in the bathroom, I wasn't sure whether to beg him not to, or beg him to do it. Even now, sitting here in the car, my body shivers at the mere thought of him touching me. But I imagine, just like this fake wedding, sex with Kostas will be nothing like I've always fantasized about when I've thought about my wedding night with my husband. There won't be any love making or worshipping. He won't tenderly kiss and love on me. He'll be rough and mean and cruel. He'll hurt me…just because he can.

The town car stops in front of a small hole-in-the-wall restaurant. Alessandro's Urban Kitchen, the sign reads. The driver opens Nora's door, at the same time my door is opened. I'm momentarily taken aback, until I see Aris is standing there, holding the door open with one hand, his other extended to help me out.

"Thank you," I tell him with a soft smile. While Kostas is a cruel, heartless asshole, his brother doesn't seem to be anything like him.

"Did you ladies have a good day?" Aris asks, guiding his mother and me into the restaurant.

"We did," Nora says, beaming. "Everything is ready for Friday."

"Friday?" Aris prompts.

"The rehearsal dinner," Nora tells him. The hostess sits us at a small booth. Nora sits on one side and I sit on the other. Without thought, Aris slides in next to me. His leg bumps mine, and he grins playfully. Flush creeps up my neck. Why couldn't Kostas be more like Aris? Then maybe being forced to marry him wouldn't be so bad.

"Don't forget you need to pick up your tux," she says, picking up the wine menu. "And don't leave until you're sure it fits. We can't have you standing up as your brother's best man looking like a dressed up monkey." She and Aris laugh. It's light and playful, and it makes my heart both soar and hurt.

"When I was a teenager, Mom ordered my suit for a dance," Aris explains. "I told her I tried it on, but I lied. When I got home, it turned out I had had a growth spurt, and the arms and legs were all two inches too short."

"I told him he reminded me of those monkeys in the circus," Nora adds with a laugh.

The waiter comes over, and Nora orders us a red wine, while I eye the menu. It's Mediterranean and everything looks delicious. We spend dinner talking and laughing. Nora talks about her sons, and two things become apparent: one, she loves them with every ounce of her being, and two, she either has no clue who Kostas really is, or she's deep, deep in denial.

"Aris, *agóri mou*, would you mind bringing Talia home with you? The time has gotten away from me and I really need to get home. Your father will be home shortly, and you know how upset he gets if I'm not home to sit with him while he eats." Nora smiles, but it's not as bright as it's been all day, and I have to wonder, if maybe the reason she focuses so heavily on her relationship with her sons is because her marriage is lacking. When my parents were going through their divorce, my mom made it a point to smother me with love and affection. I didn't understand it at the time, but maybe it was out of her guilt of not giving her children the perfect family.

"Of course, Mamá." Aris stands and offers his hand to his mother as she exits the booth. The three of us walk outside, and after Nora makes me promise to not be a stranger and reminds me that she'll see me Friday evening, we part ways.

Aris's car is brought around by the valet. It's a shiny gray two-door Porsche sports car. After opening the door for me, Aris walks around to the driver side and folds himself into the car. "It's a nice evening," he says. "How about the top down?"

"Sure." I shrug. Aris's lips curl into a handsome grin as he presses a button that has the top lifting.

"Buckle up, *agapiméni.*" *Sweetheart.* Aris winks, and a giggle bubbles up and flows out of me at his playfulness. Aris speeds through the streets just like his brother, wild and reckless, only it's different, because Aris's version is fun and exciting.

Too quickly we arrive back at the hotel, and my mood immediately drops. Aris gives me a speculating look, and it's as if he can read my thoughts because he says, "Why don't we go for a swim? I heard Kostas is working late anyway…something about a business associate not cooperating."

A chill races down my spine at the last *business associate* of his I met.

"A swim sounds really good," I say, then remember I don't have a suit. At least I don't think I do. "Can we go by the shop so I can grab a bathing suit?"

"Sure," Aris says, placing his hand on my lower back. "I need to get changed, so I'll meet you over there."

After finding a cute bikini and matching cover-up and flip-flops, I head out to the pool. Aris is already there, with a beer in his hand, sitting along the edge of the pool. "I got you your favorite," he says, holding up a glass of lemonade.

"Thanks." I set the bag of my clothes next to a lounge chair, kick off my flip-flops, and take off my cover-up.

When I catch Aris eyeing my body, my neck and chest both heat up. The bikinis were all super skimpy, and even though I picked the one with the most material, it still shows off *all* of my assets.

After taking a sip of my lemonade, I glance around the area. The last time I was here I was upset and didn't really pay close attention. On one side of the pool is the tiki hut and bar. On the other side, though, is a massive rock waterfall with something running through the middle of it. "Is that a waterslide?" I ask Aris, who laughs.

"Yep, you want to go?"

I haven't been to a waterpark since I was a child. My mom and Stefano brought me, and we had a blast. "Sure!"

Aris laughs some more. "C'mon, *agipénos*."

I can't help my grin at his new nickname for me. *Sweetheart.* It's not so different from what Kostas calls me, but when Aris says it, it feels sincere, sweet, genuine. He's not trying to taunt me with his words, or scare me with his actions.

We race up the rock steps to the top of the waterfall. I didn't realize just how tall it was, until we're standing at the top where the entrance to the slide is. My step falters slightly, and Aris chuckles. "You're not getting cold feet, are you?"

"No," I sass. "But…you go first."

Aris throws his head back in laughter, and I find myself smiling hard. It feels good to smile. "Okay, fine," he says. He drops onto the beginning of the slide. "Come here real quick. I want to show you something."

Stepping toward him, I lean down to see inside the tunnel, but it's too dark. Before I can tell him that, he grabs my hips and throws me onto his lap. "Hold on!" he yells as we descend down the dark tube of flowing water. I scream and squeal the entire way down, and Aris laughs, holding on to me tightly.

When we reach the bottom of the slide, we fall a foot or so into the water. Our bodies splash and sink, but Aris never lets go of me. We both ascend at the same time, and my laughter can't be stopped. "You're such an ass!" My hair is a mess, all over my face, and I'm sure my makeup is running. I probably look like a drowned rat, but I don't care.

"You liked it," he says with a flirty grin. "You should see our other hotel on the other side of the island. It has an entire water park." Aris runs his fingers through his wet hair.

I don't mean to, but my eyes linger on his face. On his brown eyes, that are darker than Kostas's, yet seem so much lighter. The water drips down, and his tongue darts out to lick the liquid that's landed above his lip. His sweet lips that curl into a playful smile.

My heart pounds against my ribcage, and I have to force myself to look away. I can't be crushing on Aris. He's Kostas's brother. He's going to be the best man at our wedding in five days. I've seen what Kostas has done to a man who wasn't loyal to his family. What would he do to me if he even thought I had feelings for Aris?

"I need to go," I blurt out, and without waiting for a response from Aris, I swim over to the stairs and get out. I grab a towel and wrap it around myself. When I turn around, I find Aris standing in front of me.

"Did I do something?" he asks, his brows furrowing in confusion.

"No." I shake my head to emphasize my answer. "I just...I should probably get home."

"Okay." He nods in understanding, only he doesn't really understand. "Just let me grab my stuff and I'll walk you back."

"Oh, you don't have to do that." The last thing I need is Kostas to spot the two of us together. Something I probably should've thought about before I agreed to go swimming with Aris.

"It's no problem." Aris shrugs. "My villa is right next door." He winks, and I flinch. He's not implying what I think he is, right? He's just being his usual playful self. He doesn't mean anything by it. It's all in my head.

We grab our stuff, and I throw my cover-up over my still wet bikini. We walk in silence until we reach the door to my villa.

"I'm assuming my brother told you the code," Aris jokes.

"Yeah." I type it in, then turn around. "Thank you for…" I wave my hand toward where we came from. "I had a good time."

"You're welcome," Aris says back. He steps forward and into my space. Several long seconds pass as we stare at one another, neither of us saying a word. My breathing becomes labored. Heat radiates from him, nearly luring me closer. If it weren't for the chill of worry creeping over me that my fiancé might show up, I might just chase that warmth. But just as quickly as it came, the heat disappears as Aris takes a step back. "Anything you need…I'm here," he says before he turns and walks away.

chapter
eleven

Talia

I ROLL OVER FROM MY SIDE ONTO MY STOMACH AND SEE Kostas's side of the bed is empty. My hand brushes along the sheets, feeling the coolness. Every day this week it's been the same thing. He comes home after I'm asleep and leaves before I wake up. I spend my days walking the property, swimming, and hanging out with Aris when he's not working. But today is different because today is Friday. Our wedding rehearsal and dinner. A smile stretches across my face at the thought. Not because I'm going to have to walk through the steps of marrying Kostas, but because I'm going to get to see my family, specifically my mom. At that thought, I throw my covers off my body and stretch my legs, ready to get the day started. Kostas told me I could drive with Adrian to pick them up at the airport.

After taking a shower, I head over to Aphrodite's, a restaurant on the hotel property that serves the best breakfast and coffee, and eat by myself. Then I take a stroll over to the library—yes, the hotel has an actual library where one can read, and the shelves are filled with every type of book imaginable. I get comfy on the couch, reading *The Scarlet Letter* until Adrian lets me know it's time to go. I never tell him where I'm going, but somehow he always knows where to find me.

Freaking Kostas. He couldn't care less about me, yet he still has to make sure he's always in control of my life. Stupid, possessive asshole.

When we pull up to the front of the airport, it's just after two o'clock, and their flight has already arrived. Adrian insists we wait in the car, but I can't help myself, so I get out and wait on the sidewalk. Several people are exiting at the same time. My eyes dart all around in search of her, my feet bouncing in place in anticipation, and when they finally find her, tears fall.

"Mom!" I throw myself into her arms and nuzzle my face into her neck. I can smell her signature perfume she's been wearing for as far back as I can remember. It's sweet and comforting and smells like home. The bag she was carrying hits the ground and she wraps her arms around me.

"Oh, *cara mia*," she cries. "Let me see you." She pulls back slightly, but still keeps her hands in mine. "You've gotten a tan." She smiles, but it's not real. It's her version of making the best out of things. "The sun agrees with you."

"I missed you, Mom." I pull her back into a tight hug.

"We must go," Adrian points out, and I mentally roll my eyes.

After my mom and I separate, I give Stefano a hug. Nonno and Nonna each take turns giving me a hug, but it's awkward. Everything has changed. My grandfather used to be a man I thought was invincible, but not even he could save me from this forced marriage. And our last conversation ended with him yelling at me. Something he's never done before.

"I spoke with Phoenix," Mom says as we all climb into

the limo. "He and your father will be arriving shortly and will meet us at the church."

I still at her words. I didn't even think about *him* coming.

"He's not my father," I hiss. "And he's not welcome anywhere near me, especially at the wedding he's forced me into."

My mom's brows rise in concern, but she doesn't argue.

Pulling my cell phone out, I send a text message to Kostas. I've had his number but have yet to call or text him.

Me: I don't want Niles at the wedding.

Not even a minute later, he replies.

Kostas: None of this is about what you want.

Ugh! He's such an asshole. I don't even bother to respond.

"Is everything ready for tomorrow?" Mom asks. She pushes a wayward strand of hair behind my ear and gives me her motherly smile. I hate that Niles will be at the wedding, but I'm so thankful my mom will at least be there.

"Yes, Nora and I got everything done. The seamstress will be available at the church in case any of the bridesmaids' dresses don't fit." I've spoken to my mom every day on the phone, so she knows how nice Nora has been to me. Nora came to the hotel yesterday and we had lunch to go over everything.

"I'm sure it will be a beautiful wedding," Mom says. "Have you spoken to Kostas about finishing school in the fall?"

I shake my head. My goal these past few days has been to speak to him as little as possible. I imagine once we're married tomorrow, everything will continue as it has been. He probably won't even notice if I go to school as long as I'm in bed at the end of the day.

Forty minutes later we arrive at Saint Nicholas's church. Several vehicles are parked in the parking lot, including Aris's Porsche and Kostas's Maserati. My stomach roils in fear and anticipation. I can't believe this is really happening. This time tomorrow I am going to be Mrs. Kostas Demetriou. The thought has me wanting to highjack this limo and take off in the other direction.

My mom must notice the sudden shift in my mood because she wraps her arm around me as we all walk toward the entrance to the church. The moment we're inside, I spot Nora. She's dressed in a simple yet elegant cream-colored dress with nude heels. When she sees we've arrived, she comes over to us.

"Talia, my darling girl, you look beautiful." Her eyes run up and down the simple floral dress and heels I'm wearing. And then her eyes look just past me and her smile falters slightly.

"Nora, this is my family," I say, making introductions. "This is my mom, Melody, my stepdad, Stefano, and my grandparents, Emilio and Vera."

"Yes, of course," Nora says. "Your grandparents and I have met at the occasional dinner. It's nice to see you both again." She gives each person an air kiss to their cheeks and a hug. "Everyone is waiting to begin. Victoria, Paulina, and Jacqueline have all tried on their dresses and they fit beautifully."

Nora guides us inside where the ceremony will be held. We've already gone over the details with the priest when we were here earlier this week, but she goes over it all again.

"Your family will sit on the left." Nora points out. "If you would like to have a seat, Father Nicholas is just going to go over what to expect during the ceremony tomorrow, and then we'll head over to Hēdonē for dinner," she says to my family, who all have a seat where she's pointed.

When I step up onto the altar, my eyes first find Aris's. He's standing next to his brother and three other men I've yet to meet. They must be family or friends of Kostas's. Aris gives me a small nod, and his lips curl into a half-smile half smirk. The familiarity and comfort his smile brings helps me to breathe just a little easier.

My eyes next land on Kostas. His eyes are gleaming and his wicked smirk does nothing to calm my nerves. He steps forward, and I almost take a step back but quickly stop myself.

He pushes a strand of hair behind my ear and whispers, "If you're done eye-fucking my brother, I'd like to get this over with so I can once and for all make you mine."

chapter
twelve

Kostas

THE NERVE OF THIS WOMAN. SHE MAY BE MARRYING me tomorrow, but it's my younger brother whom she smiles for. It's fucking Aris who she's been spending all her time with. Maybe no one else sees the way she looks at him, but I certainly do. And it pisses me right the fuck off.

Her face blanches at my words. "Kostas..."

"Yes, my bride," I say lowly, a hint of danger in my tone. "What do you have to say for yourself?"

All eyes are on us, but our voices are low enough only for us to hear.

"I, uh, you're being ridiculous," she murmurs. "I wasn't eye-fucking him."

It's like she's already forgotten what happened to the last person who lied to me. A hard look from me to her passes between us, making her tremble. Looking down, I nod at her strappy sandals.

"Lovely shoes. Did you get your toes done?"

She snaps her eyes to mine, her blue eyes flickering with

horror. "I'm not a liar," she chokes out, understanding dawning on her. "You're just a jealous fiancé."

I reach up to cradle her cheek with my palm. "Perhaps."

"And an asshole," she hisses, earning a chuckle from me. "Let's get this over with."

I smirk at her. "So I'm not the only one looking forward to the honeymoon it would seem."

"Go to hell," she growls.

"Of course, Talia," I say, stepping closer, our mouths nearly touching. "But you're going with me."

The rehearsal was boring as fuck. Wedding shit always is. It doesn't matter if it's my wedding or one of my several girl cousins I've chosen for bridesmaids. Weddings are a fucking snooze. What's entertaining, though, is watching my fiancée squirm now every time Aris tries to talk to her.

That's right. I'm watching. Always fucking watching.

He finally gives up and walks over to talk to our father, who as usual, barely acknowledges he exists.

After we finished at the church, we came back to Hēdonē for a private dinner. According to Mamá, it's all part of the tradition. The two families breaking bread before the big day tomorrow. While we wait for dinner to be served, everyone enjoys a drink while they socialize amongst each other.

I watch as my father's gaze darts between Niles and Melody, as if bringing the two exes into the same room to watch their daughter be forcefully married off is the most entertaining thing he's ever seen.

It shouldn't be.

That's what has me on edge.

My marrying Talia should please Father because he loves revenge, but that's it. It shouldn't be ongoing like this. I'm pissed that I feel in the dark about the whole situation.

My eyes zero in on Mamá. At the rehearsal she seemed so happy, but right now as she sips on her cocktail and speaks to Melody, something is off. Sure, she's wearing her signature Demetriou good wife smile, but the light that's usually in her eyes is snuffed out.

Melody is probably tattling to her about how her daughter was forced to marry a horrible Demetriou man. Unfortunately for Melody, my mother knows all about bad men. And she loves her son. If she thinks she'll sway my mother, she has another thing coming. Mamá's gaze darts my way, a pained expression on her face.

Enough.

I stalk over to them and Mamá's face brightens. Melody is polite enough to end whatever line of conversation she initiated.

"Would you know I forgot my gift for Talia in the car?" Mamá says, her features tight. "I'm going to just run out and grab it real quick before dinner begins."

"What about my present?" I tease, smiling at her.

She laughs and kisses my cheek. "You're spoiled, son."

As soon as she rushes off, Melody clutches my bicep. "Kostas."

"Yes?"

"It's not too late." Her lips purse together.

Irritation burns in my gut. "Not too late for what?"

"To back out of this," she utters. "You have to know you're making a mistake."

I grit my teeth. "We both know what this marriage is."

"Yes," she bites back. "Punishment against my ex-husband for screwing your family over." She lets out a heavy sigh. "Please, Kostas, I know you're a good man. Don't make her the consequence of her father's actions."

Stepping away from her, I shake my head. "Sorry, Melody, but I'm not a good man. I'm marrying your daughter and it'd be in your best interest not to intervene."

I walk away without saying another word to her.

When Mamá gets back, we're going to need to have a chat.

I'm just seeking out Talia when someone clears their throat.

"Good evening, everyone, your table is now ready," Vince, the restaurant manager, announces. He opens the doors leading to the private dining room, and everyone herds in like cattle. My cousins, aunts, and uncles all find a seat on one side of the table, along with my brother. Father sits at the head of the table, and Mamá, who has just now returned, sits to his left, next to Aris. I notice that Niles and Phoenix are wisely standing away from the table, waiting to be asked to join.

Talia practically clings to her mother and stepfather while her grandparents remain polite and stoic beside them, on the other side of the table. I've allowed her to avoid me by riding with them from the chapel to the restaurant, but I'm done playing gracious host. I want my woman at my side. Where she belongs.

"Talia, come," I bark out, making her jolt and her stepfather glower at me. "It's time to make some toasts."

She grimaces but doesn't argue. I hold my hand out and wait for her to take it. A server walks by and begins handing out glasses of our house chardonnay. I release her hand so we can each take a glass.

"You can't hide from me forever," I taunt lowly, pressing a kiss to the top of her head.

"I'm not hiding. I was spending time with my mom. You should try it sometime."

I wince at her low blow, darting my gaze over to Mamá. Aris seems concerned as well, which has my nerves ratcheting up. When I catch my mother's gaze, I expect to see her eyes light up like usual. Instead, she tears up and looks away.

What the fuck? Is it possible she's really that upset over what Melody might've told her? She knows the score, and while she might've thought Talia and I are marrying for love, deep down she has to know nothing we do is without motive.

"Did you say something to upset her?" I demand, turning to look at Talia. Maybe it wasn't Melody, but Talia who upset her. She's gotten close to Mamá this week. If she's using her to punish me, she *will* regret it.

She seems offended because she huffs. "No, if anything, I've done the best job of convincing that poor woman that I'm madly in love with you."

"Obviously not convincing enough," I mutter, sliding my palm to her cheek. "Maybe you should practice." I press my lips to hers in a slightly provocative kiss meant to serve three purposes.

Piss off her family.

Make my mother happy.

And remind both Talia and Aris I'm the fucking fiancé.

Talia grips one lapel of my suit jacket and starts to pull away, on the verge of saying something. I deepen the kiss, lashing out at her tongue with mine. My free palm slides to her ass and I give it a little squeeze before breaking away. She shoots me a flustered, go to hell look, before draining her chardonnay. I chuckle and sip mine, assessing to see if our kiss did what it was intended.

Her family is pissed. In fact, I'd say her brother and step-father would love to take turns pummeling my ass. And Aris looks jealous as fuck. Good. But my mother?

Hot tears roll down her cheeks as she shakes her head at me. Her bottom lip trembles. What the fuck? Is she ill? What have I done to upset her? And then her gaze darts over to Melody, confirming my suspicions. Meddling bitch. I'll have to remind her she has a reason to keep her mouth shut. I know she doesn't want her daughter to pay for her sins. Poor girl is already in a life sentence from her father.

"The toast?" Father urges, from the head of table looking regal as a king. "We're all waiting."

I clench my jaw and motion for Niles and Phoenix to join the table. Phoenix sits beside his mother in Talia's vacated seat with his father beside him. The weak Nikolaides all sitting in a row are fucking pathetic.

You're marrying one, asshole.

And she'll become a Demetriou.

Demetrious are not fucking pathetic.

"Tomorrow, Talia and I will become one," I say with a smile. "I'm sure the wedding will be a beautiful, extravagant affair because my mother has the magical touch when it comes to these things." I implore my mother to look at me, but she remains staring at her lap. Unease coils in my gut, but I continue. "I'm looking forward to marrying the most exquisite prize in all of Greece."

That jab is for Niles.

A jab that makes my mother flinch.

Fuck.

Talia grips my bicep and shoots me a stern look. As

though she disapproves of my speech. But I can't help and agree with her. My mother is disgusted with me.

"I…" I trail off, unable to find the right words. Nothing is genuine because this entire thing is a fraud. Sure, I'm getting the good end of the deal, wrangling a hot-ass wife, but it's not real. And my mother knows it. Either she heard it from Melody or she can sense it. Either way she knows. This isn't some business that gets taken care of in a dank cellar with a sharp knife—business my mother never has to see. No, this business is infiltrating our personal lives. Her life.

"We just want to thank you all for coming," Talia says, saving me from utter humiliation. "Nora and I have tirelessly planned a gorgeous wedding. I'm thrilled to wear the loveliest gown to ever be created. Marrying Kostas will be quite the adventure, I am sure. Here's to adventures and new memories."

Everyone but my mother raises their glass. Since Talia's glass is empty, I hand her mine before stalking over to Mamá. I grip my mother's shoulder and lean down.

"Everything okay?" I demand, shooting Aris a worried look.

She reaches up to grab my hand and then takes my brother's hand with her other. "Just feeling a little emotional. I love you boys very much. Not a second of regret when it comes to my love for you both."

O-fucking-kay.

"We love you too, Mamá," Aris and I both say in unison.

"Good," she chokes out. "Make sure you keep on loving those who deserve it, so you don't end up like your father."

Talia's eyes meet mine from across the table where she must choose to sit beside her father or mine. In the end, her hatred over what her father has done to her wins out because she sits directly across from my mother, at my father's side. Weirded out by the whole thing, I walk back over to her and take my seat between the slimy Nikolaides and the beautiful one who'll shed that last name soon. The servers begin bringing out food. My stomach is in knots. I busy myself with a Mediterranean salad, stirring it up to coat each piece of lettuce with the dressing. Everyone is talking loudly and the restaurant buzzes with voices and laughter.

Glancing up at my mother, I realize she's left the table to stand directly behind my father. She rests a hand on his shoulder.

"Everyone," Mamá calls out. "I'd like to say something."

A polite hush falls across the table. I meet Aris's stare and he's getting the same weird-ass vibe from our mother because he's tense as fuck. Father stares directly ahead, the amusement gone from his face.

"I have something to say, and it will be in everyone's best interest to let me say it. Understood?" Mamá's eyes are slightly wild. She's normally serene and calm. Currently, she's in a manic state. Her body trembles and her face is red. Sweat beads at her temples and above her upper lip.

"Mamá," I start, but she cuts me off with a sharp look I remember from my childhood.

"Especially you, my son. You need to hear what I have to say the most."

I stiffen and slide my gaze to my father. His nostrils flare, but he remains tightlipped. Since when does my father not put my mother in her place if it means she'll embarrass him. Since he's not coming to my aid, I simply nod at her.

"You know," she says bitterly, "when I saw this beautiful woman who was to marry my son, I was thrilled. Beyond thrilled. I thought, perhaps, my boy had enough of me in him to break the horrible Demetriou curse. To be anyone but his father."

"Mamá," Aris mutters.

She shakes her head at him. "Let. Me. Finish."

Talia of all people should enjoy this and be gloating, but she's tense beside me.

"I thought things were changing for our family," Mamá says, tears welling in her eyes. "I thought we'd moved past all the hate from our past, Ezio." She edges closer to my father, patting his shoulder and making his eyes widen. "But you didn't forget the affair, did you? No, you held onto that revenge and waited all these years to get back at me."

What?

I glower at my father, who won't even look at me. Again, I'm in the fucking dark and I hate it. Aris shoots me a confused look.

"Father," I growl. "Shut this down. Now."

"Your father won't say a goddamn thing, Kostas," my mother bellows and waves a gun in the air before pushing it against my father's back.

Fuck.

No wonder he's being quiet. She's holding him at gunpoint.

"Your father tortured me for years, Kostas," Mamá explains, the tears rolling down her cheeks and ruining her makeup. "Years. While you looked up to your father and wanted to be just like him, I hated him with every ounce of my being. I stayed for my boys."

"You stayed because you had to," Father growls, consequences be damned.

Mamá pushes the gun harder against his back. "I stayed for those boys," she hisses. "Don't think for a second you had me chained to you out of fear. I don't fear you, Ezio, I hate you."

A warm hand slides into mine and I realize it's Talia offering me comfort. Her of all people. My hand is cold in hers. I can't bring myself to squeeze it back. I certainly don't pull the fuck away, though.

"I am so sorry," Mamá says, turning her attention to Melody. "I was in love with Niles for over a decade, and selfishly, I hoped I could escape from my cold marriage and into the warmth of his arms indefinitely. I didn't think about what it did to your family and your marriage. Please forgive me."

It all makes fucking sense now.

"Nothing to forgive. I have Stefano now," Melody says politely, a tremble in her voice. The woman who stole her husband has a gun. I'd be polite too.

Mamá turns her animosity on Niles. "You used me," she chokes out. "I loved you and you used me. When it came down to it, and I was ready to run off with you, you abandoned me. You allowed Ezio to find out about the affair and then you left me to deal with the aftermath alone." Mamá swipes a tear away. "He was cruel to me, Niles. He hurt me and belittled me. He punished me—alone—for crimes we committed together. And yet I took it all for my sons and for the love I still held onto for you."

"You weren't the only one punished," Niles argues like the stupid fucking fool he is. "I'm broke because of you." Being broke is going to be the least of his concerns if he doesn't shut his fucking mouth.

I catch Adrian's stare from across the room as he slowly inches closer and closer. I'm caught between wanting him to stop my mother and telling him to back the fuck away from her. Adrian is loyal to the Demetriou men, not the women.

"Talia," Mamá says sadly, ignoring Niles. "I'm so sorry. I hoped it was a coincidence when I discovered you and Kostas were to be married. My past was a shadow that was creeping up on you, ready to shroud you in darkness as well." Mamá looks pointedly at me. "Don't give up on true love. If you find it, take it, and get the hell out of here, consequences be damned."

A mixture of shame and fury rushes through my veins. Talia squeezes my hand again, and this time, I thread my fingers with hers.

"Mamá, may I speak?" I demand in a low, deadly tone.

She shakes her head. "No, you may not. You will sit and listen to every word I have to say."

I'm not a child and yet she's treating me like one. I glance at Aris, expecting a satisfied smirk on his face, but he's furious too.

"Kostas, you can't turn out like him. Your father is a monster. I know you have enough good in you that you can do better than that," Mamá chokes out, her voice pleading. "Aris will be fine. He's like me. Not so hard around the edges, but it's you I worry about. I worry you'll destroy this poor, sweet girl like your father destroyed me."

"Mamá," I snap, losing my cool. "That's enough."

Talia leans in, her shoulder brushing mine. "Kostas, calm down," she whispers, looking up at me. "She has a gun. Just let her say what she has to say. It'll all be over soon."

Absently, I kiss her lips and nod before looking at my mother. Mamá stares at me, her eyes empty and her features tired. She ages ten years before us.

"Talia and you both deserve more than this," Mamá says, her voice devoid of emotion. "You deserve to make your own choices about love, not be forced into it because of the actions of your parents." She regards Aris with a soft look that used to bother me when we were kids because I assumed it meant he was her favorite. "Aris, my boy, I'm sorry if I inadvertently hurt you by my actions. Your father enjoyed punishing me, and unfortunately, you were too much like me."

Aris clenches his jaw and his eyes glass over with tears.

"And, Kostas, my boy," Mamá utters, her eyes still soft as she regards me. "I'm sorry if I've embarrassed you or hurt you. I love you and your brother both. Equally. I always have."

Talia squeezes my hand again, a reminder that even though we're on different teams in this shit show, she's offering her support. Confusing emotions war within me, but gratitude that she can put down our differences to comfort me wins over. Maybe this marriage will work out after all. Mamá has said her piece and embarrassed the shit out of everyone. Now, we can get back to dinner and Mamá can take a Valium.

"It's time to put an end to this," Mamá utters. "And the only way to do that is to eliminate the person who is the root cause of everyone's pain."

Pop!

Father's eyes widen as his chest blooms red.

"Mamá!" I roar, rising to my feet as Aris does.

Adrian rushes forward and several women at the table scream in horror. I'm already stalking to my mother when she mouths, "I'm sorry," before sliding the barrel of the gun between her lips. My eyes slam shut at the same time another pop is heard. Chaos ensues around us. When I reopen my eyes, my mother lies on the floor, a large pool of blood already forming around her head.

No.

No. No. Fucking no.

Something hot trickles down my cheek and I hastily swipe it away. Aris slides across the floor on his knees to pull Mamá into his arms. Her brain is blown across the wall. She's fucking dead. I turn away from the horror scene and catch Talia's horrified stare. When I see Talia's grandfather, Emilio, and Adrian hovering over my father, speaking in low, calming tones, I realize he's not dead. Yet.

"Father," I choke out, rushing over to him and kneeling.

His face is pale. Adrian holds a dinner napkin to the wound to staunch the bleeding where the bullet came through his chest. I grab my father's hand, another hot tear leaking from my eye.

"Father, don't leave me too."

He flutters his eyelids, but he doesn't close them. No, he locks his gaze with mine, harnessing his inner Demetriou strength, and holds on.

"Stay with me, *Patéras*," I plead, sounding every bit like his little boy. "Just fucking stay with me."

"An ambulance is on the way," someone shouts.

"Get everyone out of here," Emilio barks out to Stefano. "Now."

The room empties out save for the ones trying to keep my father alive and the ones sobbing over my mother's death.

My only focus is my father.

I won't lose them both.

chapter
thirteen

Talia

THE VISUAL OF NORA PLACING THE GUN INTO HER mouth and pulling the trigger is imbedded in my brain. Everywhere I look, all I can see is crimson. There was so much blood everywhere. The walls and the floor were all streaked with red. I've seen people shot on shows, and every time it's gory, but I had assumed it was done like that for show. To make everyone cringe. I never imagined, in real life, one gunshot could create so much red. So much blood.

I stood frozen in place, watching as Aris held his lifeless mother in his arms the same way my mom would hold me when I would scrape my knee from falling off my bike. He brushed her hair off her face, not caring that it was mangled and bloody. Almost unrecognizable. Begging her to wake up. Pleading with God to bring her back.

Kostas focused on his father, who was hanging on by a thread. He barked out orders. None of them made any sense, but it didn't matter. Kostas just needed to feel in control in a situation that was completely out of his control.

I wasn't sure who to go to. Before that moment, going to Kostas wouldn't have even been an option. The only thing I wanted to do was run from him. But as I watched the drops of grief race down his face, all I wanted to do was hold him. Tell him, even though it was a lie, that everything would be okay.

At the same time, I knew Aris needed someone. He was clutching his mother's body like she was his lifeline, and I wasn't sure he would be able to let her go on his own.

But before I could decide who to go to, my grandfather took control, demanding everyone leave. He ushered us out the door, and Phoenix walked us to the room my mom and stepdad were staying in. It wasn't until we were inside, with the door closed, and the silence overtook, that I realized I was trembling. Mom pulled me into her arms and held me while I cried into her chest. I cried for the two boys who lost their mother. For the woman who felt she had no choice but to take her own life. I didn't know her well, but from the short time we spent together, I know she loved her sons more than life itself. And when the tears began to slow, and it felt as if my tear ducts were drying out, my sadness began to turn into anger. And that was when everything Nora said hit me like a wrecking ball.

"Niles cheated on you," I say to Mom, sitting up. Her body stills, and her arms tighten around me. "He cheated on you with Kostas's mom."

My glossy eyes meet hers, and she nods once. "I didn't know it was her, though." Her voice chokes up. "It's all my fault." A waterfall of tears falls down her cheeks. "I approached Nora and begged her to speak to her husband."

A knot forms in the pit of my stomach. "About what?" I ask, but I already know the answer.

"To try to make him see reason. To stop you and Kostas from marrying." A sob breaks through, past her lips. "I didn't know she didn't know you two weren't really in love. I'm the reason she was so upset."

Oh, no. It's not my mom's fault. I should've told her. It didn't even cross my mind she would approach Nora about it. Now, though, it all makes sense. She told Nora the real reason why Kostas and I are marrying and it broke her. It broke her because our marriage wasn't just a debt to be paid. It was revenge. It was personal. Because Niles couldn't remain faithful to his wife! Because he couldn't be satisfied with what he had right in front of him. My mom wasn't enough. My brother and I weren't enough. Nothing is ever fucking enough for him. It's why he is where he is. He's a greedy, selfish asshole.

"It's not your fault," I say, trying to soothe her.

"I approached Kostas too," she adds, and the small hairs on the back of my neck rise. "I begged him not to make you marry him. He warned me not to interfere…"

"You were just trying to be a good mom," I tell her, but even as I speak the words, I know Kostas isn't going to agree. The minute he calms down and thinks, he's going to put two and two together, and he's going to want revenge. Just like his father. And when it happens, my mom can't be here.

"You need to go back to Italy," I blurt out.

Her brows knit in confusion. "With you?"

"No." I shake my head. "You need to go. Now. If Kostas finds out you were the one who told Nora about our wedding being a sham, he's going to go after you. He thought I said something to her and he was livid." I stand abruptly. "You need to go. Take Nonna and get on the first flight out."

I look around, realizing Stefano isn't here. "Call Stefano and tell him you guys need to leave."

"Talia," Mom pleads. "I can't just leave you here."

"Yes, you can, and you will. I can't risk Kostas hurting you. Please." Needing her to leave right away, I grab the bags the driver left in the corner of the room and roll them to the door. "Nonna!" I call out. With everything that happened, she lay down for a nap when we got here. "Nonna, wake up!"

My hands are shaking, and my legs are trembling in fear. I've seen what my fiancé is capable of, and I don't doubt for a second he won't hesitate to torture and kill my mom if he believes she's the reason his mother shot herself.

As I'm helping my grandmother to her feet, Stefano and Nonno walk in. They both have blood on their clothes and frowns on their faces. Without waiting for them to speak, I rush over to them. "You have to leave."

Both men look at me in confusion, and Nonno speaks. "What's going on?"

I quickly explain to them what my mom said to Nora and Kostas, and my grandfather agrees it's best for them to put distance between them. "He left in the ambulance with his father," Nonno says. "I imagine he'll be there for some time."

"What about Aris?" I ask.

"The police forced him to let go of her and he took off," Stefano says.

Oh, God! Poor Aris. I need to find him.

After wrapping my mom up in a tight hug and telling her to call me once she's home, I see them out and then head over to Aris's villa to find out if he went there.

After banging on the door several times and no one answering, I begin my search of the property. I check the tiki bar to see if he came here for a drink but don't find him. I dial his cell number, but he doesn't pick up. Maybe he went to the hospital…I call Kostas, but he doesn't pick up either. I spend the next couple hours combing through every inch of the hotel. The restaurants, the bars, the pools. I go by his office, but nobody's there. I check the parking garage and see his car is there, so he has to be somewhere.

Before giving up and heading home, I try his place one more time. "Aris!" I shout, banging on the door. "If you're in there, please open up. I just want to make sure…" I stop myself before I finish my sentence. Of course he isn't okay. His mom just killed herself. His father, who she blamed, was shot. He's the furthest thing from being okay. "Aris, please." I pound on the door, refusing to give up. What if he's hurt himself?

Finally the door swings open and Aris stumbles out slightly. "Talia," he slurs. The blood from his mother is still covering his entire front. "Sweet, sweet Talia." He smirks, but it's not playful. It's sad and despondent.

"Oh, Aris." I pull him into a hug, and it's then I notice he's holding a bottle of liquor. It drops to the floor with a bang, and liquid sloshes out, spraying my feet. "Let's get you cleaned up."

"She's…she's dead," Aris whispers. His mouth is so close to my ear, I can feel and smell his cool, liquor-covered breath.

"I know. I know," I tell him, having no clue what to say. Nothing I say is going to make this better. He's just lost both his parents. His mother literally, and his father…how will he ever get past it, knowing his father is why she killed herself?

"C'mon." I wrap my arm around Aris's waist and help him walk to the bathroom, so I can get him into the shower and clean him up. I let go of him momentarily to turn on the water, and he slumps against the wall, his body sliding down into a heap on the floor. His eyes close, and his head bangs against the wall.

"She's dead," he murmurs.

"Here, let me help you," I tell him, needing to get his crimson-stained clothes off him. His eyes are still closed as he extends each arm so I can pull his suit jacket off. Next, I unbutton his shirt, then peel it from his body. His limbs are limp, and his breathing is almost nonexistent. "Aris," I whisper, needing to know he's still awake. His brown eyes open. His lids are hooded over, and his pupils are slightly dilated. He looks devastated and lost, and my heart breaks for him. I can't imagine losing my mom, let alone watching her kill herself.

Reaching out, he pushes several strands of my hair out of my face and whispers, "She's gone."

"I know. I'm so sorry." I yank each of his loafers off his feet, then pull his socks off. "I need you to stand so we can get your pants off." The front of his pants, where he laid his mother's head in his lap, is drenched through from the blood.

Aris swallows thickly, and his Adam's apple bobs slightly. His eyes gloss over, and he nods once but doesn't make any move to get up. Kneeling in front of him, I position my hands under each armpit and attempt to lift him. He's too heavy and doesn't budge. "Aris, please," I beg. This time when he nods, he presses his hands against the marbled floor and stands. He's shaky on his feet, but he remains standing while I unbutton and unzip his pants. I push them down and consider removing his briefs but don't want to go there.

"The water is warm and will feel good," I tell him as I guide him into the walk-in shower. The water rains down on his face and back, dripping down his body. The clear liquid turns red as it circles the drain and empties. I'm about to go find him a towel, when his hands grip my hips and he pulls me into the shower with him.

"Aris…" I begin, but he stumbles forward, pushing me against the shower wall. His face finds the crook of my neck and he nuzzles into it. The only sound is the water hitting the marble. For a second I think maybe Aris has passed out standing up, but then I feel it. His body trembling against mine. His shoulders shaking up and down. He's crying. I don't know what to do or say, so I do the only thing I can do. I wrap my arms around his torso and I hold him tight as his silent sobs rack his body. We stay like this until the water turns cold, and then Aris lifts his head.

"Let me grab us a towel," I tell him, turning the water off. I find a couple towels under his sink and snag them. I hand one to him and keep one for myself. Without caring that I'm in the room, he pushes his briefs down and wraps his towel around his waist. Diverting my eyes, I say, "I'm going to get these wet clothes off. Can I borrow some clothes?"

"Yeah." He nods once and steps out. "I'll leave them for you on the bed."

After stripping out of my wet clothes and wringing them out in the sink, I wrap the towel around me and then walk into Aris's room. He's in there, still in his towel. He's sitting on the edge of his bed with his head bowed and his face in his hands. I've never felt so helpless.

"Hey." I step in front of him, and he lifts his head slightly. "I don't know what to say," I admit. "Do you want me to take you to the hospital? I think that's where Kostas is…"

Aris's eyes bulge out of their sockets and then form into thin slits. "He killed her," he hisses. Of course he blames his father. I don't blame him. Everything she said. She might as well have handed Ezio the gun. "No, I don't want to go to the fucking hospital, and you shouldn't either." He glares at me, and his hands grip my forearms.

"It should've been him, not her," he sneers. "He should be fucking dead."

"I know," I agree. "I hate this for you." My cell phone rings out somewhere in the villa. "Let me go grab that. It could be Kostas."

"Kostas?" Aris spits. "Who fucking cares?" We're both silent for a minute and then Aris says, "You're not thinking of still marrying him, are you?" He stands from the bed, now towering over me.

"It's…it's not up to me," I tell him. He knows this. He knows I'm being forced. He was there when my fate was sealed.

"That was before!" he roars. "Everything has fucking changed." He stalks toward me and I back up, my lower back hitting the edge of the dresser. I wince in pain. "You can't marry him, Talia! Didn't you hear my mother's dying wishes? To you? To me? To Kostas?"

"I know." I nod emphatically. He's starting to scare me. His chest is heaving in anger, and I'm trapped between him and the dresser. My phone continues to ring, but I can't answer it because it's in the other room. "I know what she said," I tell him softly, hoping to calm him. "And I want to give her what she asked. But in order to do that, I'm going to have to talk to Kostas. That might be him calling."

Aris flinches at Kostas's name. "He's not going to listen. He always does what our father says. He's going to make you marry him. And then my father will get what he wanted. You can't marry him. You can't." He shakes his head. His eyes bore into mine, and he almost appears to be possessed. My hands shake at my sides. I need to figure a way to get to my phone, or get out of here. Something's not right. Something is off.

"I understand," I say to Aris to placate him, "I will—"

Aris cuts me off. "No, there's nothing you can do. There's only one way to stop Kostas. There's only one reason he would call off this wedding." His eyes rake down my body, stopping when they get to the knot holding my towel together. Reaching forward, he tugs on it enough to loosen it, but not enough to make it fall. "If you're tainted…then he won't want you, and my dad won't get his way."

"Then I'm as good as dead too," I choke out, pushing at his chest. "You know that."

Another sob makes his entire body shake. "Fuck, Talia, I'm sorry."

Relaxing in his arms, I gently hug him. "It's okay."

"He doesn't deserve you," he murmurs, his breath hot against my ear. "He doesn't deserve you."

A shiver runs down my spine when his lips latch onto the side of my neck. He sucks on my flesh in a reverent way. My towel slides down, exposing my breasts.

"Aris," I whisper. "Aris, stop."

He pulls away enough to look me right in the eye. His are bloodshot from crying and drinking. Before I can grab the towel, his lips crash to mine in a demanding kiss. I abandon trying to keep the towel on in an effort to push him away. Turning my head, I manage to break the kiss.

"Aris," I whimper. "Please—"

His grip finds my jaw as he guides my face back to his, attacking my lips once more and silencing me. As he kisses me, all I can think about is how bad this is. If Kostas finds out his brother was kissing me, it's not going to end well for me.

He'll kill me.

My thought has me frozen in fear. Distracted. Worried. Confused. Hot skin against my own has me crying out in shock.

Holy shit.

Aris is naked and he's rubbing his erection against my stomach. This is bad. Really bad. I have to put a stop to it. My hands find his chest and I push against him to no avail. He's strong. Really strong. Oh God.

Kostas will kill me.

He. Will. Kill. Me.

Aris's strong hands bite into the backs of my thighs as he lifts me. I scream against his mouth as terror floods through me. His mouth consumes mine as he shoves my ass against the dresser.

No. No. No.

I claw my fingers down his chest, trying to stop him. My lips finally break from his and I scream. But that one small moment allows him to nudge the head of his cock between my spread thighs and he thrusts.

One thrust to destroy my world.

Another scream rasps from me as everything spins around me.

Numb. Darkness closes in on me and numbness takes over. Pain tears at me from the inside out while I try desperately to block it out.

He will kill me. Kostas will kill me.

Oh, God.

What have I done?

A loud, ugly sob rattles from me and my body goes limp.

I don't want to die. I don't want to die. I don't want to die.

"You're not going to die," Aris growls, dragging me to the heinous act, making me realize I'm chanting those words.

I squeeze my eyes shut, blocking out the way he drives into me in a painful way. I try to ignore the way he kisses my neck and grips my breast.

This can't last forever.

This. Can't. Last. Forever.

I'm crying so hard I can't breathe. Loud hiccups resound from me and snot runs down my lip. Everything aches, but it's my heart that hurts.

Why did he do this?

Why?

He makes a grunting sound and then heat floods inside me. A burst of elation rushes through me. He's done. He's fucking done.

"You're not going to die," Aris says again, swiping away the snot from my lip with his thumb. "I won't let him hurt you."

His cock softens and he pulls out of me before stumbling over to the bed, falling face first onto it. I stand staring at him, my entire body shaking uncontrollably as his semen runs down my thigh. For far too long, I gape at the man in horror, until his breathing evens out into soft snores, jarring me from my frozen state.

Oh God.

I need to get the hell out of here.

chapter
fourteen

Kostas

BACK AND FORTH.

Back and forth.

My cousin Victoria yammers on the phone loudly to her husband, and I want to tell her to shut the fuck up. Instead, I grit my teeth and continue to pace the floor.

Back and forth.

Back and forth.

She's dead. My mother is dead. I'll never hear her laughter again. See her smile. I'll never be able to tease her about being the favorite son. I'll never again smell her lovely floral perfume scent she's worn since childhood.

I pause my pacing as a violent tremble shakes through me.

"Kos, hon, you okay?" Paulina, my other cousin, asks.

"I'm fine," I growl.

But I'm not fine. Everything is a fucking mess.

I need for my father to be okay. I can't lose both my parents in one day. I'm barely holding on to my sanity, which means Aris has probably gone off the deep end. He was a momma's boy, and he, like me, watched his mother blow her head off right after she shot our fucking father.

Fuck.

Paulina hands me a tissue, but I wave it off, opting to swipe at the rogue tear with the palm of my hand.

I should have pressed Father on the Nikolaides issue. I'd known something was fucking wrong, but I ignored it. I hoped Father would come out and tell me why he was obsessed with making Niles pay.

Revenge.

My mother is a cheater, and he wanted to make them all pay for it.

An ache forms in my stomach. How could I have not seen this? All these years, I thought my mother and father loved each other. Sure, he was an asshole, but he would kiss her and occasionally playfully carry her up the stairs. I took it for face value. I'd never dreamed she hated him and was only staying with him because of us. He spent years tormenting her over this shit.

I want to be angry with him, but I understand his need for revenge. He loved his wife. They had a contract—that's what marriage is after all—to love one another. She was the mother of his children. And she stepped out of the marriage. With Niles fucking Nikolaides of all people. He conned her like he tries to do everyone else.

I'm going to end that motherfucker.

String him up by his goddamn ballsack.

"Kos," Paulina says, "are you sure you're okay?"

"Fucking go away," I snarl. "I just watched my mother blow her fucking brains out. How the hell do you think I'm doing?"

Paulina gapes at me and Victoria quickly ushers her

away from me. I continue my pacing. Father has to be okay. We'll get through this and make a plan to get Niles back.

My blood turns icy.

Melody.

If she'd kept her damn mouth shut, my mother may not have lost it like she did. But she didn't. Melody blabbing to my mother was the catalyst for the events that took place. As soon as I can fucking think clearly, I'll send Adrian to fetch them for me. Melody, her pussy husband, her prissy parents. I'll fucking destroy their entire line in one swoop. Phoenix too. But Niles, I'll save him to torture him slowly.

And Talia?

I stop pacing and retrieve my phone. She's tried to call me. I'm reminded of the way she held my hand at dinner. Hearing her voice might bring me some peace at the moment. I sure as fuck need it.

I dial her back.

It rings and rings and rings.

Did she leave? She better fucking not have.

I'll drag her back kicking and screaming.

She's mine.

"Mr. Demetriou," a doctor calls out, rushing over to me. "I have good news. He's stable. Your father is going to live."

I let out a heavy sigh of relief. "I want to see him. Now."

chapter
fifteen

Talia

WITH NOTHING BUT A TOWEL WRAPPED AROUND my body, I run home. My bare feet trip and stumble over the rocks that have been kicked up onto the pathway, but I don't stop until I'm standing outside my door. With shaky hands, it takes me four tries to get the code right so the door will unlock. The house is pitch-black, and I breathe a sigh of relief that Kostas isn't here.

My first thought is that I need to get *him* off of me. Rid myself of the evidence of what he did. Turning the shower on, I set it to as hot as it can go. I drop the towel and step inside, the steam hitting my senses and allowing me to take my first deep breath. For several minutes I just stand here. I'm not sure if I'm in shock, but I can't find it in me to move. And then I remember why I'm in here. To rid myself of him.

With my mind and body completely numb, I work the soapy loofah over my flesh. Scrubbing. Cleaning. Getting him off me. I scrub my face where he kissed me. My neck where he bit me. I scrub my arms and legs where he grabbed me. But it doesn't feel like it's enough. I scrub and scrub and scrub, but I can still feel him on me, over me, in me.

When I spread my legs and wipe between my thighs, the loofah turns a light shade of pink. And it's then the reality of what he did to me hits me full force. My already shaky hands begin to tremble, and my knees go weak. My body gives out, and I fall into a heap on the floor of the shower as grief pours down my face in a flood of uncontrollable tears that mix with the pink water. I watch as my blood and tears run down into the drain and disappear, reminding me that only a couple short hours ago I was in the shower with *him*. Trying to comfort *him*. Washing the blood off *him*.

How could he do this to me?

He took something from me I can never get back.

Something that wasn't his to take.

It was mine. Mine to give. Mine to share.

And now it's gone, and it feels as though a part of me is gone as well.

I scrub my body until my skin is bright red and hurts to touch. Until the water turns ice-cold and runs clear once again. Until I have no choice but to get out and deal with what he did to me.

Feeling exposed and wanting to hide my body—as if hiding it will make what he did to me any less real—I find a pair of sweatpants and a hoodie and throw them on. When I go back into the bathroom to brush my teeth, I spot the towel on the floor. Needing to get rid of it, *to get rid of the evidence*, I scoop it up and bring it into the bedroom with me. I light the fireplace, not caring that it's nowhere near cold enough to justify having a fire going, and when the room dances with bright reds and oranges, I throw it into the fire. Grabbing the blanket off the bed, I wrap it around my body like a cocoon, then I lie down in front of the fire and watch the fabric burn, until my eyelids can no longer stay open, and I allow myself to shut down.

chapter
sixteen

Kostas

I'VE WATCHED HER SLEEP FITFULLY FOR FUCK KNOWS how long now. Hours maybe. Sometime during the early morning hours when the moon was still out, I left the hospital and came home intent on crashing. The events have worn me the hell out. But finding Talia looking so broken and fragile gave me pause. A frozen sliver in time where everything stilled and elusive peace washed over me.

I don't move.

I don't speak.

I don't do a damn thing except stare at her sleeping form as I sit on the edge of the bed. Her silky blond hair has dried into messy waves and her plump lips pout out as though her dreams are horrible. For her, they probably are. She was dragged into Greece's most ruthless family and forced into a marriage with a monster.

Monsters aren't always as horrible as they seem.

One day, maybe she'll see that.

Like Mamá did?

The thought hollows me out. My mother clearly put on a

show for all of us. A show Father was a star in. I feel betrayed by them both. For my mother stepping out on my father, and for him playing this fucked up game with our lives as payback.

Would Talia eventually come to love me like I thought my mother did my father, or will she feel like she's trapped with a monster, always seeking for a chance to escape?

Irritation churns in my gut.

My instinct is to drag Talia up by her hair, force her to look deep into my eyes, and explain to her that if she even thinks about pulling a stunt like my mother, I'll destroy her in every way possible. The monstrous beast inside me begs to do just that, fueled on betrayal.

But all it takes is a little whimper in her sleep to have me backtracking.

Talia isn't my mom.

And I'm not my dad.

I scrub my palm down my face and let out a huff. I'm still marrying her because that's clearly the play destiny has set for us. It's something my parents and her parents paved the way for. Sure, it was done to us as some sort of punishment, but it doesn't mean we can't take control from here.

Rising from the bed, I make my way over to her and kneel. My fingernails are still caked with my father's blood and a shower is long overdue. But as the sun peeks in through the windows, signaling the start of a new day, I can't help but take action.

Take what's mine.

"Morning," I say, my voice rough from leftover emotion and lack of sleep. "Talia, wake up."

She jolts, a scream of terror ripping from her lips, as she tries to scramble away. I grab her shoulders and pin her down on her back.

"Calm down," I growl. "It's me."

Her lashes flutter and then a mixture of relief and worry swims in her sleepy blue eyes that are bloodshot. "Kostas," she croaks. "You're home."

Something about the way she says home has my chest tightening in response. "I am. We need to shower and get ready. I have a big day planned for us."

She furrows her brows together as she studies me. "Are we going to the hospital?"

"No, *moró mou*, we're getting married. Remember?"

"W-What?" she screeches, sitting up and looking around frantically. "We can't. Your mom just died and your dad is in the hospital. And my parents…" She trails off, more worry flashing in her eyes.

"Your parents what?"

"I sent them away," she breathes.

Smart girl. There's no telling what I'd do to Melody if I saw her right now.

"It'll be better as a private affair." I rise and walk toward my bathroom, shedding soiled clothes along the way. I've just turned on the shower when I sense her nearby.

"Kostas," she whispers, her hand touching my bare back. "Are you sure this is a good idea?"

I swivel around to look at her. Genuine concern gleams in her eyes. Her chin is lifted, and even in her disheveled state, she's beautiful. And mine. Soon, in the eyes of God and the law, legally mine.

"It was always the plan," I remind her, tucking a blond strand behind her ear.

She trembles visibly and curls her arms around her waist. A pitiful look crumples her pretty face. I really am a monster to her. A prison sentence. Torture. I grip her wrist—the hand that wears my ring shining brilliantly—and bring her palm to my bare chest where my heart thunders.

"Feel this?" I rumble, searing my gaze into hers. "This thinks it's a good idea."

Her eyes well with tears, and her bottom lip trembles. "But…"

I lean forward and kiss her soft lips. "There are no buts, Talia. Just the plan. Follow the plan."

A tear snakes down her cheek, making my heart pound harder. Everything in me screams to strip her down and tug her into the shower with me so I can give her a preview of exactly how good of a plan this is. But the utter fear on her face is enough to have me pulling back.

"Go eat some breakfast," I grunt out as I unbuckle my slacks. "We'll leave in an hour."

She bolts from my presence before I even get the words out of my mouth.

As we drive to the church, I expect Talia to argue, or ask me to check on my brother, or beg me not to make her go through with this marriage, but she doesn't. After my shower, she quickly took her own. Then, she fixed her hair and put on makeup before donning a simple, silky white dress I laid out for her. She's being ridiculously compliant, which makes me feel uneasy.

I'd thought about calling Aris, but I know how he is. He was a momma's boy. If I know him, he's gotten wasted, cried his eyes out, and fucked his way into oblivion. His villa is probably destroyed due to one of his tantrums. And with time, he'll get better. I'm not the person to help him out of his sea of grief. I'm treading water as it is. Thank fuck I have Talia as a lifeline, breathing fresh, healing water into me with every breath I take.

She's quiet when we arrive and doesn't pull away when I take her hand before walking inside. I'd called ahead to tell the priest it'd be a private wedding with just the bride and groom. I'm sure news has spread about my mother and he wisely didn't ask. I simply instructed him to be ready for us, not wanting to waste another minute.

Father Nicholas greets us once we're inside the empty cathedral that's already been decorated. Talia's heels clack along the marble floors as we follow him down the center aisle to the altar. Once up front, I take both her hands while Father Nicholas flips through his Bible.

"Ready?" I ask Talia.

A line between her brows deepens. "Not really."

I rub my thumbs over the backs of her hands. "Too bad."

Her nostrils flare, giving me a preview of the fiery woman she can be when she's not overcome by fear of her situation. One day, I'll pull her from her fear that has its steely hold on her, and into my arms, where she can be herself all the time.

One day.

"Okay," Father Nicholas chirps. "And so let us begin…"

As he recites verses from the Bible, I admire Talia's pretty features. Wide, brilliant blue eyes that say so much all at once. A petite, slightly upturned nose that begs to be kissed. It's her lips, though, that always steal the show. Full, naturally dark pink, glistening and parted as though she's desperate to be kissed.

I'm going to kiss you a lot, *moró mou*.

"Talia," Father Nicholas gently urges. "Here's where you state your vows."

Her eyes widen as she gapes at me. "I didn't know we were writing vows."

"It's okay," Father Nicholas says. "Repeat after me."

As he recites words from the Bible that Talia breathlessly repeats, her cheeks blaze red. Shame. I think she might be embarrassed that she didn't come up with her own vows. Not that I expected her to. She's made it clear she thinks this wedding is a sham. I don't hold her responsible for thinking that way. When they finish, I clear my throat.

"Talia, you were born to be a Demetriou. Fate knew it, I know it, and one day you'll know it, too. Too many things over the past decade have happened to lead to this exact moment for us to believe otherwise. At this point, we not only must accept it, but we must embrace it." I pin her with a fierce look that I hope she can feel down to her pretty toes. "I, Kostas Angelo Demetriou, vow to protect you always from yourself, from others, and from me. When you take my name, you take a part of me, and I will treat you as though you are a valued piece of me. The truth you'll come to learn is that I am yours now as much as you are mine. I vow to learn every part of you in hope you'll want to learn every part of me. If you ever lose your way, I vow to find you and guide you back to a place where we can be truly happy. By taking my ring and my name, you're taking me too. We're bound in more ways than either of us can count. For me, it will be until death. And I vow to never let you go, even then."

Tears slide down her red cheeks as she regards me with a mixture of confusion and worry. It makes me want to lick the tears right from her face and vow to her what I'll do to make her scream a little later on. But, alas, Father completes the ceremony by asking us to exchange rings. She seems surprised when he hands her my titanium band that says Demetriou carved along the outside of the band. Inside, it has our initials and today's date. Once she shakily slips my ring on my finger, I place a platinum one beside her massive diamond. Her ring, too, has the same inscriptions.

"By the powers vested in me and God, I now pronounce you Mr. and Mrs. Kostas Demetriou." He smiles at me. "You may now kiss your lovely bride."

Sliding my hands into her silky hair, I grip her and tilt her head back. Her lips part and a gasp escapes her. I brush my lips across hers in a warning kiss a second before I sear her with a claiming kiss. My tongue slides out to lash with hers. Eagerly, I devour her sweet moan of surprise. We kiss with me owning every breath and mewl until I decide we've given this old man enough of a show for today. Besides, I want to spend the entire day with my wife, making her whimper in other ways.

"Come now, wife, it's time to go home."

I hang up with room service and track Talia as she exits the bathroom. Like a good wife, she obeyed me when I told her to put on her swimsuit. Since the wedding, she's not spoken a word to me. It's like she's shut down and closed me out.

Time to open up, *zoí mou. My life.*

While she looks out the window, I quickly change into some swim trunks and then walk over to the door in my room. I open it and grab her hand before guiding her out the back of the villa, to the secluded pool. In one corner of my private yard, beside the outdoor expandable daybed, a man from the hotel staff is setting up a small table with a pitcher of ice water. I give him a nod of my head before walking Talia over to it. The daybed is shaded from the bright sun with a white canopy.

"Thirsty?" I ask, nodding to the pitcher. "They're bringing out food and some proper drinks soon."

She shakes her head. "I'm fine."

But she's not fine. The poor girl is shaking like a leaf despite the hot sun blazing down on us. I take her hand again and guide her to the stairs of the pool.

"What are we doing?" she bites out.

"We're going swimming."

"Obviously. But what are we doing? I thought…you know…"

I step in the cool water and cock my head at her. "That we'd get right to the fucking?"

She scowls at me. "You're an asshole."

"You married me."

Before she can huff and puff any more, I grip her hips and pull her back with me into the chilly water. She screeches, her hands going to my shoulders as though she can climb on top of me to keep from getting wet. A laugh rumbles from me as I dunk us both. When we reemerge, she sputters and gives me the worst go to hell look, which only makes me laugh more.

"What?" I ask innocently. "I prefer a little foreplay before I bed a woman."

"You're disgusting."

I grip her ass in a hard, punishing way as I urge her to wrap her legs around me. Fear once again contorts her features. But, with firm urging, I manage to get her to lock onto me. She's tense and her fingernails dig slightly into my shoulders.

"Relax," I croon, walking her to the edge of the pool. "You don't have to hold on so tight. I won't let you go."

She rolls her eyes, but my taunting her seems to have her losing some of her tension. Once I don't think she'll take off, I gently massage her ass.

"Kostas," she mutters. "What are we doing?" she asks again.

I lift a brow as my gaze travels to her pouty mouth, then give her the same answer I already gave her. "Swimming."

"But why?" she demands. "Your mom…your dad… You have a funeral to plan."

Gritting my teeth, I look past her to where another hotel staff member walks over with a tray of food and begins setting it on our table. "I'm trying to enjoy the moment."

Her wet palm slides to my face as she turns my attention back to her. "It won't make what happened go away."

"No," I agree, stepping closer so that she can feel my erection pressed against her. "But it can freeze time and give me a fucking break."

My harsh words make her flinch. "I'm scared," she whimpers. "I'm scared you'll hurt me."

I press my lips to hers, kissing her softly and in a teasing way. "I'll make it feel good."

She opens her mouth to accept my demanding kiss. I gently grind against her cunt, wanting to tease her in every possible way. A whimper travels through her, more fear than excitement. With a sigh, I pull away and carry her out of the pool. She frowns at me the entire walk over to the daybed. I set her to her feet and then drape a large towel over her.

"Sit," I command.

She rolls her eyes at me but curls up on the daybed. I fill up a plate with meats and olives and cheeses and crackers before handing it to her. Then, I wrap a towel around me and grab another plate. She scoots over and gives me room to sit. A warm breeze tickles around us as we eat in silence.

"I meant what I vowed," I tell her when I finish up my food and set the plate down.

She frowns and hands me her plate. "Why, though?"

"Because marriage, to me, isn't what they told me it had to be." I know I sound like a pouting schoolboy, but I don't care. I make my own destiny, not my father. Not Niles. Me.

A hotel staffer walks over to us with a chilled bottle of chardonnay. He pours us a couple of glasses. I instruct him to bring something a little more stout. I'm going to need it to get through today. After handing Talia her glass, I clink mine to hers.

"To us."

She acts like she wants to say something, but in the end, she utters out, "To us."

We spend the entire day eating, drinking, and swimming. Talia doesn't say much, and frankly, I'm not in the mood to talk. She allows me to touch and kiss her, but always freezes up when she thinks I'll do more.

"You're drunk," I state when she stumbles slightly on the way back to the daybed.

The sun is setting and the breeze has picked up. I smell rain in the air.

"No, I'm not," she sasses as she pours more ouzo into her tumbler. Someone really likes her ouzo.

I climb out of the pool, prowling after her. This time, when I touch her hips, rubbing against her from behind, she doesn't flinch. She simply sucks down her ouzo instead. I pull the drink from her lips, not allowing her to finish, and scoop her into my arms. She lets out a shriek, clawing at me, but then relaxes when I settle us on the daybed.

This time, when we kiss, she puts more effort into it. Her fingers explore my wet chest, and her breaths come out unevenly. Needy almost. I kiss her hard, twisting her until she's pinned down on the cushions. She moans when I kiss along the column of her throat. Another sound of pleasure resounds from her when my lips meet her nipple over her suit. I kiss her and then bite at the hardened nub over the fabric.

"Ohhhh," she cries out, her back arching up.

Taking that as permission, I peel her suit off to the side. She mewls when I lick her bare nipple.

"Kostas."

I smile against her nipple. She's drunk as shit. It's nice seeing her so relaxed, though. Trailing my kisses south, I linger at her belly button for a moment. The thought of filling her up with my kids is thrilling. A possessive need courses through me. She makes a garbled sound when I tug at the strings of her bikini bottoms. With a few short pulls, I reveal her pussy with trimmed, golden-blond hair.

"You smell good," I murmur, inhaling her scent of arousal.

She lifts her hips up. "I do?"

I lick her slit, causing her to groan and her fingers to latch onto my wet hair. "You taste good, too."

"Oh, God," she whispers.

"We left him back at the church," I growl. "It's just us now."

Using my thumbs, I part her lips so I can find all the delicate pink she hides beneath. Suddenly feeling starved despite the fact I've eaten all day, I lick and suck and nip at her sweetness. It doesn't take long before she detonates. Loud, explosive, without warning, like a bomb. I lick at her clit as she rides out her orgasm. When she's down from her high and can't take any more teasing, I kiss my way back up her body.

Her eyes are closed, a serene smile on her face. My pretty, drunk wife. She'll hate herself when she sobers up. Hate that she gave up control to me. I smirk, imagining how her face will turn pink. The same color as her needy cunt.

I pull her to me and drape the towel over me. Within seconds, her soft breathing evens out. My dick aches for attention, but I ignore it for now. I'll wear her down eventually.

It might take some time, but we have the rest of our lives.

She's stuck with me now.

chapter
seventeen

Talia

MY EYES ARE CLOSED, BUT I CAN FEEL THE LIGHT flooding in through the window. I'm no longer outside on the daybed with Kostas. I can feel the cool air in the room. The soft bedding wrapped around my body, and the plush pillows under my head. The last thing I remember was Kostas's mouth on me. Bringing me to orgasm. Making me scream in pleasure. It was the first orgasm I've experienced by the hands—or I guess I should say mouth—of a man. Why was he making me scream in pleasure? And why was I letting him? Oh, God! Because I married him. I'm his wife. I'm Mrs. Freaking Kostas Demetriou.

And he was unusually sweet. The vows he spoke, telling me he's mine as much as I'm his. Promising to protect me until the day he dies and even then after. His eyes when he spoke were warm. Sweet. Determined. Honest. As if he was a different man. Not the monster who kills, but a man capable of loving. *A man I could see myself falling in love with.* My chest tightens at the mere thought. A choked sob escaping past my lips. A throat clears, and my eyes pop open, realizing I'm not alone.

"Good morning, wife," Kostas says, his voice almost sounding playful. He's lying on his side, shirtless, with his hand holding up his head. He looks so normal like this. Like a husband. The thought makes me smile, which has Kostas eyeing me warily.

"We're married," I blurt out, the reality of yesterday hitting me again. I *married* Kostas. I am a Demetriou.

"I was there." He chuckles in amusement and holds up his hand, showing me his wedding band. The one he had engraved to match mine. He reaches over and brushes a strand of hair behind my ear. The gesture is so sweet. So unlike Kostas.

His tongue darts out to wet his lips, and I'm reminded of where that tongue was yesterday. Licking my nipples. My neck. Between my thighs. When my thighs clench together, remembering how good it felt, I feel the dull ache between my legs. The ache that wasn't caused by Kostas's mouth, but by his brother.

A cold sense of dread chases away the surprising warmth I'd been feeling. My heart rate speeds up. When my eyes meet Kostas, he's assessing me closely. I feel too vulnerable under his careful scrutiny. Like if he looks too hard, he'll see the pain that's bubbling beneath the surface. His lips are turned down in a frown. He knows my thoughts have taken a wrong turn. I need to tell him. He needs to know what his brother did to me.

"Kostas," I begin, as he sits up, throwing the blanket off his body, and then stands. For a second, I'm distracted by his hard body. He's in nothing but his boxer briefs, his full body on display. His intricate tattoos. His rock-hard abs. The trail of hair leading downward…

"As much as I'm enjoying the way you're looking at me right now," Kostas says, ending my moment of ogling, "you need to save your *eye-fucking* for later. I need to get going." He shoots me a knowing smirk and then starts for the bathroom. I cringe at the word eye-fucking. The same word he flung at me at the wedding rehearsal.

"Kostas," I yell, flinching when I realize my voice came out louder than I planned. "I need…"

Without looking at me, he says, "Whatever you need will have to wait. I need to get to the hospital to see my dad and plan my mother's funeral."

"Wait!" I shuffle out of the bed and stumble toward him. He turns around in the doorway, his eyes meeting mine. Burning fiercely. He's back to himself. The sweet man from yesterday is gone. The monster is back. He stares at me for a long beat, his eyes narrowing, and his nostrils flaring.

"I need to talk to you," I croak out. *I need to tell you that your brother raped me…please don't cut off my feet and beat me with them.*

"We can talk tonight," he says, his tone final. "Be ready at seven for dinner. We'll talk then."

Knock. Knock. Knock. Knock.

My eyes flutter open when I hear the sound of someone knocking on the front door.

Bang. Bang. Bang. Bang.

The knocking turns into banging. I rush out of bed, worried Kostas might've forgotten his key. But when I swing the door open and see it's Aris standing on the other side,

I remember the door has a damn code, so Kostas can't be locked out.

Shit.

Panic swells up inside me like a tidal wave. Fast. Unexpected. Terrifying.

My heart hammers in my chest as I'm frozen in terror.

"Hmm…in my brother's shirt. Looks like you two have gotten cozy," Aris accuses with a wicked smirk that sends chills up my spine. He grips the bottom of the shirt, tugging on it slightly, and I slap his hand away. I didn't even realize I was wearing Kostas's shirt. He must've put it on me last night after I fell asleep. The last thing I remember wearing is my swimsuit. Before he removed it…

I lift my chin, facing off with the man who raped me, praying I don't burst into tears. I need him to know I'm not afraid of him. The slight wobble in my bottom lip suggests otherwise.

"I figured you would want this back," Aris says. He extends his hand, holding my phone out for me to take, but when I reach out to grab it, he brings it back in. "We need to talk." He steps forward, and I take one back, bumping into the door.

"We can talk out here." I push his chest with enough strength, he's forced to take a step back. There's no way I'm letting him anywhere in my home.

"What's wrong?" he asks, tilting his head to the side slightly. "Are you afraid to be alone with me?"

"Can you blame me?" I glare at him. "The last time we were alone, you—"

Aris cuts me off. "Had sex with you?"

"More like you raped me," I hiss.

His eyes go wide, and he takes a menacing step forward

into my space. He drops his voice low to a frightening growl, as though he fears we might be overheard. "What the fuck did you just say?"

"I said you raped me." I cross my arms over my chest. "Or were you too drunk to remember?"

"Like fucking hell!" he booms, pushing me into the villa and slamming the door behind him. My back hits the table in the foyer, and Aris towers over me. "I don't know what game you're playing at, but I suggest you think twice before you make that kind of accusation."

Accusation?

He's delusional.

Not one bit of what happened was consensual.

"It's not an accusation," I choke out. "It's the truth! And we both know it." This time, I can't keep the tears at bay. They burn my eyes.

Aris's hand comes up, and I flinch, thinking he's going to hit me, but instead he grabs something on the table. A paper crinkles. "You and Kostas got married?" He holds the marriage paperwork Father Nicholas gave us in my face.

"Yes, yesterday," I admit.

Aris drops the paper back onto the table and barks out a humorless laugh. "So, let me get this straight. You fuck me Friday night, and the next day marry my brother. And now you're crying rape?"

"I'm not crying anything. You *did* rape me."

"Do you really believe my *brother* is going to believe that? I'm his flesh and blood. You're a fucking Nikolaides. You're a liar by birth. It's in your blood. You came to my villa to comfort me, we ended up having sex, and now that you're married to Kostas, you want to cry rape, so he doesn't kill you for sleeping with his brother." At his version of what happened, my bones grow cold as fear slides through me. He's right. Kostas isn't going to believe me. I'm my father's daughter. The man who had an affair with his mother.

"I like you, Talia," Aris says. "And I don't want to see you die, so you don't have to worry. I'm not going to tell him what happened between us." He leans in close, until his body is flush against mine, and then he whispers into my ear, "It will be our secret."

A shudder ripples through me. Sharing secrets with this monster is the last thing I want to do, but what choice do I have? If Kostas finds out…

He can't.

He simply can't.

Aris backs up and extends his hand, offering me my phone, but before I can grab it, he drops it onto the table. "Welcome to the family, *sis*."

The moment he leaves, I lock the door behind him, then attach the chain just to be on the safe side. The nerve of that asshole! And to think I thought he was the nice one. The one with a heart. He's nothing more than a wolf in sheep's clothing. At least Kostas owns the monster he is.

Grabbing my cell off the table, I check to see if Kostas has called or texted. He hasn't. He's busy dealing with the shitstorm that's become his life. His father is in the hospital. His mother is dead.

It's only ten in the morning, and we're not meeting for dinner until seven. I glance around the room. It's quiet. Empty. It's only me here. I consider calling my mom, but what would I say? Do I tell her I got married? Will I be able to keep it together enough that she won't know how upset I am about Aris?

Needing to calm the blood that's boiling beneath my

skin, I take a cool shower, taking my time to wash and shave every part of me. My thoughts go to yesterday with Kostas. He could've easily taken advantage of the fact I was drunk, but he didn't. We've yet to consummate our marriage. At one time I would've been dreading it, but now I just want to get it over with. I want to replace the horrid images of Aris with Kostas. I wonder what kind of lover Kostas will be. I assumed he would be rough. Ungentle. But the way he made me feel by the pool was the complete opposite. Maybe I have him all wrong. Maybe he's not the monster I've made him out to be. But then I remember the way he tortured that man for lying. Would he torture me like that if he believes I'm lying about Aris raping me? A body trembling shiver runs down my spine.

Turning off the water, I step out and wrap myself in a towel. It's the same towel from Aris's villa. They all have the same towels. Because they live on the same property. The thought has my heart rate picking up and my chest heaving. I was hoping a shower would calm me, but it only had the opposite effect. Maybe I just need to get out of here. Get some fresh air. It will help me take a deep breath.

After blow drying and straightening my hair, and applying a little bit of makeup, I feel a little more like myself again.

Just as I'm finishing getting dressed, my phone rings. It's my mom. I hit ignore. At the same time, my stomach growls. I consider taking a walk to the restaurant but stop myself. The last thing I need is to run into Aris. Space. We need space. Out of sight, out of mind. Right?

Instead, I place a call to room service and order breakfast and coffee. I glance at my phone again to see if maybe Kostas has texted. He hasn't. It's only eleven o'clock. It's only been an hour. I need to get out of here.

Remembering the patio that Kostas and I passed through to get to the pool yesterday, I head out back. The patio looks out at a beautiful, private flower garden. There are two Adirondack chairs and a matching table. They look untouched. I laugh, imagining Kostas coming out here to lounge out on his day off. Does he even get a day off? I doubt crime organizations have a set of working hours.

Dropping into one of the chairs, I take a deep, calming breath and then dial my mom's number. She answers on the first ring, her frantic voice bringing tears to my eyes.

"Talia!" she screeches. "I've called you so many times, but you haven't answered. Please tell me Kostas hasn't hurt you because of me. I've been so worried!"

"Oh, Mom," I choke out. "I'm okay. I miss you. Kostas hasn't hurt me. I'm sorry I haven't called. A lot has happened. I have so much to tell you."

"Talk to me, *cara mia*. Tell me everything."

"Well, for starters, Kostas and I got married." There's a deafening silence, and for a second I wonder if she's hung up on me. But then I hear a sniffle through the line and I know she's still there. She's crying.

"Don't cry, Mom. Please don't cry."

"I just always thought I would be there when you got married. And I had hoped…with everything that happened, maybe there was a chance he would let you go." She sobs through the phone.

"It's okay," I tell her, realizing I need to hear it myself. "It will be okay."

I hear a rustling in the bushes, and a sudden sense of unease washes over me. Remembering room service will be delivering my breakfast soon, I stand to head inside, when the sound of several branches cracking sounds through the air.

And then a man in a black ski mask is coming at me. With my phone still in my hand—my mom still on the line—my fight or flight instinct kicks into gear. Grabbing the chair, I kick it toward the man. It causes him to momentarily stumble, and it's enough time for me to get inside and lock the doors.

"Mom!" I scream. "Someone is here. I need to call you back." I hear her yelling over the phone, but I hit end and dial Kostas's number. The doorknob on the French doors rattle, and I know it's only a matter of time until the man gets in.

"Talia, I'm going to need to call you back," Kostas says, his voice calm.

"Kostas! Someone is here. He's wearing a mask, and I think he's trying to get to me." The nob begins to turn, and I run to the front door.

"Where are you?" Kostas demands.

"At home! He's trying to come in from the back." I stand against the front door, watching the French doors, when the front door begins to shake, causing me to jump back.

"He's at the front door!"

"There's a gun in my nightstand, Talia. Go grab it! I'm going to call Aris right now. He should be close by."

I sprint into the bedroom and find the gun he mentioned. "No, Kos, I need you! Not him," I cry. "Please come home! Please."

I can't chance going out the front or the back. So instead I find a spot in the corner of the closet to hide, and with Kostas's gun in my hand, I wait.

chapter
eighteen

Kostas

"**I**'M SCARED."

My heart thunders in my chest as I excuse myself from the hospital room where my dad sleeps in a medically induced coma. As I talk to her on speaker, I text my men on the hotel grounds. This ski mask fucker won't touch a hair on her head.

"I know, *zoí mou*, but you're safe," I assure her. "Just stay quiet. Did you do as I told you? The safety is off?"

"I t-think so," she whispers.

"Check it again," I instruct.

"Y-Yes. It's ready to fire."

"Good, now keep it trained on the door. Aim high and for the chest if anyone comes through the door."

Her breathing is erratic. "Are you coming home? Please come home."

The terror in her voice—begging for me—claws inside me. I hate to hear her so terrified. Once the threat is eliminated, whoever thought they could try and hurt my girl will fucking pay.

"I'm coming—"

Pop! Pop! Pop!

It takes me a second to realize the gunshots aren't coming from her end, but here at the hospital. What the fuck?

"Talia, listen to me," I growl. "Hide behind the clothes and shoot anything that comes for you. There's a shooting in the hospital. I need to go."

"Kostas," she sobs.

"I'll be home soon."

Hanging up with her makes my chest ache, but I need to focus. Another shot. I take off running, drawing my H&K .45 from my holster inside my suit jacket. Nurses and employees run toward me, so I head in that direction, passing my father's room door. Two men in suits round the corner holding MP5s. A spray of bullets mows down a handful of people. I slam my back against the wall and retreat into my father's room.

Where the fuck are my men?

Pop! Pop! Pop!

Responding fire to the spray has my heart ratcheting up. My guys are out there. Shouts can be heard. I back up, putting myself between my father and the gunmen. When the door flings open, I shoot.

Pop!

The headshot sends the man flying back and the door closing again. Another loud spray of bullets shatters the door to pieces, but then I hear several pops. Moments later, Adrian flies in, disheveled and breathing heavily. That'll teach him to take a shit break.

"Sir," he barks out. "You okay?"

"Yes," I grunt and check over my father. "So is Father. Did you get them?"

"There were two and they've been eliminated. I've called for more men and the Minister of Public Order. He'll sort it out from his end," he assures me.

Thank fuck Father is friends with Josef, otherwise this shooting at the hospital would look bad on the Demetrious.

"Any word on Basil?" I demand.

Adrian pulls out his phone to check his texts. "Threat has been eliminated. Talia won't open the door, but there are no signs of forced entry into your villa. The men are in Basil's custody."

"Men?"

"The one who was trying to get to Talia was wearing a ski mask. The other two wore suits. They seem like two different operations."

Could be a coincidence. With my father on death's door, it wouldn't take long for our enemies to come up with a plan to try and take out the Demetrious while we were down. Too bad for them, we fight fucking better when we're down.

"Deal with the shitstorm here," I order as I move past him. "I'm going back to the hotel."

I slam my Maserati into park and fly out of the car on one mission. Get to Talia. My men are posted around my villa, angry scowls on their faces. This attack is personal. These people waited until we were weakened by grief and pounced. Lowlife motherfuckers. I'll hunt them all down and make them pay.

After.

Right now, I must console my frightened wife.

I punch in the code on the front door, but the chain is hooked. Good girl. Walking around to the back patio doors, I punch in the code and slip inside. The villa is quiet and I creep through it in case anyone is hiding inside. When I make it to the closet door, I call out her name as I open it.

Bam!

A huge hunk gets blown out of the door, sending me stumbling back.

Bam!

Another blast.

"Talia!" I roar. "It's me, Kostas!"

Bam!

Enough of this shit. I crawl on my knees and yank open the door. Pressed against the far wall with her knees to her chest and the Glock wobbling in her hand is Talia. Crying, terrified, trembling. Her eyes are wild as she aims for me. Not giving her a chance, I pounce on her, grabbing for the gun as she fires again. I wrestle the gun away from her and toss it away. Then, I grab her ankles, dragging her toward me. She screams and kicks until I pin her body with mine. I hold her wrists together with one hand and grip her jaw with the other.

"Look at me," I demand. "It's me."

She blinks away her daze before crumbling. Heavy sobs rack through her. I release her to hug her on the closet floor, nuzzling my nose in her hair that's sweaty. I kiss her cheek and whisper assurances until she calms, no longer crying.

"I almost shot you," she whispers hoarsely. "I'm sorry."

I lift my head to look at her. "You did great, *zoí mou*."

Her fingers find my head and she pulls me closer. Our lips meet in a soft kiss that soon turns ravenous. I bite on her bottom lip and tease her tongue with mine. She whimpers when I nestle on top of her between her thighs and grind against her. My dick is aching to be inside her, but now's not the time. Not when I have to get answers. She claws at my tie and manages to loosen it. Banging can be heard at the front door, but I ignore it for a few more seconds with my wife.

"Mr. Demetriou," Basil bellows. "We heard gunfire. Are you okay?"

I groan, pulling from Talia's lips. "I'm fine," I call out. Aside from the fucking blue balls. "I'll be out in a minute."

My lips meet Talia's once more for a brief kiss. "I need to take care of business."

"What business?"

"Interrogate the man who tried to take you," I snarl.

Her brows furrow. "Like Cy the liar?"

"Probably more intense of an interrogation. Cy was a liar. This motherfucker tried to hurt my wife. It carries a heavier offense."

She nods as though she approves of my monstrous intentions. "I want to come with you."

"It's probably best if you stay and rest."

Tears flood her eyes. "Please don't leave me again."

Fuck.

"Fine," I relent. "Let's get this over with. I have a big fucking PR mess to deal with."

"Your dad?" she croaks.

"Alive. They didn't get to him, but they shot a lot of people at the hospital."

"I'm sorry."

I kiss her once more. "Come on. Let's get this over with."

Once I coaxed Talia out of the closet, I changed out of my suit into something a little more comfortable. A pair of navy shorts and a red T-shirt. No sense in dirtying up one of my good suits. Talia also changed from her dress into something that looked better suited for the beach—a pair of jean shorts and a black tank top. Now, we probably look like a tourist couple who got lost and ended up in a torture cellar.

Lucky for us, we're the torturers and not the other way around.

Three men sit in chairs, tied tight by my men. The one who tried to take Talia has his ski mask sitting in his lap. My men wanted me to know which one should get the most of my attention. This is why I pay them well. They know my preferences.

"Care to sit, *zoí mou*?" I ask, lifting a brow at her, motioning to the sofa where Aris is already seated wearing a hateful scowl.

She shakes her head and reluctantly releases my hand. "I'll stand here."

I kiss her cheek before turning to regard the hunks of shit tied to the chairs. They stink and I want them gone. But I want answers first.

"Names," I bark out. "I want your names."

Nobody responds.

Okay, I suppose we'll do this the hard way.

Walking over to the guy on the far right, I slam my fist into his throat. He gasps and chokes for air, struggling against his restraints. When I pull back my fist, he sputters out a name.

Gio.

"Next," I state in a bored tone.

The middle man, also wearing a suit, scowls at me. His

body tenses as he awaits my blow. I give Basil a hard look and he tosses a knife at me. When I catch it by the hilt, the middle man tenses.

"We both know I'll do whatever it takes to get your fucking name," I growl. "One, two—"

"Jordan," the man barks out, sweat beads racing down his forehead.

Turning my attention to the asshole who tried to take Talia, I give him an expectant look. He trembles like a motherfucking girl at a horror flick. When I'm done with him, he'll be less than a man and there'll be enough blood. I can see where he'd be confused. He must sense my malevolent intentions because he pisses on himself. The middle man, Jordan, curses in disgust.

"P-P-Pauly," the wannabe bitch cries out.

"Okay, P-P-Pauly," I taunt. "Why the fuck were you trying to steal my goddamn wife?"

He sobs. "I fucked up, man."

He fucked up.

This pussy has no motherfucking idea how badly he fucked up.

"Hmmm," is all I say as I approach him.

The man stills when I run the blade along his carotid artery, cutting just deep enough to open his skin. One wrong move and I'll puncture the vein that keeps him alive. He cries out in pain but doesn't move a muscle. Crimson runs quickly from the cut. I take a step back and admire my handiwork.

"I need more of an answer than 'I fucked up' because that's not a fucking answer. I want to know who hired you."

He trembles, his dark eyes darting all around. "Niles Nikolaides," he blurts out.

Talia gasps from nearby. Betrayal cuts deep. I cut fucking

deeper. This motherfucker is about to learn: you mess with a Demetriou and you'll pay the hard way. Talia Demetriou is mine to avenge.

"Niles Nikolaides wanted you to what? Kidnap his daughter and be a hero? I'm sorry," I tell him, shaking my head. "Seems a little out of character for that worm."

"H-He thought with you d-distracted by your f-father, he could sneak in and sneak out with her."

"So he sent a pussy to do his dirty work?" I demand. "A little bitch who pisses himself in the face of true danger? A cunt of a man who thought stealing a Demetriou would make him a tough guy?"

"N-No," he whimpers. "I had other plans. I wasn't going to hurt her. I was g-going to contact you. Return her in exchange f-for more cash and offer up that N-Nikolaides was behind this."

I set my knife in his lap on top of his mask and dig my fingers into his cut. He howls in pain when I rip open his flesh, baring his veins and muscle. "So you thought you could blackmail me, bitch? Is that what you thought? A little Nikolaides errand runner thought he could go toe to fucking toe with me?"

The man screams and squirms in pain. I push my fingers into the meat of his neck, rolling my thumb over his carotid that pulses furiously. His head lolls as he nearly passes out, but when I spit in his face, he jolts awake.

"Apologize to my wife," I snarl, massaging his fat vein.

"I'm s-so sorry," he moans.

"Sorry for what?"

"F-For trying to steal her."

"Tell her you're just a little bitch who couldn't even capture a woman right. Tell her you're a fucking failure. Tell her you're a piece of shit who doesn't deserve to share the same motherfucking air she breathes," I roar, inches from his face.

"I, uh, what was the first part?"

I yank hard on his slippery vein, breaking it like a piece of liquorish. Blood sprays outward in a high arc, and I sidestep it to avoid the mess. I grip his chin and make him look at my wife.

"Talia, he's sorry."

The man twitches and convulses as his life bleeds out of him. Too easy. Too quick. But the fact he's denying me of time with Talia pisses me off.

"Now," I growl, turning toward Jordan. "I want to know why you thought you could try and kill my father. Who fucking sent you?"

Pop! Pop!

Talia screams, pressing her back against the wall. I jerk my head over to my brother, fury rising up inside me.

"What the hell, Aris?" I bark out. "I wasn't done interrogating them!"

Aris's chest heaves and his eyes are wild. "They tried to kill Father. Kostas, they tried to kill our dad." His eyes glisten with tears.

Weak.

Always so fucking weak.

"Find out who they are and who sent them," I snap at him. "And next time you interfere with one of my interrogations, it'll be your last."

He winces at my words. "Shit, man. I'm sorry. I was just so angry."

"Make sure this gets cleaned up," I hiss as I storm past him to Talia. I grab her hand with my blood-soaked one and haul her upstairs. We barely make it out of the groundskeeper's house before she mauls me.

Her lips crush to mine in a breath-stealing kiss. I grab her ass and lift her, carrying her to my car. Pressing her ass to the door, I deepen our kiss, my hands roaming all over her.

"Kostas," she pleads. "I need you."

And right now, I'd love nothing more than to rip her shorts down her tanned thighs, flip her around, and fuck her hard against the side of my Maserati.

But there are cameras and men stationed nearby and I don't fucking share.

I grind my hips against her, loving the sound of her whimper. Trailing kisses from her mouth along her jaw, I find her ear and bite hard enough on her earlobe she moans.

"I'm going to fuck you, *zoí mou*, and soon."

She squirms in my arms, her nails digging into my shoulders. My fingers bite into her ass as I rub against her until her breathing becomes shallow and ragged.

"That's it," I croon. "Come like a good girl and get it out of your system."

Her head tilts back as she lets go. I latch onto her sweaty flesh and suck hard. She convulses with an orgasm simply from being dry humped. I can only imagine how she'll explode when I'm deep inside her needy cunt. As soon as she comes down from her high, I bite her neck hard enough to leave a bruise. On the same spot I just flayed a man. My girl is brave because she slides her fingers into my hair and holds me to her, unafraid. I smile at her growing trust in me before pressing a soft kiss to the bite mark.

"Let's get cleaned up. I owe you a nice dinner."

chapter
nineteen

Talia

I WAKE TO FIND KOSTAS'S SIDE OF OUR BED EMPTY, AND I scramble up, needing to find him. Not wanting to be alone. It's been three days since I was nearly stolen from our back patio and I'm still shaken by the events. Before that day, I never so much as touched a gun, let alone shot one. But that day I not only shot one, but almost killed my husband, who up until recently, I wouldn't have minded being shot. But now, well, things are changing at such a rapid speed, I feel as if my head is spinning and my heart is being pulled in a million directions. When I saw the way Kostas killed the man who tried to take me, two things became clear: Kostas would do everything in his power to keep me safe, and if you fuck him over, he won't hesitate to end your life. I also learned a couple things about Aris down in that cellar: he won't hesitate to shoot, either, and he's a loose cannon. A piece of information I would be stupid to ignore.

"Kostas!" I call out, my heart pumping against my ribcage. For the last few days, since I was almost taken, I haven't allowed Kostas to leave my sight, and surprisingly, he's been extremely patient about it, allowing me to stick to his side without making me feel as though I'm a burden. While he's had his father brought home from the hospital and hired a couple of nurses to care for him while he recovers, I've helped him plan his mother's funeral.

Which is today.

"Kostas!" I call out again, climbing out of bed to find him. He wouldn't have left without me, right? When I hear his commanding tone through the walls, I take a breath of relief, knowing he's here. I round the corner and find him standing in his home office, already dressed in his black suit. I swear the man practically lives in suits. Not that I'm complaining. He looks hot as hell in them.

When he sees me approach, he tilts his chin down, indicating for me to join him, without stopping his conversation. When I get over to his desk, where he's sitting, he pats the top of the oak desk, silently telling me to hop on, so I do. Coyly, I spread my legs wide, placing one foot on each arm of his chair, giving him a full view between my legs. Kostas smirks, knowing exactly what I'm up to. I swear the man has the patience and restraint of a saint. If it weren't for the way he's constantly touching and kissing me, I would have quite the complex by now.

"I will speak to my father and let you know," he tells whoever he's talking to. "Today isn't the day to discuss it." His hands run up my bare thighs and under my silky pajama short bottoms, near where I want him, without actually touching me there. When I scoot closer, trying to trick his hands into touching me, he chuckles under his breath and shakes his head. "Very well. I will see you in a couple hours."

He hangs up and sets his phone down, giving me his undivided attention.

"I got worried when I didn't see you in bed." The corners of my mouth turn down into a frown.

"I'll never be far from you, *zoí mou*." He leans in and captures my mouth with his own. When my arms wrap around his neck, and I pull him closer to me, he breathes out a laugh and backs up. "Not now, *moró mou*. We need to leave soon for the funeral." When my lips purse together in displeasure, he lifts me off the desk and swats my ass. "Go get ready. Now."

Stepping into the limo that's going to take us to the church and cemetery, where the funeral is being held, I'm momentarily taken aback when I see Aris is already in the limo waiting. I should've expected him to be here, but I've made it a point to think about the man as little as possible.

"Talia," Aris says with a wicked smirk. The same smirk I once thought was playful. How could I have been so stupid to believe he was a good guy? A man I could consider a friend?

"Aris," I say dryly, scooting to the other side of the seat.

Kostas slides in next to me and pulls me into his side. The ride there is silent. Kostas is on his phone doing business, and I'm checking out my social media accounts in an attempt to avoid Aris, but to also get caught up with my friends. As I'm scrolling through my newsfeed, I spot a picture of Alex with his arm around a pretty woman. He's grinning from ear-to-ear, and while I should be upset or jealous, I find myself smiling, happy he's having a good time in Chicago.

"Who's that?" Kostas's demanding voice asks. I jump in shock, my phone falling into my lap. I didn't realize he was paying any attention to what I'm doing. "Who. Is. That?" he asks again, his tone telling me he's about three seconds from losing his shit.

"Alex," I admit. "He's still on my social media."

"Do you still talk to him?" he asks, taking the phone from my lap and clicking on the picture.

"No, I haven't talked to anyone except my mom," I tell him, flinching slightly when I mention her. The last thing I want is for her to be on his radar.

"Hmm..." He hands me back my phone. "I don't think it's appropriate for you to have your ex on your social media. It looks bad." In other words, delete him now before I make you.

Remembering Aris is in the car with us, I glance over at him, embarrassed that Kostas is telling me what to do like I'm his puppet. I expect to find him smirking at me, enjoying Kostas giving me shit, but instead I find he has his arms crossed over his chest and his eyes are pointed narrowly at Kostas as if he's silently cursing him. It's no secret they have some weird love-hate relationship going on, but the way he's glowering at his brother looks a hell of a lot more like hate than love.

At the church, Kostas and Aris stand just inside the doors, greeting and thanking everyone for coming as each person walks through and extends their condolences. I stand by Kostas's side as he introduces me to several people as his wife. Some look shocked, but most congratulate us. He explains who some are to me, and others, who I assume aren't important enough in his eyes, he doesn't bother.

When his father arrives, a nurse wheels him up the ramp in his wheelchair and then Kostas takes over, pushing him to the front row, leaving him to sit at the end of the pew. The funeral service is being held in the same church as our wedding. Father Nicholas speaks about love and loss, and the entire time, Kostas's fingers stay intertwined with mine. He doesn't shed a single tear, but I can feel it in the way he squeezes my hand when Father Nicholas talks about her going to heaven, he's barely keeping it together. I can practically feel the sadness radiating off him, and I wonder if, at some point, he's going to finally lose it. In the short time since I've known Kostas he's never once lost it. He's the epitome of put together all the time. Aris, on the other hand, gets so upset, he ends up walking out of the church.

The funeral moves to the cemetery for the burial, and once again, Kostas pushes his father down the sidewalk to the spot where the earth is open and Nora's coffin is waiting to be lowered into the ground. There's a tent set up so everyone can stand in the shade while Father Nicholas says a few more words, and then the casket is lowered.

When Father Nicholas calls on the family to step forward to throw the dirt onto her coffin, Kostas pushes Ezio over and helps him gather a handful of dirt to throw in. Aris and I go next, and then the other family members follow. Everyone circles back around under the tent while Kostas remains in the front with his dad.

Kostas's gaze meets mine, and I try to convey through my gaze how sorry I am for his loss. As if he knows what I'm trying to say, his eyes go a little softer, and the smallest hint of a smile appears.

And then they go dark. And hard. I have no clue what's going on until I feel someone's hot breath at my ear. "I know you married him because you thought you had to…because you're afraid of him."

With my eyes locked on Kostas still, I do my best not to make a scene or show any emotion. I will not let Aris get to me.

"You can't deny we have something. From the moment I saw you in the bar, to the night we fucked…"

My chest heaves at his words, and Kostas's eyes narrow as he pushes his father's wheelchair toward us, his eyes never leaving mine.

"Just because you're married now, doesn't mean we can't explore those feelings. I could make you happier than Kostas ever could," Aris says.

And just when I think he's finally done, he grabs my ass.

Panic rises inside me.

I feel sweaty and dizzy.

I'm thrust back to the night he shoved me against the dresser and took what wasn't his to take. It's difficult to keep my emotions in check.

My lip wobbles slightly, and I pray Kostas doesn't notice.

Leave me alone! I want to scream at him. Push him away. But there are people all around us, and I don't want to cause a scene at Nora's funeral.

Unable to stand this monster's hand on me for another second, my self-preservation wins out. My eyes leave Kostas's and meet Aris's, and my hands comes out, grabbing Aris's hand to remove it off my ass. "What the hell is your problem?" I seethe. "We're at your *mother's* funeral, for God's sake."

Aris simply shrugs a shoulder and smirks, not even bothering to argue. When I scan the area to find Kostas, hoping he didn't see what Aris did, I find him standing directly behind Aris. His fists are clenched at his sides, and his eyes are pointed down at my hand, which is still holding Aris's. Oh, shit!

"Kostas," I begin, unsure how to even explain what he's seeing. But he doesn't give me a chance. Because when Aris spins around to face his brother, Kostas cocks his fist back and clocks Aris directly in the jaw. His head whips to the side, and he stumbles back. The hit is so loud, everyone turns to see what the commotion is.

"You ever put your hands on my wife again, and you will lose them," Kostas roars, his body trembling with rage.

Aris, the instigator he is, just laughs and walks away. It's like he has a death sentence he gleefully awaits.

"Kostas." I step toward him. "Please let me explain."

"Go home," he demands, his eyes cold. "I'll see you when I get there."

"But—"

"Now, Talia," he seethes, and I don't dare to argue.

I nod in understanding, and on shaky feet I walk back to the limo. When I get there, I'm terrified Aris will be in there, waiting, but thankfully he's not. The driver returns me to the hotel, and I head straight back to our villa to wait for Kostas. The entire time I'm waiting for him, I pace the room. Back and forth. Rehearsing what I'm going to say. How I will explain. I'm not sure if he saw Aris grab my butt, or if he just saw what looked like we were holding hands. If he didn't see him grab my butt, I don't want to tattle on Aris. Based on the shit he was word vomiting, he's either seriously delusional or scarily cunning. Either way, the last thing I need is to fuel whatever is motivating him.

An hour later, the door clicks open and in walks Kostas. I stand frozen in place, waiting for him to speak first. His tie is now unknotted, the top several buttons undone, and his hair looks disheveled as if he was running his fingers through it in irritation.

His eyes meet mine, and I look to see which man I'm dealing with. Warm. Sad. Soft. I take in a breath of relief. I can deal with this man. He will see reason.

"I'm sorry about earlier," Kostas says, cupping my cheeks with his hands. My features must convey my confusion over his apology because he adds, "Aris explained that he was only asking if you were okay." He told Kostas he was seeing if I'm okay? What the hell is Aris playing at? "He seems very concerned about you almost being taken." I search his eyes to see if there's any hint of disbelief in them, yet I don't find anything but worry. Wow, Aris is fucking good. And that seriously worries me.

"I shouldn't have punched him," Kostas grumbles. "At least not at our mother's funeral. But as I told him, I don't care what the reason is, he never has the right to touch you in any way. He's lucky the only thing he was doing was holding your hand." His lips descend on mine and he kisses me deeply. "You're mine, *moró mou*. Only mine to touch."

He releases my face and steps around me. "My father was supposed to head over to the other side of the island to handle some business, but because he's out of commission, he's asked me to go. The business will probably take a week." I follow him into our bedroom as he pulls out some luggage from the closet and sets it on the bed.

"You're leaving?" My heart begins to race, and my head goes fuzzy. A heaviness in my chest weighs down on me, and I have to grab the side of the dresser to steady myself.

Kostas is leaving me here.

For a week.

Alone.

No, not alone.

With Aris.

"Kostas, you can't leave me." I cut across the room and grab ahold of his hand, yanking him toward me. "Please," I choke out. "Take me with you." Hot, wet tears fill my lids.

Kostas brows dip low. Still allowing me to hold on to his one hand, he lifts the other to wipe the liquid from my cheeks. "Calm down, *moró mou.* Of course you're coming. You don't really think I'd leave you alone again, do you?"

chapter
twenty

Kostas

THE FARTHER AWAY WE GET FROM AGIOS NIKOLAOS, the lighter I feel. I opted to take my Range Rover versus the Maserati because after the shit that went down a few days ago, there's no way I'd go anywhere without bringing a small arsenal with me. The hour plus drive has flown by because Talia's mindless chatter passes time in the best possible way.

"I think I can see the ocean," Talia says, leaning forward toward the windshield. "Where are we going again?"

"Agia Fotia Beach. And we're close. The cliffside home I reserved is about five minutes away."

She smiles at me. "Will you have to work right away or can we explore?"

"Work can wait until tomorrow." I'm chasing down a lead per my father's request. He's certain Estevan Galanis was behind the attempt on his life. Estevan has been known to hole up in one of the hotels on Agia Fotia Beach when things heat up. I'm about to bring motherfucking hellfire to his doorstep.

She sits back and returns to looking out the window, a pleased smile on her face. I don't think I've ever seen her so relaxed and happy. Getting away is exactly what we both needed.

"Kostas," she chokes out. "Someone's following us."

I glance in the rearview mirror to see a black SUV behind us. "It's Adrian and a few of my men. Basil is holding down the fort back home."

"Oh," she mutters. "Duh. Wherever we go, they go."

Reaching over, I clutch her thigh over her dress. "Not everywhere."

She lets out a breathy laugh before covering my hand with hers. "I can live with that."

Adrian is droning on about the hotel Estevan is staying at and I'm trying to stay focused. It's just Talia has changed into a skimpy bikini and is rooting around in the refrigerator looking for something. Adrian, a wise man, keeps his gaze averted. I, however, can't take my eyes off her ass that's barely covered in the white fabric. When she finds a bottle of water and closes the door with her hip, making her tits jiggle in the tiny triangles, I've had enough.

"Time to go, Adrian," I growl.

"Yes, sir," he responds with a chuckle and slips from the kitchen without another word.

"Can we go swimming now?" Talia asks, her blue eyes flickering with wickedness despite the innocent look she has plastered on her face. As if she didn't just seduce my dick into canceling my meeting to go chase after her fine ass.

"We can," I say as I stand. "I need to change first."

The dirty girl watches me with rapt fascination as I trade my three-piece suit for a swimsuit. It's fucking cute when her cheeks burn bright red when I give her a preview of my dick.

"Keep looking at me like that and we'll never get to swim."

She bites on her bottom lip. Adorable as hell. "I mean, we can swim later."

"Nah, it'll get cool. Let's go down to the ocean before the sun sets."

Grabbing her hand, I guide her out of the small house and down the series of wooden staircases on the side of the cliff. As soon as our feet hit the small round rocks, I inhale the salty air and exhale the past week's worth of stress.

Even villains need a fucking vacation.

Talia kicks off her flip-flops and gingerly runs along the rock-covered beach to the cerulean water. The waves lap at the shore in a soft, rhythmic way. Her blond hair flutters in the wind and she looks over her shoulder, smiling at me. I wish I could capture this moment. Freeze it into a frame to look at when the world is weighing heavily.

She makes me soft.

Inside.

My dick is achingly hard.

But my heart? I'm drawn to her. I want to own and spend hours exploring her. I'm happy as fuck that she's mine now.

"Come on, Kostas," she calls out before turning back to stare at the Mediterranean Sea.

I kick off my boat shoes and prowl after her, the rocks making me wince each time I step on a sharp one. She's already knee-deep in the ocean by the time I make it to her.

"It's warm," she tells me when I wrap my arms around her from behind.

"Want me to make it hotter?"

She laughs, tilting her head to allow me access to her bare neck. I kiss her soft flesh. "By all means, make it hotter."

I nip at her throat as my palms slide to her breasts. Her breath hitches when I pull the tiny triangles of fabric down to reveal her hard nipples. A small moan escapes her when my thumbs run over the hardened nubs.

"It would seem that we're both very hard for one another," I tease as I pinch her nipples and rub my erection against her ass.

"Very," she breathes.

"Your body is practically begging for mine." I bite her neck again. "Don't you think?"

"It is. But you never give in. In a couple of days, if you still haven't, it'll be too late."

I slide a palm down her flat stomach and inch my middle finger down into the fabric of her bikini bottoms. She sucks in a harsh breath of anticipation. Before I go any farther, I find her ear with my mouth.

"Why will it be too late, wife?"

She groans, rubbing her ass against me as if to encourage me. "B-Because."

I slide my finger farther down, just between the lips of her pussy to tease at her clit. "Hmmm?"

"I'll be on my period then," she murmurs. "You can't have sex with me then."

Biting on her earlobe, I sink my finger farther down and push into her soaked opening. A kitten-like mewl purrs from her. Fuck, she's tight around my finger. She's going to strangle my cock.

"You think a little blood scares me off?" I rumble, finger-fucking her in a teasing way.

"I, uh…"

I slide my finger out of her and rub the wet tip over her clit again. Her hips rock in tandem with my movements as she eagerly seeks release.

"What, Mrs. Demetriou? Please enlighten me with your answer."

"It doesn't gross you out?"

"Nothing with you will gross me out. I already wiped away the only gross thing about you when I wed you in that chapel. Your last name. The new one is pretty fucking fabulous if I do say so myself." I suck on her neck and then let go with a loud popping sound. "I'm going to fuck you whenever the need arises, *zoí mou*."

She whimpers when I bring her right into an orgasm. Her body trembles and shakes so much that I have to keep her standing with my free arm. When she finally comes down, I slide my hand from her bottoms and twist her to face me.

"I'm going to fuck you now," I growl.

She blinks rapidly at me. "Now, now?"

I point at the never-ending staircase. "I don't have the energy for that shit right now. I'm going to fuck you on those rocks, Talia. It's going to hurt."

Her brows furrow and she looks away, a slight tremble wracking through her. "Will I bleed again?"

I sense a shift in her mood. True fear practically seeps from her pores. If I find out this Alex fucker hurt her taking her virginity, I'll drag him to my cellar and make him bleed.

"You bled your first time?" I ask, gripping her chin and tilting her face to meet mine.

She blinks away tears and tries to avert her gaze. I keep her pinned so I can study her face. "Y-Yes. My, uh, my first time was painful and traumatic."

I suppress a growl low in my throat. "That first time… did you want it?"

Her head shakes from side to side vehemently. "No, Kostas. I didn't."

Fury swells up inside of me. One day she'll tell me who the motherfucker was who hurt her. "Listen," I say harshly. "If you didn't want it, it doesn't fucking count. Understand? What we're about to do fucking counts. That's your first time. Are we clear?"

Relief floods her features. "But you said it would hurt."

I smile wolfishly at her. "Because I'm going to fuck you on a beach of rocks. Your back is going to be pissed."

"Oh," she utters, a shy smile on her lips.

Grabbing her ass, I pick her up and carry her to a part on the shore where the rocks are smaller and finer. Gently, I lay her back as the ocean laps at our feet. With my eyes searing into hers, I peel away her bottoms, revealing her sweet cunt to me. Once they're gone, I toss them farther up the beach. She unties her bikini top at her neck first and then undoes the one at her back. The moment it loosens, I rid her of that too. I stare at her perfect body, drinking in every tanned curve of her.

"Beautiful," I praise, skimming my palm down her thigh. "Mine."

A sweet smile tugs at her lips. "Your turn, husband."

My dick does a jolt at her words. I untie the top of my trunks and shed them faster than a teenage boy about to get laid for the first time. When I fling them up the beach, she laughs, her tits jiggling in a delicious way.

"Come here, wife," I growl, pouncing on her.

Her laughter fades to uneven breaths as I kiss her hard. My cock rubs against her clit. At first, she's stiff, but the more I rub on her, the more eager for it she is. Her legs gingerly hook around my waist and soon she's digging her heels in, silently begging for it.

"It's not supposed to hurt," I whisper on her supple lips. "It's supposed to feel good."

"I want to feel good," she pleads.

"Are you wet enough?"

She nods rapidly.

"We'll see," I mutter with a wicked grin.

I grip my dick and tease her slick opening. She's more than wet. Her body practically weeps with need. I rub the tip of my dick up and down along her slit from her clit damn near to her asshole. Up and down. Up and down. Up and down.

"Kostas!" she cries out, the need making her fussy.

"Yes, *zoí mou*?"

"I need you."

Her breath sucks in sharply when I press slightly into her. Our eyes meet, and though hers are wild and frantic, they're begging me to erase whatever fuckface who hurt her before. Fucking gladly. I thrust into her deep, loving the way her eyes bulge in shock. My lips meet hers and I kiss her deeply, keeping my hips still so she'll adjust to my size.

I kiss along her cheek to her ear. When I nibble her lobe, her cunt clenches around me.

"Ahhh," I croon against her ear and then nip at her throat. Her body tightens around me once more. "You like being bitten as much as I like to bite. What a match made in hell we are, woman."

I slide my palm to her hip, gripping her tightly. Possessively. I'll never let her go. Not now. Not after I've had her as mine.

One of her hands claws at the rocks as though she's trying to get away, but we both know she loves being in my grip.

"Do you believe Pluto was hurting Proserpina now, my wife?"

"Kostas," she whines.

"He couldn't let her go," I murmur, clutching her hip hard enough it'll certainly bruise. "But he would never hurt her."

"You think?" she chokes out. "You think he loved her?"

"I think she loved him too."

She moans and digs her nails into my shoulders when I thrust hard. Again and again. Her slick juices provide the most delicious lubricant. I want her coming with me, though, and with rocks digging into her spine, I don't know if she'll reach that height by my dick alone. My hand slides between us and I rub at her throbbing clit, loving the way she clenches around me with each rub. It doesn't take long until she's squirming and screaming my name. As soon as she comes, I buck into her wild and hard. When my nuts seize up, I latch onto her neck with my teeth and growl against her flesh as my release floods inside her. My hips flex a few more times until she's milked every ounce of cum from my dick. Feeling boneless, I relax against her and kiss her neck.

"I'm going to have to carry you up those motherfucking stairs, aren't I?"

She laughs, breathless. "That's what good husbands do."

"What if I'm a bad husband?"

"Save being bad for when we make it to the hot tub on the deck. Then you can be the bad husband all you want."

Her fingers thread into my hair, making my softening cock twitch back to life. "Now carry me out into the ocean so we can swim. I have about four hundred rocks that need removing from my ass."

Sassy fucking girl.

chapter
twenty-one

Talia

THE EGGS ARE FRYING IN THE PAN, THE BACON IS sizzling in the oven, and the bread is toasting in the toaster. While I move the eggs from one side of the pan to the other, my eyes are stuck on the window just above the stove. The one that overlooks Agia Fotia Beach. The crystal clear blue water turns darker and darker the farther out it goes until it's the darkest shade of blue-black. Not quite black, but not blue either. The perfect mixture of dark and light.

It reminds me of my life. In Italy, it was the lightest shade of blue. The shallow parts of the ocean, where you can see. Where it's safe. My mom. Alex. School. My friends.

Here, in Crete, I'm swimming in the black waters. The darkest, deepest part. Where you can't see inside the water. Where it's dangerous. Aris. Niles. Ezio.

And then there's Kostas. He's the blue-black. The mixture. Not quite dark, but not light either. He's the part just after the shallow waters, where you step down and are shocked by just how deep it is, but you're still able to stand.

Your head is just above the water, and you can still breathe. It's the best part of the ocean. The water is warm, and you're fully emerged. You're comfortable. Far enough out to make you feel like you're dangerous, but still knowing you're safe.

That's what Kostas does to me. He makes me feel safe.

"Your eggs are burning," a deep, throaty voice says from behind me, bringing me back to what I was doing. Kostas's hands encircle my waist, and his lips find my neck. Nibbling on the sensitive part of my flesh. I find myself leaning into him, soaking up his warmth, his depth. "Good morning," he rasps before stepping back and leaving me alone in the shallow end, where it's cold. I used to like the shallow end. It was safe. Now, I suddenly find myself craving deeper, warmer waters.

Clicking the stove and oven off, I move the pan of eggs off the heat and take the bacon out of the oven. Grabbing the toast out of the toaster, I make us both a plate of food and set them on the table, along with two coffees and orange juice.

"Good morning," I say back.

Kostas finds his seat first, and when I'm about to sit across from him, he grips the curve of my hip and pulls me into his lap.

"Kostas!" I squeal at his playfulness. He situates me so I'm sitting bridal style with my arm around his neck. Taking a forkful of eggs, he brings them to my lips before he takes the fork away and takes the bite of food, moaning dramatically.

"Give me some!" I smack his chest, and he chuckles darkly. The sound does strange things to my body. He piles some more onto his fork and this time slides the fork past my lips.

"I have some business I need to take care of today," he says, taking a piece of bacon and running it along my bottom lip before I take a playful bite, nipping at the tips of his fingers. He growls lowly but also smirks playfully. *The perfect mix of blue-black.*

"How long will you be gone for?" I ask, picking up a piece of bacon and feeding it to him. He takes the entire slice into his mouth like the damn caveman he is.

"I should be back by dinner time. Adrian will be around watching you." He pulls my face toward his and traps my bottom lip between his teeth before he licks across my flesh. "Behave, and I'll take you to dinner when I return."

After cleaning up after breakfast, I throw on my bathing suit, a pair of cut-off jean shorts, and flip-flops, then head down to the beach for a walk. With Kostas renting us this home, the beach we're on is private, cut off from the rest of the world. With the only sound coming from the waves crashing against the shore, it's serene and peaceful. My own little piece of heaven.

Unrolling the towel from the bag I've packed, I lie down on it and pull up my Kindle app on my phone so I can get some reading in. The sky is shining down, and the wind is whipping around my face, calming my heartrate, and before I know it, my eyes are fluttering shut.

Ring. Ring. Ring. Ring.

My eyes pop open, and for a second I forget where I am. That is until I feel the salt sticking to my limbs and remember I'm on the beach in southeast Crete.

Ring. Ring. Ring. Ring.

Grabbing my phone from where I left it next to me, I answer the call without looking to see who it is. "Hello."

"Talia, *cara mia*. How are you? How was the funeral?" My mom. I spoke to her briefly after I was almost taken so she knew I was okay. She cried and begged me to come home, but she knew it wasn't happening. I haven't spoken to her since the funeral, and I know she's concerned about Kostas. More about his reaction than how he's handling his feelings toward his mother's death. I haven't brought my mom up to him, and he hasn't either. I don't know if that's a good or bad thing. Eventually, I'm going to want to visit my mom, or have her visit me, so I imagine I'm going to have to broach the subject and see where he stands, but right now, it's too soon. His wound is still too deep.

"It was okay," I tell her. "Sad, of course. How are you? How's Stefano?"

Mom breathes out a sigh, her telltale sign she's about to tell me something I'm not going to like. "We're okay. But… we…umm…received your bill for your classes for next semester." The classes I signed up for just before I was taken to Crete and told I would be marrying Kostas.

"I'll go online and cancel them," I say, each word getting caught in my throat. "I don't want to waste your money when we know I won't be back." *And I won't be graduating.* Tears of hopelessness fill my eyes.

"I looked online," Mom says. "Did you know there's a college near you in Agios Nikolaos?"

My chest blooms with hope. I didn't even think to look at colleges here. I was too busy fighting off psycho rapists and potential kidnappers.

"I can email you the info," she adds.

"That would be great. Thank you, Mom." I miss her so much. Her hugs and kisses. Her comfort.

We talk for a few minutes about the school, and the more information she gives me, the more I want to check it out. After we hang up, I click on the email she sent and browse the online catalogue. It has all the classes I need to finish my degree. Now it's just a matter of convincing my thick-headed husband to let me go.

And then an idea blooms…

The door slams shut, and I quickly light the candles I found at the market to create a romantic ambiance. Standing, I run my sweaty palms down my tiny black dress—another find at the market—and quickly fluff my hair as I wait for Kostas.

There's a crash and a bang and then a "Fuck!" followed by "Talia! Why the fuck is it so dark in here?" Kostas enters the dining room and stops in his place. The brightness of the candles hit his eyes and I can see the irritation in them. He's had a bad day. And my heart sinks. This isn't going to go over well.

"What's all this for?" he asks, taking in the candles and dinner and me in my dress.

"Surprise." I shrug, attempting to smile even though my nerves are getting the best of me and my entire body is now trembling. "I made you dinner." I lift the metal lid, exposing the chicken parmesan, pasta, and broccoli. Kostas eyes me speculatively but doesn't say a word, sitting in his seat.

"It's Italian," I tell him, taking his lid off, and then filling his glass with an Italian white wine I found.

"It smells good," he says with a small smile. "Thank you."

I sit adjacent to him and we begin eating in silence. When I can't take it anymore, feeling as if this night is going to shit, I break the silence. "How was your day?"

His fork, which was halfway to his mouth, stops, and he sets it down. His jaw ticking. "Talia, what is this all about?" he asks, waving his hand over the table and ignoring my question.

I could lie and tell him this was just my way of being romantic, but something tells me that Kostas will appreciate my truth more than my lie. "I spoke with my mom today," I say, watching his face for any reaction. His hazel eyes go the tiniest bit darker, and his teeth clench together. Both signs he's not a fan of my mom. Both signs it's probably best to keep her out of our conversation for the time being.

"And?" he prompts dryly.

"There's a college—"

"No," he says, cutting me off.

"You didn't even let me finish!" I screech, already losing my patience.

"I don't need to. You're not leaving me, ever. End of conversation."

"Well"—my eyes narrow on his, hitting him with my fiercest glare—"if you would let me finish, I was about to say the college is in Crete."

Kostas's eyes soften a notch, and I take in a deep breath.

"I only have one year of school left. I've already completed three years, and I would really like to finish. It would mean a lot to me."

I wait with bated breath for him to say something. Anything. But when he finally does, I want to reach over the table and choke him.

"We'll see."

We'll see? *We'll see?* Is he freaking serious right now?

"That's what my mom used to tell me when I was a child and she didn't want me to throw a temper tantrum over her telling me no."

Kostas lifts his gaze from his plate, raising his brows slightly, and then goes back to eating, as if that look is the end of the conversation.

"That's it?" I hiss. "You have nothing else to say? Just 'we'll see?'"

Kostas drops his fork onto his plate, and it makes a loud clanging sound that causes me to flinch. "I've had a shit day, and the only thing I want to think about right now is sinking my cock into your tight cunt and getting lost in you. But you made this dinner, so I'm trying to enjoy it so I don't hurt your feelings. So, yes, Talia. 'We'll see' is the only answer you're getting from me right now."

I'm not sure whether to gasp at his dirty words, or swoon over the fact that even after he's had a bad day, and the last thing he wants to do is sit at this table and eat dinner with me, he is just for the sake of my feelings.

Leaning across the table, I blow out the candle, then stand, making my way around the table and extending my hand. "How about we skip the dinner and move onto the dessert?" I hit him with my most dramatic Marilyn Monroe wink, and Kostas grants me the smallest smile.

With our hands entwined, I walk us outside and onto the deck where I've already turned on the hot tub and have the jets and bubbles going. Kostas stands near the edge, eyeing me with lust-filled eyes as I shimmy off my dress, leaving me in only a super-tiny white bikini that *barely* covers the important parts.

"Did you wear that anywhere other than under that dress?" he asks, his lids hooded over. For a brief moment I want to lie and tell him I have, just to see what he'll do, but instead I go for the truth. My goal is to calm him down, not rile him up more.

"Nope, only for you." I saunter over to him, adding a bit more sway in my hips, and he groans lowly, liking what he sees. "Your turn." He's dressed more casual than usual, in a button-down shirt and dress pants. No tie or jacket. And he's barefoot. He must've taken his shoes off at the door.

After removing his shirt and pants, and setting them on the lounge chair, I reach for his briefs. Hooking them around my thumbs, I pull them down slowly, bending with them until my face is eye level to his dick. And holy hell, is it a nice dick. It's the only one I've ever seen—Aris doesn't count because he never gave me the opportunity to take a look before he brutally shoved it inside me—so I have nothing to compare it to. But Kostas's is neatly trimmed and smooth. He's already hard, and a tiny pebble of pre-cum is lingering on the tip of his mushroom head.

According to my Cosmopolitan article online, the key to giving good head is to tease, so that's exactly what I plan to do.

I back up until I'm at the edge of the hot tub, and then I step down inside, taking a few seconds to adjust to the hot water. I pat the edge of the porcelain, indicating for Kostas to join me. Once he's sitting on the edge, with only his feet in the water, I spread his thighs and grip his shaft lightly with my fingers. He watches me intently but doesn't say a word as I lift up until I'm hovering over the top of his dick and then take him all the way into my mouth. Remembering the article said to use tongue, I run my tongue along his smooth skin. He tastes like a mixture of salt and soap.

"Jesus, woman," he groans. His fingers weave into my hair, but he doesn't push down. Instead, he grips my hair tightly and lifts my chin so I'm forced to look at him. "Keep that up and your 'we'll see' may be upgraded to a maybe." He smirks devilishly, and my thighs clench in need.

He releases my hair, and I go back to what I was doing. My tongue darts out and swipes across the tiny slit of his swollen head, the saltiness of his pre-cum hitting all of my senses. I lick and suck. Taste and tease. And then wrapping my lips around him, I take him all the way down. Kostas groans, then pulls me off his dick, my lips making a popping sound from the saliva.

"I wasn't done," I whine, at the same time Kostas growls, "Need to be in you. Now," as he lifts me by my hips and drops his body into the water. His hand finds the material of my bottoms, and with one tug, he yanks them off my body and pulls me directly onto his dick, filling me to the hilt.

"Fuck. Yes." His head goes back, and his eyes close. His hands are still holding on to my hips, but he doesn't move, seeming content to just sit here with his dick buried inside me.

After a long beat, his head lifts, and his eyes meet mine, reminding me of the ocean this morning. Warm honey around the edges with cool shades of green mixed in. Dark meets light. Dangerous meets safe.

"Ride me, baby," he demands, and even though I have no clue what the hell I'm doing, I do exactly what he asks, suddenly wanting—no, needing—to please him. Not so he'll say yes to me going to school. Not to calm him down after his shitty day. I need to please him because pleasing him means pleasing myself.

With my hands firmly gripped onto Kostas's shoulders, I begin to ride him. Up and down. Side to side. I get lost in the feeling of Kostas deep inside of me. He nuzzles his face into my hair, biting and nibbling on my neck. And then his thumb is at my clit, and with a couple of swipes to my already swollen nub, I'm exploding around him. My head falls onto his shoulder, and he takes over, his fingers digging into my hips as he pumps into me from the bottom until he finds his own release.

"Congratulations, *zoí mou*, you just earned yourself a definite maybe."

chapter
twenty-two

Kostas

School. She wants to go to fucking school. It's like she forgets who I am. The enemies who lie in wait, desperate to grab something precious to me and tarnish it. Talia is a good girl. Sheltered despite being born to a shady Nikolaides. I'm the bad guy...*whom she fucks*. So the lines are blurred for her and the threat is confusing at best.

She doesn't understand what's out there.

What they'd do to her if she slipped from my grip.

Fuck.

But what am I supposed to do? Keep her holed away like a fucking princess in a castle?

Yes.

Of course that's what I'll do because she's safer that way.

Irritation churns in my gut. It's hard to stick to my guns with her because then she prances by in her tiny shred of a bathing suit, flashing me her fuck me eyes, and I'm giving in to her.

She makes me weak.

Weak never felt so fucking amazing.

Focus, Kostas.

Estevan. We've sniffed him out, and as it turns out, he's hiding in an apartment complex not far from the hotel. Either his money has run out, or he thinks he's clever. Either way, we have eyes on him, and I'm coming for him.

"Where are you going?" Talia asks, looking up from her phone.

I wish nowhere.

She looks hot as hell in my T-shirt and a pair of tiny shorts as she scrolls through her phone.

"To work."

"I want to come."

Is she fucking serious right now?

"No," I bark out, stalking from the room.

She huffs in exasperation and storms after me. "Kostas, stop."

"I'm going to get answers from Estevan. It's dangerous, Talia. Understand?"

Her nostrils flare. "Maybe I need a little danger in my life. You leave every day to go hunt *badder* bad guys and leave me to do what?" Her voice rises several octaves. "Watch fucking sunsets while I wait for you to come home? What century are we in?"

"Jesus, woman," I snap. "I said no."

She gapes at me, her blue eyes filling with tears, but anger makes her neck turn bright red. "Kostas…"

"Do you need more chocolate?"

Her lashes blink rapidly in confusion. "W-What?"

"To get over your hormones."

She fucking attacks me. Claws bared. Hissing. A little roar of fury ripping from her. "You fucking asshole! How dare you blame this on my period!"

I catch her before she claws my eyes out and twist her around, pinning her to the wall. Her body heaves as she breathes heavily, her cheek smashed against the wall.

"What the fuck is your problem?" I demand, holding her tighter when she tries to escape.

"You!" she cries out. "You think I'm good for nothing but a good fuck or a blow job when the need arises." A loud sob escapes her. "You don't care about what I want, though."

Jesus fucking Christ.

"You said you wanted to go to school and I said fine—"

"You didn't say fine," she argues.

"And after breakfast this morning, we decided—"

"We decided nothing!"

"—that we'd go to dinner somewhere fancy—"

"I'm tired of eating and fucking and goddamn walks!"

When she starts to sob, I groan. Leaning my hips forward, I release her hand and reach up to brush her hair away from her neck. I kiss her sweaty flesh. "I've never been married before, Talia. I'm not good at this."

Her body relaxes. "I'm not good at it either, but I know most normal marriages don't work this way. The husband doesn't lock away his bride and not expect her to go crazy from boredom."

I nuzzle her hair with my nose. "Then what do you want to do?"

"Feel normal. Nothing about this feels normal."

Sliding my palms to her waist, I pull away to twist her around. Her blue eyes glimmer with a myriad of emotions. "We're not normal, Talia. You're married to me. A fucking mobster. People hate me. People want to destroy what's mine. You saw this firsthand at the hotel when that asshole tried to take you."

Her brows furl together. "Staying locked up by myself all day long isn't safe either."

"And why not?" I demand, scowling.

"Because I can't be happy that way. If I can't be happy…if I don't have family or friends…if I can't go to school or fulfill my sense of purpose, why am I even here?"

I grip her jaw and glower at her. "What does that mean?"

"It means nothing," she says gently. "But your mother was unhappy. Unhappiness is a poison that eventually will kill."

As though she's struck me, I stumble back. She lifts her chin, not backing down on her stance. I pace the floor, glaring at her. So what? She'd fucking off herself like my mother did? Because she's fucking bored?

"We'll talk about this later," I snarl, stalking toward the door.

A loud crashing sound fills the room. When I glance over, I see pieces of ceramic shattered across the floor. She threw a fucking vase. At my head. Luckily for her, she missed.

"Kostas, so help me, if you walk out now…"

She doesn't finish that statement.

"I don't take lightly to threats." I turn and narrow my gaze on her. "Are you threatening me?"

"I'm educating you."

"Go to fucking school. You happy?"

"In August I will be," she says softly. "But what about now? Today?"

Thunder rumbles in the distance as though pleading her case.

"And, Kostas, so help me if you tell me to watch the storm roll in…"

I smirk. "Thunderstorms are beautiful."

"So are long walks on the beach." She smiles. "Maybe I want to see something not so beautiful."

"You're serious about going with me?"

"It sure beats sitting here by myself."

I scrub my palm over my face. Adrian will give me his stupid little smirk when he sees I've given in to Talia and taken her on business. Women don't go on business. But Adrian likes her sassy mouth, and if he were here right now, he'd probably help plead her case.

"Fine."

"Fine?"

"You can go with me," I agree. "But you listen to me. You don't step out of line. It's dangerous."

She suppresses a squeal like torturing fucking Estevan is an exciting item on the honeymoon itinerary. "And then?"

"Dinner," I growl. "I'll take you to dinner where we can discuss whatever it is you did for enjoyment back in Italy that kept you from driving the ones around you crazy." It would seem I need to spend a little more time getting inside that pretty head of hers that apparently runs constantly with all the things she'd rather be doing than being treated like a mafia queen who wants for nothing.

"I enjoyed pickling," she deadpans, the corners of her lips twitching.

Cute, fucking sassy as hell girl.

"Go get dressed, smartass."

"You don't believe me?"

"Five minutes, Talia, and I'm leaving you."

"Fourth floor," Adrian says from the passenger side.

Talia remains quiet in the backseat, but I can hear her fingernails tapping on her phone. I look in the rearview mirror. Her blond hair is pulled up in a neat bun. She wears a black T-shirt, jeans, and tennis shoes. Hot as fuck wannabe bad guy killer who's going to sit in the car and play Candy Crush. As though she senses me watching her, she lifts her big eyes to mine.

"I'm not sitting in the car," she sasses.

I roll my eyes and Adrian chuckles.

"Give her a gun, Adrian," I growl out. "She knows how to use one."

"I do," she assures Adrian.

"Yeah, I heard. Basil said you almost took out our boss."

"Save your girl talk for later, ladies. We have an interrogation to attend. Are Felix and the team inside yet?"

Adrian nods. "They've staked out the whole building and have it surrounded. We have a clear shot to go inside on your call, Kostas. Room 414."

"Let's go," I command, climbing out of the car and pulling out my H&K .45. The wind is whistling harder now as the storm rolls in, and rain sprinkles on my face.

Adrian stalks forward and I step aside to let Talia come between us. Her eyes are wide and worried, but she's also eager too. I guess she really was bored as fuck if she'd rather come do this. As we creep down the hallway toward the stairwell, I can't help but replay our fight.

My parents never fought.

At least not that I knew of.

Clearly, their fight was more like a war. Long lasting, no one wins, everyone damn near dies.

Mother is dead, Father nearly died, and Niles will die.

Whatever my parents had wasn't normal. A small glimmer of delight flitters through me. The stupid as shit argument Talia and I had was as normal as they come. My entire life I've lived an extraordinary life—one written in other men's blood and my father's endless supply of money. I used to watch the kids who'd come to the hotel with their families and they were happy. They were free to splash around at the pool, surf, and play sports. Aris and I? We watched as our father lectured about the importance of organized crime, dressed in our expensive-ass suits, and secretly wished for one day to be normal kids.

I never thought much about my future or my own kids. But the more I allow my mind to wander there, now that I have Talia as my wife, I can't help but want them to have some normalcy. Talia grew up with her mom and was happy. I'm sure she did what all teenage girls did—crushed over boys, went shopping at the mall, and watched rom-coms. She very well could have been one of the carefree girls at the hotel diving into the pool hunting for plastic rings at the bottom.

I'm tired of being an outsider.

I want something genuine.

Fighting with Talia is both maddening and refreshing. She runs her mouth in ways that would get most men killed, but with her? I fucking stare at her, imagining all the naughty things I could do to her sassy mouth.

What was I thinking bringing her here?

As we reach the fourth floor, she smiles over her shoulder at me. So out of place. She looks like a fucking college girl on her way to toilet paper a frat house. Fuck. This is a mistake. I grab her bicep, ready to turn her back around, when Adrian wastes no time kicking the apartment door in.

"Stay close," I bark at Talia, shoving her right behind me as I raise my weapon.

Her fingers clutch the back of my shirt as we stalk along the hallway toward the doorway where Adrian went inside. As soon as I creep around the corner, I see he's in a scuffle with a tubby fucker.

They're grunting, but Adrian has two hundred pounds of solid muscle on this big boy. Adrian clocks him hard in the jaw, sending the man stumbling back onto the bed.

"That's Estevan?" I ask, walking inside the room, curling my lip at him.

"Yep," Adrian grunts out.

Estevan swipes blood from his lip and glowers at me. For a man in his position, he should be begging, knowing what's coming to him. "You killed my brothers," Estevan sneers, confirming his identity.

"Fire killed Bakken," I say, holding up one palm in defense, my gun still trained on him.

"Fire that *you* ordered," Estevan hisses. His eyes dart just past me and his brows furrow. "Who the fuck is this bitch?"

I tense and crack my neck. "A ghost. Someone you can't fucking see or talk to. You keep looking at her and I'll relieve you of your goddamn eyes."

Estevan snorts out a laugh, his attention back on me. "You're going to kill me anyway, Demetriou."

"I might let you live," I taunt. "For the right information."

"You. Killed. My. Brothers."

"Technically, Cy did it to himself," I say with a smirk.

Talia makes a small choking sound behind me, earning Estevan's creepy stare.

"Listen," I say as I walk into the room, nearing the bed. If he moves, I'll put a bullet through his throat. "I just want answers."

"I'm not talking to you."

Petulant fucking man-child.

"Tell him what I did to Cy, *moró mou*." I turn and give her a nod.

"He, uh," she stammers. "H-He cut off his foot and beat him to death with it."

Estevan's face turns purple. "You motherfucker."

"*The* motherfucker," I correct. "*The* motherfucker who can end you with a bullet to the head before you can even glance at my wife one more time. But I'm giving you a chance here, man. Tell me who put the hit out on my father. You do that and I'll let you go." I motion toward the balcony.

"Your *wife*," he grunts, licking his lips as he eye-fucks her just to piss me off. "It may not be me, but someone is going to use that to your disadvantage." He lifts his hips in a salacious way as he stares her down. "And it's going to hurt, baby. So goddamn—"

His words are cut off when I fire a round into his crotch. Blood blooms from where his hopefully mutilated cock lies in his jeans. He clutches the area in horror.

"Y-You shot my dick, you sick fuck!"

"I know it was the Galanis behind the hit, but I want to know who ordered it," I bark out, stalking right up to him. "Tell me and I'll allow you to die quickly unlike your rotten brothers. Keep evading the fucking question and you can live as a cockless roach never to fuck again."

"You're fucking blind, Demetriou," he hisses. "Blind and a damn fool dragging your motherfucking wife here."

I put another bullet in his thigh. He screams in pain,

clutching both his thigh and his dick. "Tell me who ordered the hit."

"Fuck you."

Cocking my head at Adrian, I point at Estevan with my gun. "Pull his intestines out through the hole I made in his crotch. Then hang him with them."

Talia gapes in horror, stumbling back a few feet.

Adrian starts forward and Estevan shakes his head.

"Just shoot me," Estevan howls, waving his bloody hand in the air at us. "Fucking psychopaths."

"Okay, then." I pop off another round, blowing out a huge hunk of flesh in the middle of his palm. "Any more requests, Galani?"

He rolls on his side, writhing in pain. Felix stomps through the door, scowling. "Police are on the way."

I nod at him. "Deal with them."

"Sir," he says before rushing out.

"You're lucky they're on their way," I tell Estevan. "I was going to make you scream a little more before I put you out of your misery."

"Just s-shoot me," Estevan says through gritted teeth. "In the fucking head."

"Tell me what I want to know," I growl. "And the police won't have to wonder how to put your mangled cock back together. I imagine they'll be able to staunch the bleeding and get you to a hospital in time."

"No," Estevan moans.

"They'll try to put it back together, but what a fucking mess, man. You really want to live your life with that messy meat show in your trousers?"

Estevan sobs. "P-Please, Demetriou."

"Tell. Me."

"Nikolaides," he says, darting his eyes to Talia.

She gasps behind me, but I'm not easily fooled.

I won't be played. So he figured out who she was. Big fucking deal. Not rocket science. She looks just like Niles. I'm not stupid like Estevan thinks.

"Have it your way," I tell him. "Come, *moró mou*. Let's go."

"No! Kill me, motherfucker! KILL ME!" Estevan cries out. "I told you what you wanted to hear!"

I glower at him. "Exactly. I didn't want you to tell me what I wanted to hear. I wanted you to tell me the fucking truth."

He can bleed out or live for all I care. Estevan Galani is a roach. I will squash him eventually, but right now, I'm hunting a rat.

chapter
twenty-three

Talia

"WHAT CAN I GET YOU TO DRINK?" THE bartender asks with a flirty grin. Kostas and I have been back home for three days and I've had enough of hiding from Aris and being stuck in that damn villa, so I've ventured out. The hotel has six pools, each one with its own tiki bar. Aris favors the one on the east side, so I'm at the one on the west side.

"Can you make a strawberry lemonade vodka?" Maybe adding some alcohol to my usual lemonade will help to suppress the constant sense of boredom.

"I can make anything you'd like," he says.

"And you'll do it without ogling my *wife*, or I'll fire you and then kill you," Kostas says, having a seat next to me.

The bartender's eyes widen, and he nods several times. "I'm sorry, sir. I didn't know she was yours."

He stumbles over something behind the bar and then goes about making my drink.

"Must you threaten every man who speaks to me?" I twist my head to the side, narrowing my eyes at Kostas. "At this rate, I'll have nobody to talk to but you."

"Is it really wise to start drinking at ten in the morning?" he asks, ignoring my question as the bartender sets my drink on the coaster in front of me.

"Would you like anything, sir?" he asks Kostas, who simply waves him off.

"What else do I have to do but drink?" I stand, and taking my drink with me, walk down the cobblestone walkway. I hear Kostas groan in irritation behind me, but I pay him no attention.

"I'm bringing in your father later to speak to him. Would you like to join me?"

"He's not my father," I correct. "And yes, I would like to join. Do you believe he put the hit out on your father like that fat man said?" I take a sip of my fruity drink. It's delicious.

"No, I don't believe Niles is stupid enough to do something like that. Try to steal you, yes? That was his way of trying to apologize to you. But hire men to try and kill my father, no. However, I would be a stupid man not to consider all the possibilities."

"It's too late for him to apologize," I say. "I'll never forgive him for what he did."

We walk down a pathway I've yet to take, along the side of the cliff. The hotel is so big, I could probably take a different direction every day for a month and still not cover the whole property.

"Is being married to me so bad, *moró mou*?" Kostas asks.

I glance over at him, and for the first time, his eyes scream something that looks like vulnerability, maybe even insecurity. I must be seeing things because Kostas is the strongest man I know.

"It's not the point," I tell him truthfully, stopping and facing him. "If I had a child, I would do everything in my power to protect him or her. If I was dumb enough to have an affair with a powerful man's wife and then drum up a debt worth millions of dollars, I would *never* hand my child, my own flesh and blood, over to him to save myself." I don't realize tears have begun to fall down my cheeks until Kostas steps closer and swipes one away. "I would protect my child," I say through a sob. "A parent is supposed to protect their child." And then I add, "Like what your mom did for you."

Kostas flinches. "She killed herself. How is that protecting her children?"

"Didn't you hear everything she said, Kostas?" I take his hand in mine and he lets me. "Her warnings and apologies? It might've not been right the way she went about it, but it was her way of putting you first. All she wanted was for you to fall in love and be happy. While she wanted more for you than this life, mine was handing me over to it."

"This life is all I know, Talia. You understand that, right?" Kostas's eyes plead with me to understand. "What my mother said. It's not going to happen. I will live and die in this life, and now as my wife you will too."

The burning in his eyes tells me what he says is the truth. And at one time, this life would've scared me, but now, I've accepted my fate. "I'm okay with that," I tell him honestly. "I just…I'm just trying to find out who I am in this life. Before you, I was Talia, the college student in Italy. During the week, I attended classes and studied. On the weekends, I attended parties and shows and visited art museums. I just don't know where I fit in, in this world. Your world." I raise my barely drunk glass. "I'm not a girl who drinks at ten in the morning."

Kostas stares at me for a long moment before he takes my glass out of my hand and sets it down on a table. "Come with me," he commands. Pulling me down the sidewalk, we end up in front of an area of the hotel I haven't been to yet. It's quieter over here. The pool isn't open. The rooms look as if they're all empty. "Come." He unlocks a door to the building, and just like the outside, it's quiet on the inside. Empty.

"Before my mother died, we were expanding. She handled all of the interior design. The rooms are just about done, but the restaurant isn't yet. We were planning to open in the fall, but we'll need everything to be finished before we do."

Confused as to why he's brought me here, I ask, "What does this have to do with me?"

"You're an art major, right?" he asks. "You know style, and you're educated about Greek mythology. You said you're bored. I'm giving you something to do." When my brows rise, still needing further clarification, Kostas adds, "I want you to finish what my mother started. The restaurant. You can design it however you want. Money is no object."

My heart expands at his words. Finish what his mother started. Sure, he could hire someone to finish it, but he listened to me. I told him I needed a purpose and he gave me a solution. I turn in a circle, taking the massive empty space in. It's filled with so much potential. I can make it anything I want. I can spend my summer creating a masterpiece.

"So," he prompts. "What do you say?"

"Yes." I nod emphatically. "I'll do it."

"Good." He threads his fingers into mine and walks us back out, locking the door behind us. "I have time before my meeting, so we can quickly go over the details."

When we get back to the main hotel, he stops in front of his office but doesn't go in. Instead, he makes a left and… walks into Aris's office. Oh my God. Why are we going in there? It's been over a week since I've last seen him. I've done a stellar job at avoiding him since we've been back.

"Aris," Kostas greets his brother, gesturing for me to have a seat.

"What can I do for you?" Aris asks, tilting his head to the side in annoyance. "I'm busy…working."

"As I am." Kostas grins. "Meet our new interior designer. Talia has agreed to finish the restaurant Mamá had started. The unfinished expansion on the west side that's due to open in the fall."

Aris glances from Kostas to me, a sly grin splaying upon his lips, and my heart sinks. What does Aris have to do with the expansion? The only time the guy leaves his office is to go to the bar near his villa.

As if Kostas can hear my thoughts, he says, "Aris is in charge of the money."

"I thought you said I don't have a budget," I choke out as all the pieces slowly come together.

"You don't, but Aris is who you will get all your money from. He also knows who all the vendors are. Anything you need to get the restaurant done, just ask him and he'll be able to help you." In other words, I'm going to be forced to go to Aris every time I need money. And I can't change my mind now because that will raise a red flag.

"Okay, will do," I say. "If you don't mind, I'm going to head home to think about what I would like to do with the restaurant, and then I'll meet with you."

"I look forward to it," Aris says with a knowing smirk tugging on the corner of his lips.

"Can you see yourself back, Talia? I have some things to discuss with my brother. I'll meet you at home."

I nod my understanding. Just as I'm about to exit Aris's

office, I'm gently tugged into Kostas's arms. He cups my cheeks in his strong hands, and his mouth, oh so gently, presses against mine. "I'll be home in a little bit, and then we can spend the afternoon together...in bed." He sucks my lower lip into his mouth and bites down, not enough to cause any pain, but enough to send shivers down my spine, momentarily making me forget we're standing in front of Aris.

And then a throat clears, reminding me that we are in fact in Aris's office. I will my eyes not to glance over at Aris, but I can't help it, and when I do, I see he's staring at us, his jaw clenching, his smirk wiped clean off his face. I need to get out of here, away from him.

Pulling out of Kostas's arms, I give him one last chaste kiss before I turn around and leave. I practically run the entire way home. Only slowing down once I'm safely back in our villa, with the door locked. I don't know how I'm going to get out of this, but I can't work with Aris. I can't sit in his office and have meetings with him. I have to find a way around this.

As I climb into bed, curling up into a fetal position, I think about everything Aris has said to me. It's clear he's jealous of his brother. He wants what Kostas has. Kostas is closer to his father. He runs the majority of their business. He was chosen to marry me. And the entire time, for the most part, Aris keeps his mouth shut. He didn't threaten to tell Kostas that we, according to him, slept together. No, he agreed to keep it a secret. And then it hits me. Even if Kostas believed Aris didn't rape me, and what happened between us was consensual, Kostas would kill his brother for having sex with me. Aris knew we were supposed to marry. We were engaged. And yet he still went behind his brother's back and had sex with his now-wife.

And now, every time I see him, he gets off on my being scared of him. Of Kostas finding out. Well, fuck that, and fuck him. I'm not going to let him victimize me. We both know what he did, and if I told Kostas, sure, he might not believe me, but regardless he would end Aris's life. Which is why Aris will never tell him himself.

I'm going to design that restaurant, and I'm going to go to those meetings with my head held high, knowing Aris is a piece of shit, coward rapist. And I'm going to turn the table on him. He wants to threaten me, well, two can play this game.

No more scared Talia. I'm the wife of Kostas Demetriou, the biggest mobster in Greece, and it's time I start acting like it.

The door opens and in walks Kostas. Once he's in our bedroom, he sheds each article of clothing from his body until he's naked. His beautiful, masculine body completely on display. "I see you're waiting in bed for me, *zoí mou*." Kostas grins devilishly as he stalks over to the bed, his thick cock bobbing between his muscular legs. I find myself salivating like Pavlov's dog at the sight of him. "I don't have a lot of time before my meeting, but we have just enough for me to make you come a couple of times."

And with his words, all thoughts of Aris are pushed out of my head. I'm back in the warm, safe waters with my husband, right where I want to be.

chapter
twenty-four

Kostas

"I'M COMING WITH YOU."

I stare at my wife with her mussed up blond hair and swollen lips. I thought I could distract her into staying, but I should have known better. She looks good in my bed. Sated, just-fucked, relaxed. Her tits are on full display, proudly showing off the red and purple marks I left on her with my mouth.

Claimed.

She looks claimed and owned.

The possessive animal within me roars with pride. It also wants to chain her to the bed and leave her there until I'm ready for her again.

But Talia has an animal of her own and it hates to be caged. Her animal likes to prowl about trying to see what sort of trouble she can drum up. If she's going to be out of my bed, then she may as well be with me.

"It could get messy," I challenge with a hard glare. No matter how much she thinks she wants to watch her father suffer, it's always different when it comes down to it. My methods are brutal and unconventional. I won't go easy on him.

"I've seen messy," she huffs out as she climbs from the bed.

My dick jumps in my slacks at seeing her naked body prancing in front of me like a little treat just begging to be devoured.

"You've seen messy with work shit. But you haven't seen messy from personal shit," I grind out, my eyes fixated on her ass as she bends to pull underwear from her drawer. Red marks from my fingertips still dot her tanned skin at her hips where I held on tight as I fucked her hard.

She slides on the silky white panties that look virginal on her, and she frowns at me. "He put me in this situation and then paid to have me kidnapped. If you're going to interrogate him, I want to come with. I have questions of my own." Her chin lifts in a regal way that makes me want to kiss the fire out of her.

"Fine, little badass. Get dressed and let's go." I cock my head to the side as I admire her marked flesh since it's proudly being shown to me. "He won't get any favors from me simply because he's your dad. You do realize this."

She pulls on some yoga pants, still leaving her tits for me to salivate over. "Kostas, I know you. I know what you're capable of. And I'm still going."

Sadly, she pulls on a bra and then a tank top. Her sexy curves are not hidden behind fabric. If I didn't have this motherfucker waiting on me, I'd rip her clothes off again and fuck her until she passes out.

"Stop looking at me like you're going to eat me," she grumbles. "My thighs are raw from your scruff. No more eating."

I snort and motion for the door. "That's a promise I can't make. When it comes to you, I'll never get enough."

She slides on her tennis shoes and shakes her head at me before taking my hand. "You say that super sweetly, but it's kind of psychotic if we're being honest."

"What you see is what you get with me," I remind her. "Psychopath and all. And if you're not only married to me, but also enjoy getting fucked all hours of the day by said psychopath, what does that make you, hmmm?"

"Dumb."

I let out a chuckle as we step outside. "It makes you a psychopath too, *zoí mou*. Own it. You're not the same woman who stepped onto Crete." I give her hand a squeeze. "You're one of us now."

She doesn't argue, simply rests her head against my arm as we walk.

The drive to the groundskeeper's house isn't long, and soon we're walking down into the cellar hand in hand. When we reach the bottom, anger bursts up inside me to find the chair empty and no one tied to it.

"What the fuck?" I roar, my fury aimed at Basil.

Basil scowls and points to the corner where Phoenix stands smoking a cigarette. "I said I had Nikolaides."

"You implied it was Niles," I snarl. I yank my hand from Talia's grip, eager to fuck someone up.

"Good afternoon to you too, Kostas," Phoenix says coldly, dropping his cigarette to his feet and stubbing it out with his shoe. "Talia. Good to see you. Do I get a hug?"

Before I can forbid her to see him, she rushes over to him and hugs him. Jealousy lashes at me, which is fucking stupid. She's his sister. They're not long lost lovers finally reunited. Not one single thing about their hug should I be jealous about.

And yet I am.

I grit my teeth and level Basil with a hard glare. "You know better than this shit," I growl at my family's long-time bodyguard.

Basil has the sense to look ashamed. "He wanted to talk to you and—"

"You report to him now?" I demand, a tsunami of rage consuming me.

"No," Basil grits out.

"He reports to me," Aris says, clomping down the stairs. "I told him to keep it vague. We need answers, and you'd be pissed if you learned we didn't have Niles. This conversation still needed to happen, and if you knew we didn't have Niles, you would've stayed holed away doing your husbandly duties." He smirks at the last part.

Talia clings to her brother, frowning at me.

"Then start fucking talking," I bite out, my eyes on Phoenix. "Where's your father?"

Phoenix's eyes flare with anger. "Underground."

"Where?" I seethe.

"That, I don't know," Phoenix grumbles. "He won't even tell me."

"Put him in the chair," I bark at Basil.

Basil starts for them, but Talia clings harder to Phoenix.

"No, Kostas," she begs. "He's telling the truth!"

Fucking woman.

I knew I should have left her fine ass in bed where she fucking belongs.

"He's telling the truth," Aris agrees. "Two of our guys have been tracking Phoenix's activity and can confirm this."

"Then what the fuck is the point of this meeting?" I

hiss, seconds away from yanking Talia from Phoenix so I can pummel his smug face just for the goddamn fun of it.

Aris scrubs his face in frustration. "We need him to draw out Niles. Something he's agreed to do as long as he has contact with his sister."

The hairs on my arms rise. I don't take fucking lightly to people making plans behind my back. Basil keeps his gaze averted to the ground. He fucked up and he knows it. I'll let Adrian deal with his misstep.

"I'm supposed to believe you'd sell your father out?" I demand, glowering at Phoenix.

"I'm not selling him out," Phoenix snaps. "I'm telling you I don't know where he is and I'll give whatever information I have, which isn't much, so you can find him."

Anger rolls off me in waves hot enough to burn everyone in the room. "Why are you being so compliant?"

"Jesus, Kostas," Aris grumbles. "It's right in your face."

Phoenix tightens his hold around his sister. "I don't want to be cut off from Talia. I shouldn't have to pay for the sins of my father and neither should she."

I crack my neck, desperate to relieve some tension. "They're paying taxes to the Demetrious now?" I ask Aris. "Every penny plus interest?"

Aris nods. "Now that Niles is gone, Phoenix has been doing damage control. The money is flowing in from Thessaloniki as it should be. Numbers look good now that Niles is no longer dipping his greedy fingers in the pot."

"No more games," I growl, darting my eyes from Aris to Basil. Then, I land my eyes on Phoenix. "I want you to do whatever it takes to get Niles out of hiding."

"I will," Phoenix agrees. "And I want to freely see my sister."

The fact that *this* Nikolaides thinks he can negotiate with *my wife* has me wanting to choke the life out of him.

"Phoenix," Talia finally says. "We can have dinner together or you can come swim every now and again. But 'freely' is a little overboard. Even before all this, we didn't see much of each other."

Her brother grits his teeth. She hugs him, standing on her toes, and whispers something to him that has him relaxing. I want to rip them apart, but I keep my emotions in check.

"I want him found," I say coldly, not agreeing to his terms. "And until we find him, you can deal with me. I'll collect the taxes."

Aris scowls at me. "I can handle it. You've got enough going on now that our father is out of commission."

I'm tired of him being the middle man. The power is going to his head. My brother isn't cut out to sniff out lies and find hidden truths. I'll do this shit my damn self.

"This isn't up for discussion," I utter in a low tone.

Once Talia realizes I'm not going to kill her beloved brother, she smiles at me and pulls from his embrace to walk over to me. I'm stiff when she hugs me, still thrumming with wild energy to make someone pay.

"I'll call you and we can make a date to do something," Phoenix tells his sister as he makes his way to the stairs. "And I'll let you know if I hear word on my father."

As soon as he's gone, Aris opens his mouth, but I wave him on. "Not now. We can talk later."

Aris's jaw flexes as he bites back his words and gives me a clipped nod. He storms up the stairs. I pull from Talia and walk over to Basil. When I poke him in the chest, he glares back at me.

"Loyalty is everything," I remind him.

His brown eyes gleam fiercely. "I'm always loyal to you, Kostas."

Not my brother. Not my father. Not the Demetrious. Me.

"That's what I thought," I grind out, dismissing him with a nod.

Basil leaves without another word.

"Kostas…" Talia's hand clutches my shoulder from behind.

I shake off her hold and turn to stare at her, my icy gaze freezing her where she stands.

"You can't undermine me like that," I hiss, my anger still needing an outlet. I'd come here hoping to fuck up Niles. Instead, I made an alliance with his fucking son.

Her plump pink lips part. "I wasn't undermining you. I was protecting my brother."

"From your husband!" I roar, making her flinch. "You're mine, not his!"

She recovers from my outburst and bravely walks up to me. Her hands are warm over my dress shirt as she runs them up over my pecks. "I'm yours," she breathes, her blue eyes glimmering with conviction. "I took those vows, albeit against my better judgment, but I stand by them now. We weren't meant to care about one another, but we do, Kostas. And because you care about me, you'll protect the ones I care about too."

I clench my jaw, burning my glare into her. She's so fucking confident that I care enough about her that I'll take care of the people she loves too.

Weak.

She makes me so fucking weak.

"Underneath all this fury and aggression, you're gentle

and loving. Beneath the mob boss is my husband." She stands on her toes and kisses me.

Some of the anger melts away as my palms find her ass. I squeeze her hard enough that she gasps against my lips. When her hand slides down to my cock that's hardening by the second, I groan. Too quickly she's learning to play my body against me to get what she wants.

I've killed men for much less.

With Talia, it's like she's a seductress who gets inside my mind, no matter how dark and fucked up it is, and fills me with her sweet light. It's maddening. And exhilarating too.

"I know you hate giving in to those who've angered you, but unfortunately, these people are a part of me." She grips my dick and kisses me deeply before pulling her lips away. "Like my mother." When she starts to kneel, her motive on giving me a blow job evident, I grip her hair tight to prevent her from moving.

"No," I say lowly. "You're not going to suck my cock into getting your way. It doesn't work like that, Talia. I'm on to you."

Rather than seeming afraid or panicked, she frowns at me. "So you don't want a blow job?"

Why does she have to look so fucking cute when I'm pissed at her?

"Of course I want a blow job. But not when you're trying to secretly get your way. You want your way then you negotiate for it like a real Demetriou. Out with what you want and what you're willing to give for it." I nip at her bottom lip before giving her a sinister smile. "Let's make a deal, *zoí mou*."

She purses her lips, studying my face for a moment. "Fine. I want contact with my mom."

Anger coils inside me like a snake. "Your mother—"

"I know exactly what she did," she breathes. "And I'm sorry. I'm sorry it was her who was the catalyst for what happened to Nora. But my mom was still a victim. She'd been cheated on."

"You can't go see her," I bite out.

"I want her to come see me." She lifts her chin, fire burning in her blue eyes. "Freely."

"I don't care to see that woman," I growl.

"She's my mom," Talia bites out. "And if you care about me, you'll give this to me."

I narrow my eyes. "In exchange for what? We're negotiating. I might bite. But I want to know what I get. And don't offer me a fucking blow job."

Her lips curve up into a half smile. "I'm inviting her to the grand opening of the restaurant when it's done."

"In. Exchange. For. What?"

"I don't know," she purrs, backing away from me. "I think you're a smart man, *Pluto*, and can come up with that answer."

A chase.

She'll let me chase her down and fuck her like a god does for the one he's laid claim to.

"I agree to your terms, *Proserpina*," I growl. "But you better run fast. When I catch you, I'm going to fuck you hard, wild, and rough."

She grins and flashes me a wink.

And then she's gone.

Watching her ass bounce up those stairs, knowing I'll be ripping her yoga pants off very soon, is worth the shitty meeting I just endured.

Talia's ass makes everything better.

chapter
twenty-five

Talia

S ITTING AT KOSTAS'S DESK IN HIS HOME OFFICE, double-checking my book of ideas a.k.a. my restaurant proposal to present to Aris, my mind wanders to a recent conversation with him. When I approached Aris a couple weeks ago regarding the budget, he explained I wasn't prepared, and once I was, to schedule an appointment. Asshole.

After taking fifteen calming breaths, I knock on Aris's door and wait for him to grant me access.

"Talia, what can I do for you?" He closes his laptop and gives me his undivided attention. My heart is beating so fast you would think it was in a race, but luckily, Aris's door is open and is surrounded by other offices. Including Kostas's.

"I'm here to speak to you regarding the budget for the restaurant." I stay standing, hoping this will be quick and painless.

Aris's lips curl into a smile, and I'm taken aback. It's just like the smiles he would grant me before... "Okay. What do you need from me?"

"I guess I just need to know who I order from and how to pay for things." I shuffle from one foot to the other nervously.

Aris laughs and then starts firing questions off at me. "Have you decided what the theme will be? What the menu will look like? Contacted any chefs for interviews? Have you put together a plan? How about an estimated budget?"

When I don't say anything, shocked and dumbfounded at how formal he's behaving, he says, "I take it you didn't think about any of that?" Aris stands and walks around to the front of his desk. Instinctively, I back up so I'm almost out of the office, afraid he's going to try to close the door and trap me in here. He stops and leans against the desk, completely unfazed by my actions. "In the world of business, Talia, one must come prepared to a meeting with all the information needed. I know my brother told you there's no budget, but that doesn't mean you view it as a shopping spree. The Pérasma Hotel has a reputation to uphold. The restaurant needs to be cohesive with the rest of the wing, which will be finalized at the same time, and Hilda, who is in charge of that, actually has a budget. She's going to need to know what your intentions are so she can work alongside you. And while my brother doesn't seem to care how much you spend, we still need to turn a profit. It is a business after all."

I refrain from rolling my eyes. We both know damn well this restaurant, hell, this hotel is nothing but a front. Sure, they turn a profit, but Aris doesn't really give a shit about how much I spend. He's only doing this to stick it to me.

"Once you have all your ducks in a row, give my secretary a call to schedule an appointment and we'll sit down and discuss it." He steps toward the door, opening it wider, silently indicating he'd like for me to leave. So, this is how he wants to play this game... Fine. He might've won this round, but I will win the war.

After leaving his office, I was more determined than ever to make this restaurant a success. First step, I had to come up with a theme. Once I figured that out, I started researching everything. From paint, to décor, the restaurant kitchen appliances. I've created an item analysis of everything I'm planning to purchase and what the estimated cost of labor will be. I'll be damned if I'm not prepared for the meeting today.

Going over everything one last time, I gather everything I'm going to need for our meeting, including my big girl panties and five-inch heels, and head over to Aris's office. His secretary has rescheduled me twice now, so hopefully this meeting sticks. I could've told Kostas the games Aris is playing, but I almost think that's exactly what he wants me to do—run crying to my husband, who I know will tell Aris to stop his shit. So, I haven't told Kostas anything, except that I'm, as Aris said, 'Getting my ducks in a row.'

"Talia, how are you?" Carlene, Aris's secretary greets me.

"I'm good. How are you?"

"Ready for five o'clock to come." She laughs good-naturedly. "I have a date tonight." She winks playfully, reminding me of my friends back in Italy. Maybe Carlene and I can hang out some time. "Mr. Demetriou is ready for you. Just go on back."

"Thanks, Carlene. Have fun on your date tonight."

When I get to Aris's door, it's slightly ajar, but I still knock, not wanting him to give me another lecture on business etiquette.

"Come in."

When I enter, he stands and gives me a sincere smile. *I swear the man is bipolar.* "Have a seat, Talia. I can't wait to hear what you have for me."

Against my better judgement, I have a seat, and Aris

sits back in his. I hand him my business projection binder—I made three copies—and he starts flipping through it. He stops at the restaurant name but doesn't ask questions. Unlike Kostas, he's not educated in Greek mythology, so he won't get it. I wait with bated breath as he flips through the pages until he gets to the end. Then he closes it and grins.

"I see you've come more prepared, Talia. This is great work. We'll need to make a copy for Hilda—"

"Actually, I made one." I hand him one of the other copies I made, and he chuckles.

"Very good." He types something on his laptop and then the printer starts up. He grabs the papers and hands them to me. "These are the billing instructions and credit card info. Everything gets charged to this card, unless it's over ten thousand, then it needs to be submitted and I'll use our business account."

He circles the information, then says, "Your estimated opening date is at the end of August. That's only eight weeks. We'll need to meet every couple weeks to make sure you're on track to finish on time. We can't open the reservations if the work isn't going to be completed on time."

Mother. Fucking. Asshole. Of course he wants to meet every two damn weeks. So he can kill me with kindness.

Not letting him see that my blood is boiling, I plaster on my sweetest smile and say, "Sounds good."

After we finish our meeting, I head straight over to the restaurant to take another look at the place and begin placing orders. If I'm honest, this part of the hotel is my favorite. Unlike the other parts of the hotel, which are built up with pools and gyms and walkways, this side has a more natural feel to it. The trees cover the entire area, giving it privacy. Nora had started designing the area, so there's a few hammocks hanging from palm trees, which overlook Mirabello Bay. While I've been working on designing the restaurant, lying in these hammocks has become my new favorite pastime.

After spending the next few hours calling various places to get things scheduled, I call the contractor I've chosen to confirm a walkthrough with him and his team. I need to make sure everything can be done in time.

"Tomorrow at noon is perfect," Mr. DeSantis says.

"Thank you. I will see you then." Just as I'm hitting end on our call, a masculine voice speaks into my ear, and I jump slightly in the hammock, almost tipping it over.

"There's my wife," Kostas says, his voice deep but playful. "I was beginning to forget what you looked like." He leans down and gives me a soft kiss. "Were you planning to come home tonight?"

I glance at my phone and see it's already almost six o'clock. "I didn't realize how late it was. And you just saw me this morning...in bed...naked."

Kostas leans against the wall that separates the hotel from the bay. "I can't help that I can't get enough of my wife." Kostas hits me with a boyish grin, the one I'm beginning to think he saves only for me. It never ceases to amaze me how Kostas can be so cruel and cold one minute, and then turn around and say something so sweet.

"Who were you speaking to on the phone?" he asks, changing the subject.

"The contractor. We begin construction on Pomegranate tomorrow."

Kostas smirks wickedly at the name of the restaurant. Of course he gets it. "That's what you're calling it? Pomegranate."

I climb out of the hammock and step in between Kostas's

legs. "It seems fitting." After all, pomegranate was what the Greek god, Pluto, of the Underworld conned Proserpina into eating to keep her by his side for all eternity.

"I would happen to agree with you. Come, wife, I'm taking you to dinner." He grips the curves of my hips and pulls me in closer, his lips finding mine. My body sinks into his and he deepens the kiss before he pulls back and whispers, "And then I'm going to have you for dessert."

chapter
twenty-six

Kostas

I<small>T'S</small> <small>BEEN A WEEK SINCE CONSTRUCTION STARTED ON</small> Pomegranate. A week too long of losing my wife to the leering stares of workers as she flits about bossing everyone around in a way that gets my dick hard. She fought me on working late tonight too, but I pulled rank and told her we're dining with my family whether she wants to or not.

"You don't have to be so smug about it," she sasses from the passenger seat.

I reach over and grip her silky, tanned thigh just below the hem of her sparkly navy dress. "About what, *zoí mou*?"

She shakes her head but doesn't push my hand away. I smirk as I pull into the driveway at my father's estate. Aris's gray 911 GT2 RS sits parked crooked in front of the six-bay garage. It makes me want to park close enough that Talia's door dings the car he adores. In the end, I'm an adult and choose to park directly behind him instead to block him in.

"Close enough?" Talia asks, laughing.

"He worships that stupid Porsche. He's lucky I don't do worse just to fuck with him."

She simply smirks and climbs out. I follow after her, drinking in how goddamn hot she is today. After being on site all day, she'd scrubbed away the grime, ditched the jeans, and dolled up for me. Her long blond locks hang in messy beach waves down her back, nearly coming to her ass that has my full attention. The dress is just short enough on her long legs to seem risqué. I'm torn between wanting her to change and demanding she bend over so I can see what color panties she's wearing.

I do neither because Aris steps out to greet us. One look at the proximity of my car and the murderous scowl on his face is enough to send satisfaction thrumming through me. My pleasure at his annoyance is cut short when he rakes his gaze up and down my wife. She stalls to a stop. I prowl up behind her and wrap a possessive arm around her middle.

Aris, the little bitch, laughs. "Calm down, killer. I wasn't checking out your wife. I was thinking she and Selene must have shopped at the same boutique for their dresses."

Selene?

Who the fuck is Selene?

As though on cue, a redhead with fat lips and wide green eyes clacks over to Aris in her high heels. She's wearing a navy dress as well, but unlike Talia's classy one, Selene's looks to be painted on her curvy body. And it looks like they missed some paint on her big tits.

"Kostas, this is my girl, Selene," Aris introduces. "Selene, that's my brother, and his wife, Talia."

Selene offers her hand. Talia politely shakes it, but I don't offer my hand, just a nod of my head. Gingers aren't usually my brother's type—blondes are—but I can't say I'm complaining. Maybe he's moving on from eye-fucking my wife all the time, something I'm glad to see.

"How's Father?" I grunt out as I usher Talia past them.

"Chipper as fuck. You know Dad." Aris's dry, sarcastic tone has Selene giggling at his humor.

Ignoring her annoying laugh, I guide Talia into the house I grew up in. Since my mother died, I've tried not to get caught up in the emotions and memories. I stay singularly focused when I visit. Make sure Father is cared for and doesn't hurt for anything.

I find Father seated in the dining room. Despite the pain meds he's been on since the accident, he still remains sharp and aware. He watches us enter, irritation marring his features. I've avoided bringing Talia here because Father has no problem in telling me how much he despises her and her family. And while I can tune it out, I don't want to see how his words might affect her.

"Good evening," I greet, nodding to him.

Talia clutches my hand like a lifeline. I guide her to a seat and pull out the chair. Once she's settled, I take a seat between her and Father. Aris escorts Selene to the other side of the table, planting her beside Father, and then sitting across from Talia, much to my aggravation.

"We're in beautiful company tonight," Father says, turning his smile on for Selene's benefit.

Aris straightens, seemingly surprised and simultaneously proud that Father approves of his flavor of the week. "I certainly agree," Aris says, offering our father a smile.

I simply grunt. Talia is hot as fuck. Selene is a cheap wannabe who won't last until Saturday. She's insignificant to the Demetrious.

Before dinner starts, Father asks us to say a small prayer for our mother. I bow my head and try not to let her absence claw at my heart. His words float through the air, but I don't hear them. Talia clutches my thigh and squeezes. I grab her hand and bring it to my lips, kissing her skin.

At first, dinner is polite and conversational. We steer away from Father's "condition" even though I can tell Talia is curious. Talia sucks down the wine nearly as fast as Aris and Selene. I keep my eye on the clock, waiting for the moment we can wrap up and bail. Things between my father and me are strained. His power and influence have waned, and in his inability to lead, I've been forced to take over all aspects of the Demetriou business. It pisses him off, but there's nothing he can do about it.

"Any word on the men behind the attempt on my life?" Father grits out.

Aris lifts a brow at me. Both women are quiet as they listen for the answer.

"It's being handled, Father," I reply in a bored, dismissive tone.

"And the taxes?" Father demands.

"They're being collected, Father."

"And the Aegean Sea fleets?"

"Still floating, Father."

"And Niles?"

"We're hunting him down, Father."

"And the hotel?"

"Running flawlessly, Father."

Father slams his fist down on the table, his rage making his face burn bright red. "Stop dismissing me like I'm your fucking wife, Kostas. I want answers. Tell me what's going on with my empire."

Aris sucks down another glass of wine, too much of a wussy to get involved. Selene obviously gropes him underneath the table because he hisses at the contact.

"It's all being handled, Father," I tell him, tearing my gaze from my brother.

"You're being a disrespectful shit," Father seethes.

Aris shoves Selene's hand away, his eyes gleaming with delight to see our father and me arguing. Usually he's the one in the hot seat.

"You're acting like an old man who needs a nap." I narrow my eyes at my father. "Does the doctor need to change your medications? It's unlike you to snap and lose your cool in front of the ladies."

"I don't give a flying fuck about your fake wife and your brother's whore," Father rages. "I want to know what's going on with my businesses!"

Rising from my chair, I shake my head. "We'll talk when your head is clear," I say in a placating tone. Then, to Aris, I order him to stay. "Keep Father company through dessert and then see to it he's put to bed early. I'll call Dr. Newman in the morning."

Father huffs and puffs but wisely shuts his mouth as I escort Talia from the dining room. When we make it back outside, I let out a breath of relief. Slowly, I've had to take over in all aspects. It's what I was trained to do. Of course, we didn't expect for me to take over so soon, but that was before my mother offed herself and nearly took out my father in the process. Now, I'm forced into the position, but I'm ready. And I can't allow my invalid father to keep calling the shots from his bedroom. The Demetriou name has ruled efficiently and powerfully because we are an active participant in our business dealings. We don't send men to do the jobs we can easily do ourselves. My father is beyond that. He's no longer the King of Crete. I am.

"You okay?" Talia asks, stopping in front of Aris's car.

"Better now," I admit, brushing a strand of blond hair from her face.

"Good." She stands on her toes and plants a kiss on my mouth.

I nip at her lip and grab her ass through her dress. "Be better if I were inside of you."

Her blue eyes darken with lust. "No one's stopping you."

A shriek escapes her when I lift her by gripping the globes of her ass. Her legs hook at my waist, and her hands latch at my neck.

"I've always wanted to fuck you on the side of my brother's precious car," I rumble, nipping at her jaw and then tugging at her earlobe with my teeth. "You going to let me fuck you on his pretty Porsche?"

Her answer comes in the way of her unbuckling my slacks. I smirk as she pulls my cock into her hand.

"It'll have to be quick, *zoí mou*. He'll have a shit fit if he catches us out here doing this."

"You're the one stalling, Kos."

I grin wolfishly at her. "Pull your panties to the side and show me how wet you are."

With her eyes fiery with desire, she pushes up her dress and tugs at the tiny scrap of blue panties revealing her pink center. In the moonlight, her cunt glistens with her need. Nice and juicy, ready to take my cock. Greedy girl. I tease her opening with the tip of my cock until she's squirming, begging for every hot inch. Without warning, I push hard into her with a forceful thrust.

"Kostas!"

"Shhh," I rumble. "You'll get us caught. I don't want to have to slit my own brother's throat for accidentally seeing my wife's pussy."

Her cunt clenches around me, encouraging me to pound harder into her. I grip her breast hard through her dress as I ravish her mouth with mine. I devour each needy moan until she's trembling with a near orgasm.

"Put your foot there," I instruct, nodding to the hood of the car right beside us. "I want your pussy wide open so you can take every inch, Talia."

She unpeels her leg from my waist and spreads herself. I grip her knee and push it, stretching her. The heel of her shoe finds purchase on the hood. Her head tilts back as she breathes heavily.

"I'm so close," she moans. "Touch me."

Her hand holding her panties to the side trembles. I reach between us and finger her needy nub that's warm to the touch. My cock slides in and out of her easily as she becomes juicy as fuck.

"You're so fucking hot," I growl, pinching her clit.

"Mmm," she moans. "Oh, God. So close."

I rub her until she spirals out of control. Then, I slam into her hard. Over and over and over until she's clawing the shit out of my neck and her arousal is soaking me. She shudders again, signaling another climax, which sets me off with my own. I groan as my cum jets deep inside her. The moment my dick stops twitching, I slide out of her heat and pull away.

What a fucking sight.

My wife spread open with my cum running down her thigh, her eyes hooded with lust. I step closer and bend so I can run my fingers through our combined juices running down her leg. Slowly, with my eyes locked on hers, I run them back up her leg to her pussy. She lets out a sharp gasp when I push the cum back inside her.

"It belongs right here," I growl. "Right fucking here."

She bites on her bottom swollen lip and nods.

"Now put your panties in place like a good little wifey and keep my cum inside you."

Her fingers release her panties and then she adjusts them so they cover her again. I hook my arm under her knee and ease it down so that her feet are once again planted on the pavement. Her entire body trembles.

"Oh, naughty Talia," I rumble, glancing at the hood of my brother's car. "You've scratched his car." Gouges from the heel of her shoe mar the shiny surface. He's going to be so fucking pissed.

Her eyes flash with evil wickedness I'm sure she's learned from me. "Oops."

I grip her jaw in a punishing grip and kiss her hard until she's panting and clawing at me for more. Pulling away slightly, I grin at her.

"Are we going to fuck on your car next?" she purrs, her voice breathless.

"My car cost a helluva lot more than his." I stroke her hair. "But you can suck me off on the way home, dirty wife."

"And then you can have your dessert by the pool when we get home," she challenges back.

I reach between us and feel her up, loving how soaked her panties are as my cum drains out of her.

"A good marriage is about compromise," I tell her with a sinister smile. "And we're getting really fucking good at it."

chapter
twenty-seven

Talia

"**L**OOKS LIKE YOU'VE BEEN BUSY." ARIS STEPS through the doors of Pomegranate and eyes the place speculatively. My gaze follows his, trying to see through an outsider's eyes the finished restaurant. The rich crimson, dark brown, and black color scheme flows throughout the place. Mahogany tables and chairs matched with blood red centerpieces, which hold tiny candles that flicker against the dark walls, giving it a sensual and mystical feel. A large cut-open pomegranate custom designed and created out of crystal and wrought iron is hung on the center of the back wall to represent the symbolic meaning of the restaurant's name. It's hung just above the large stone fireplace, which was created to give the restaurant a warm and cozy feel to it.

"I gotta be honest," he continues, assessing the expansive bar just off the dining room, "I didn't really think you'd be able to pull it off, but it seems I underestimated you." His eyes land on mine, his one brow rising in a challenging way.

Every time Aris speaks to me, as if he hadn't forced

himself on me only a couple short months ago—stealing the most precious part of myself, as if it were his to steal—my stomach roils in disgust. Instead of meeting with him, like he advised, I managed to find a loophole by sending weekly emails to update him. I was shocked when I sent the first one and he replied with a simple "Thank you." My only thought is maybe having Selene around is keeping him occupied. I've seen them around the hotel on several occasions: having a drink at the bar, coming and going out of Aris's villa, going out to dinner at the restaurants on the grounds—Kostas and I even got roped into joining them once. Yuck! Maybe he's done antagonizing me. It would definitely make things easier if that were the case. Nothing is harder than trying to move forward with Kostas, while having his brother lurking in the shadows.

"What are you doing here?" I ask Aris, ignoring his backhanded compliment. With the restaurant set to open in less than two weeks, I'm meeting Rosie, who I've hired to manage the restaurant, and Angelo, the head chef, to finalize the menu. I could've left it up to Rosie to handle it since she's more than capable, with twenty years of restaurant management experience under her belt, but Pomegranate has become my baby, and I want to see it through to the final detail.

"Do I need to remind you that this restaurant is owned by the Demetrious, and therefore obligates me to make sure it meets the standards our name represents?"

I should've known when I emailed Aris to let him know the restaurant is done, and that I would be confirming the menu today for opening night, he would show up.

"My brother may be pussy-whipped and not care what you do," he continues, "but I'm not waiting until opening night to make sure everything is in order."

My stomach heaves at the mention of the word pussy out of Aris's mouth, but I choke it down. I need to get this meeting over with and then I can go home to my husband and get lost in him, erasing every part of Aris once again from my mind.

Just as I'm about to tell him to go fuck himself, the door opens again, and in walks Rosie, dressed in a professional royal blue pantsuit. Her heels *click-clack* against the wood floor. She smiles wide at me and waves as she approaches Aris and me.

"I hope I'm not late," she says, glancing at Aris, who is now standing by the table where my tablet and cell phone are at. I was working on a couple final details while I was waiting for Rosie to arrive and the chef to finish.

"Nope, you're right on time." I want nothing more than to pretend Aris isn't here, but when he clears his throat, silently indicating to make introductions, my manners win out. "Aris," I say, gesturing toward the man I despise, "this is Rosie, the restaurant manager. Rosie, this is Aris, the *bookkeeper*."

Aris's nostrils flare at my little dig. Everyone knows how jealous and resentful he is toward Kostas, especially since Kostas has formally taken over the entire organization in his father's indefinite absence.

"Aris, is there anything else you need?" I ask, hoping he'll get the hint and leave.

"Nah." He tilts his head to the side slightly and swipes his tongue across his bottom lip, hitting me with a hard stare. My stomach knots, worried I've crossed the line and angered the beast.

He smiles, his signature boyish smile I once upon a time fell for, walks around the table, and pulls my chair out for me. "If it's okay with you, I think I'll stay to try the food. I haven't had lunch yet."

"Fine," I choke out as I begrudgingly accept his gesture and sit in my seat, allowing him to push it in. He does the same thing for Rosie before he has a seat as well.

While we wait for the food to be ready, Rosie and Aris make small talk. He's sweet and polite and professional, and it makes me want to stab him in the eye with my salad fork.

The chef finally brings the sample of food out, and after going through each item—I've gone with an Italian menu—he places the tray in the middle of the table.

"Thank you, Angelo, this all looks delectable," I tell the chef. With a smile donning his face, he nods once and waits for us to each take an item from the tray. The veal parmesan looks delicious, so I decide to go with that. Bringing it up to my nose to smell it, the delicious aroma wafts in the air, and my stomach gurgles in hunger. Aris takes a piece of the chicken marsala and Rosie forks a piece of the crab stuffed parmesan shrimp.

Bringing the veal to my lips, I take a small bite, wanting to make sure I leave room to try everything else. It's scrumptious. The sauce is flavorful, the veal is tender, and the cheese is gooey.

"Angelo," I say, needing to praise him. "This is perfect."

"Agreed," Aris says.

"This shrimp is to die for," Rosie adds. "Here, try it." She forks another piece of the shrimp onto my plate. Without hesitation, I pop the shrimp into my mouth, but unlike the veal that appealed to all of my senses, the shrimp does the opposite. The moment it lands on my tongue, my stomach rolls, and then, when I force myself to swallow it down, my stomach revolts, refusing to accept the food.

Quickly excusing myself, I bolt straight to the bathroom and throw up. Just when I think I'm okay, I throw up again, losing whatever is left in my belly.

My head is halfway into the toilet when a masculine hand lands on my shoulder. Thinking it's Aris, I jump back, smacking the back of my head on the marble wall.

"*Zoí mou*, it's just me," Kostas says, his brows drawn together in worry. "Are you okay?" He kneels next to me, and lifting me in his arms, carries me over to the sink, setting me on the countertop. "I wanted to surprise you, but I got held up at a meeting. When I arrived, Aris said you ran to the bathroom." He takes a paper towel from the dispenser and wets it, then dabs it along my forehead.

"I'm okay. I think it was the shrimp." I take in a deep breath. My stomach no longer hurts. "I feel better now."

Kostas eyes me carefully. "I think Rosie and Aris can handle the rest of the menu. Let's get you home."

When we get back to the table, Aris eyes me speculatively. "Everything okay?"

"Yeah," Kostas says for me. "Talia isn't feeling well, though, so I'm going to get her home."

Not wanting Angelo to think his food was bad, I explain to him that I'm not much of a seafood person. Thankfully, he doesn't appear to be too offended. It helps that Rosie is working her way through almost every item on the tray and swears everything is perfection.

"Let's go, wife," Kostas says as he guides me down the pathway toward our home. "I was going to offer to run you a relaxing bath, but now that you're feeling better, I think a hot shower is in order." His wicked smirk makes me feel *tons* better.

chapter
twenty-eight

Kostas

I PACE OUR BEDROOM, SLIGHTLY ANNOYED BY THE FACT I'm wearing a tux rather than one of my usual Armani suits. But this is Talia's doing. The entire grand opening of Pomegranate is an over the top affair that she singlehandedly orchestrated herself. Pride chases away my irritation as I think about all the work she's put into the restaurant. It's by far the most unique restaurant at Pérasma Hotel. She's put an incredible amount of effort into it. My mother would be so proud.

Thunder rumbles in the distance. We've had nice weather all week. Of course it'd wait to rain until when we have guests coming in from all over Greece to help celebrate opening night.

"We better get a move on," I call out. "Weather's looking shitty."

She exits the bathroom in a pair of nude-colored panties and nothing else. Instantly, all thoughts of the event are erased as my hunger for her takes center place.

"No," she grumbles. "My stomach is in knots with nerves,

and I need to get dressed. We can't be late." She purses her juicy lips that have been painted the color of the skin of a pomegranate and frowns. If we didn't have this shit to go to, I'd suck every bit of the color off those perfect lips like she was my very own fruit to devour. "No," she huffs once more.

I roll my eyes but follow her into the large closet. Her long blond hair has been curled and hangs loose down her back. She locates her dress on a hanger and unzips the back. Then, she pulls it off the hanger before stepping into it. Her ass gets hugged by the material before it disappears when she pulls it up. I stride over to her and push her hair over one shoulder so I can zip it up. A tremble rattles through her.

"Don't be nervous," I tell her, kissing the top of her head. "You've done the hard part. Now it's time to enjoy it."

She turns and presses her lips to mine. "Thank you."

I step away and admire the way the crystal-studded dress hugs her luscious curves. When she'd seen the dress in a magazine and offhandedly mentioned how much she liked it, I knew the truth. It was her subtle way of asking for it. And since I'm a giving husband, I flew the designer out for a fitting. The sheer chiffon material serves one purpose—to hold the crystals in place. But in the places the crystals don't touch, I'm rewarded with tiny glimpses of her tanned flesh. It makes me want to tear the dress from her body one crystal at a time and forbid her to ever leave my sight. Just knowing both men and women will be staring at what's mine sets my teeth on edge.

"You're growling like a dog," she teases as she bends to slide on her silver strappy sandal heels.

"You're a sparkling dick magnet," I bite back.

She laughs—sweet and carefree. "I think that's a compliment, so thank you."

I stalk over to her and place my hands on her hips so I can inspect her closely. The dress is heart-shaped at the top and strapless. Her breasts fill the cups and spill over slightly. With each breath she takes, the flesh jiggles and entices. My dick fucking loves this dress.

"Still growling," she sings, flashing me a wicked grin.

She pulls away to walk over to her jewelry drawer that I've filled with gorgeous pieces that remind me of her. As she peers into the drawer to select what she'll wear, I rake my gaze down the rest of her dress. Where the crystals stop mid-thigh, the shimmery sheer chiffon goes all the way down to her ankles with only a few crystals dotting the material here and there. A long slit cuts through the fabric and ends incredibly high up her thigh.

This dress is fucking maddening.

"Can you help me with my bracelet, Fido?"

I pierce her with a hard glare. "I swear to fuck if anyone so much as touches you tonight, I'll gut them with my fork."

"Your wickedly possessive and equal parts horrifying threats are somehow romantic in a way," she teases as she hands me the thick, sparkly diamond bracelet. "I don't want anyone touching me but you, Kostas. No one."

Settled by her fierce words, I take the jewelry and connect it around her delicate wrist. Not letting go of her hand, I draw her palm to my mouth and kiss it, my eyes searing into hers. She grins at me before pulling away to put on some diamond dangly earrings.

"I'm ready," she finally says, "and you look handsome as ever."

Gently, I grip her neck and run my thumb along her throbbing vein. "Are you sure you wouldn't rather stay here instead?"

She clutches my wrist at her throat. "I'm sure. I'm excited to do this. But I'm already tired, so maybe we can cut out early."

"Deal, wife. And then you're mine."

"I already am."

I watch Talia like a hawk as she moves about the room as though she was born to do this. Eyes follow her everywhere and they all smile for her. Irritation burns inside me each time I see her mother and stepfather, but they're wise enough to avoid me. They're proud of her and that makes me happy for her. Doesn't mean I have to fucking socialize with them, though.

Aris comes to stand beside me and follows my stare, simply sipping from his tumbler of amber liquid without saying much else. After a few moments, he points at them, still holding his glass. It sloshes slightly.

"It's her fault, you know," he says, his words sharp and furious.

"Talia?"

He turns and offers me a cruel smile. "So quick to blame your wife and you don't even know what I'm talking about."

I grit my teeth. "Out with whatever the hell you're going to say, asshole."

"Not your wife." A laugh escapes him. "Her mother." He turns back to look at them and scowls. "Our mother would still be—"

"Oh, honey," Selene coos. "There you are." She bounds over to Aris, her big boobs nearly bouncing out of her dress in the process. "Been looking everywhere for you." Her gaze follows his, which is still locked on Talia, and she huffs. "That's an awfully daring dress to wear in public."

Before I can snap at her, Aris shuts her down by snagging her wrist and pulling her to him. "That mouth always gets you in trouble. Keep it up and I'm going to find something to keep it quiet."

Rather than being intimidated, she giggles and presses her tits against him as she kisses him. When they get a little too into it, I step away from them on a hunt for Talia. A waitress walks by with a tray filled with plates of dessert—pomegranate themed—and I grab one from her. I take a small bite and lift my brows in surprise. It's delicious.

Talia's eyes catch mine as her mother speaks to her. She pales at my looming presence. I don't miss the slight wobble of her feet, and the breathy way she asks for them to excuse her. Then, she makes her way over to me, forcing a smile.

"I know this is awkward," she breathes, sounding tired and overwhelmed. "But thank you for letting them come. It means the world to me."

I give her a simple nod and then grab her elbow to lead her over to an abandoned table. Once she's seated, I set the plate down and give her thigh a squeeze.

"You did a wonderful job. I'm impressed, but not surprised," I say, smiling at her.

Her smile falters and her face seems to pale more. She blinks as though she's slightly dizzy. Now that I think about it, while everyone else was eating, she made her rounds instead. When she looks down at her lap, I pick up the fork and stab at a piece of the dessert.

"You haven't eaten a thing tonight," I tell her, offering her a bite.

She lifts her gaze and eyes the food warily before darting her attention to her mother nearby. "I'm fine," she utters with a frown, not taking the bite, but instead waving it off.

"You're nervous and overwhelmed, which is to be expected," I placate as I set the fork back down on the plate. "The next restaurant opening in November will go off even smoother."

"That'll be tricky with school and all," she mutters, reaching for an untouched glass of water in front of her. "I enrolled for a full load. But I'm pretty sure I can make it all work."

Opening this restaurant took up all her damn time.

But school too?

There's no fucking way.

"Make the new restaurant your focus. We both know school was just something to pass the time for you. You have this now." I wave in the air as if to back up my words. "Now eat this. You're about to pass out."

She eyes the forkful of pomegranate dessert like it's poison. "Something to pass the time? You're being a dick, Kostas."

I grit my teeth, darting my gaze around to see if anyone heard her. Luckily, everyone is focused on chatting and eating dessert.

"Eat the fucking food," I grit out.

Her cheeks bloom red with the first flush of color all night. "No," she says stubbornly.

"You're hungry. Eat."

"I loved doing this restaurant, but I want to finish school. Something you said I could do," she bites out. "I'll figure out a way to manage both." She swats away the fork and it's really starting to piss me off.

I pin her with a hard glare. "Eat the pomegranate, *Persephone*."

"I said I don't want any, *Hades*." Her nostrils flare and she swallows hard.

Fury rises up inside of me like fire from the depths of Hell. Is this how the fabled god felt when the one he loved refused to eat the pomegranate that would keep her bound to him for eternity?

Obstinate women.

"Fine," I snap, setting the fork down with a hard clank. "Be that way."

She flinches at my tone. "I'm not being any way, Kostas." She rises quickly from her chair, swaying slightly. "I need fresh air."

"You're not going," I lash out.

"Outside or to school?" she challenges, tears welling in her pretty eyes.

I'm an asshole.

"School," I growl. "You have the restaurants, and you have me."

A tear races down her cheek as her blue eyes flash with betrayal at my words. I never said I wasn't a liar. School is a waste of fucking time and energy. She's a Demetriou now and doesn't need it.

"Then I'm going outside, boss," she sneers, her red bottom lip wobbling.

"Get your air and dry your tears." I clench my teeth before pinning her with a hard glare. "And then come back to eat your fucking pomegranate dessert."

We both know the meaning behind my words.

You eat it. You stay.

That's the end of our motherfucking story.

Five long minutes pass before my blood runs icy cold.

Fuck this.

Fuck her attitude, too.

I stalk out of the restaurant and into the pouring rain. It's cold and immediately saturates through my tux. In the dark, I scan the buildings and trees, searching for her.

Nowhere.

"Looking for your wife?" Aris asks, pressed against the wall, just under the awning of the building. "She went that way. Said she was running away from the monsters." He snorts at his joke. "Something could happen to a woman all alone…"

I'd love nothing more than to punch his fucking face in, but his words cause my anxiety to spike. I rush out into the direction he pointed along a path that leads between some villas. My dress shoes splatter in puddles on the stone in my quest to find her. As minutes pass without finding her, I'm getting more and more pissed.

It's like she forgets who she married sometimes.

I'm a monster.

She's called me this many times. It's not my fucking fault she has a hard time remembering it. I hear sobbing nearby, ratcheting up my nerves.

"Talia," I call out. "Come here."

"No," she barks out.

I see a flash of white in the darkness and chase after it. A squeal erupts from her as she tries to outrun me, which is futile. I'll always catch her. I'll always find her.

She darts through some bushes into the backyard of

someone's villa. I push through the shrubs and catch her running around their small pool. I charge after her, nearly making it to her, when she slides out of the yard on the other side. Once outside of the yard, she runs up some stone steps, but she's losing steam. I'm nearly to her when she slips and lands hard on her knee. A choked sob rattles from her, cutting me to the bone. Without a word, I scoop her soaked and trembling body into my arms. She's lost the fight.

My fight still burns inside me.

I storm back to our villa. She whimpers when I push inside and then slam the door shut with my foot. My chest heaves with fury. I just want to strip her down, fuck her senseless, and remind her who she belongs to. I've barely set her on her feet when she takes off running again. This time, she makes it into the closet where she starts angrily ripping off her jewelry.

"Calm the fuck down," I roar, stomping in after her.

Her blond hair is darker now that it's wet and plastered to her head. Black makeup runs down her cheeks and she's red-faced from crying. Lips that were once red are now looking kind of blue from the cold rain.

"Take that dress off," I command.

She needs a hot shower and a good dicking to calm her down.

"F-Fuck you," she chatters out.

I pounce on her and twist her around, bending her over the island in the closet. She screams when I unzip her dress. Forcefully, I rip the offending material off her body and it falls heavily to her feet. Her body trembles from the cold and adrenaline. I rip off her panties next and then her shoes, the entire time with her fighting me. When I've had enough, I yank her wrists back and gather them with one hand.

"Stop flipping the fuck out," I demand.

She squirms and wriggles to no avail. I press my hard dick against the crack of her ass, letting her feel through my slacks what she does to me even when she's pissing me the fuck off.

"I hate you," she sobs.

"No, you don't, goddammit."

I unbuckle my slacks and send them to the floor before kicking out of them. My boxers get shoved down my thighs and then I grip my dick before pressing into her soft, warm, and inviting body. We both hiss as I slide into her.

"I'll always be your little captive," she whimpers.

"Damn right," I growl, slamming into her.

"You're a liar," she accuses. "You lied right to my face to get your way."

I punish her hard with a thrust of my hips that makes her scream. "You said it yourself. I'm a monster."

She doesn't say anything else. Simply cries. I reach around to touch her clit. At first she flinches, but then she starts to moan when I work her into a frenzy. As soon as she reaches climax, she screams out my name, whether she wanted to or not. A sense of male pride surges through me. I groan out her name too before coming deep inside her. Her body relaxes against the island. I pull her to her feet and then turn her around.

Hopeless. Sad. Broken.

Fuck.

Maybe I'm not a monster when it comes to her.

"I'm sorry," I blurt out, cradling her cold cheeks in my palms. "I'm fucking sorry, okay."

She falls against my chest and I hug her tight. "I'm sorry too."

"You can go to school," I assure her. "I'm just a possessive asshole, is all." I kiss the top of her head. "Please don't ever run away from me again."

Her head tilts up and she kisses my lips. "I promise. Although running from you is kind of hot."

"Says the woman with blue lips and chattering teeth." I pull away and frown when I see blood from her skinned knee. "Come on. Let's get you cleaned up and warmed up and fed."

I don't let her walk to the bathroom, but instead scoop her into my arms. Her fingers push back my wet hair from my forehead as she studies me intently.

"I just didn't want that sweet dessert," she whispers, her bottom lip wobbling. "I wanted the pomegranate. I want you."

Relief floods inside me at the double meaning in her words.

She may have run, but she wants to stay.

"I know," I assure her. "I know."

Settled by my response, she smiles. I spend the rest of the night taking care of everything I fucked up.

Lucky for me, Talia's quick to forgive. She's sweet like that.

The make-up sex is even sweeter.

chapter
twenty-nine

Talia

BOOKS. CHECK. SCHEDULE. CHECK. PENS. CHECK. Notebooks. Check. I triple check I have everything I need for my first day of classes. I'm taking Theatre, Creative Writing, Art History, and Modern Greek Literature. I already know Theatre will be my favorite with Modern Greek Lit coming in second. I've read over the syllabi the professors have sent and I'm as prepared as I can be for my first day.

"Talia, I have a meeting at nine. Let's go," Kostas calls from the other room.

I roll my eyes as I gather my stuff and head out to meet him. He's been cranky ever since he realized I was set on finishing my degree, but at least he's now accepting it. That crazy man seriously thought he was going to keep me locked up here and I would be okay with it.

When I step into the living room, I find two beefed up men, both dressed to the nines in suits, with buzzed cuts, standing next to Kostas. Both share a similar scowl.

"Hello," I say, greeting them. I wasn't aware we had

company. When neither of them says anything back, my gaze goes straight to Kostas.

"This is Michael." He points to the man on the left. "And this is Tadd." He points to the one on the right. "They'll be escorting you whenever you leave the property, including to school." Kostas raises a single brow, daring me to argue, but I'm not stupid. He's looking for any excuse to forbid me from going, and I'm not about to give him one. "They'll remain with you at all times. Anywhere you go, they go."

"Including the bathroom?" I joke, not able to help myself.

Kostas's jaw clenches. I guess he's not in a joking mood. "Talia, if you don't want to take this seriously, I can tie your ass to the bed to keep you at home and call it a day."

My eyes dart over to Michael and Tadd. Neither of them even cracks a smile or flinches. Are they even human?

"I was only kidding," I defend.

Kostas steps toward me. "Your safety is not a joking matter," he says matter-of-factly. "I have a lot of enemies, *zoí mou*." He fondles a strand of hair that's fallen out of my ponytail. "Men who would do anything to get their hands on what's mine." His fingers travel down the side of my neck, and my body goes limp at his touch. "To use you as a bargaining chip. To torture you for the things I've done to them."

A chill runs down my spine, remembering when I thought I was going to be kidnapped. It turned out it was Niles's doing, but at the time, I was terrified. My face must show how I'm feeling because Kostas gives me a knowing look. "Every time you step foot off the property, you are in danger. These men are trained to keep you safe. They know your schedule and will escort you to every class, every day. Understand?"

"Yes." I glance over at the men, who are still standing in place as if they aren't even really here.

"Very well," Kostas says. "I'll see you at home tonight. We'll go to dinner so you can tell me all about your day."

I find myself sighing in relief. He may not be happy about it, but he really is going to let me go.

"Have a good day," I tell him. Standing on my tiptoes, I give him a chaste kiss, unsure if he's okay with kissing me in front of my new bodyguards. Kostas must not care because he turns my quick kiss into something deeper, devouring me as if it's the last time he'll see me. For a split second, I consider skipping my first day of classes and spending the day in bed with him. But then he pulls away.

"Behave," he warns.

In the town car, I sit in the back, while Michael drives and Tadd sits shotgun. Neither of them says a word as we drive out of the resort and toward the city.

"Can you please stop for coffee?" I request when I notice we're going to be passing by my favorite coffee shop. Michael nods once. Since I'm not allowed to go anywhere alone, they both accompany me into the coffee shop. I offer to buy them something, but they shake their heads. Their loss. The coffee and pastries here are to die for.

When the barista calls my name, I grab my coffee and croissant, thanking her. I take a sip, but it tastes off, bitter, causing my stomach to churn.

"Everything okay?" Tadd asks.

"Yeah, I think the coffee is bad." I try another sip, but when the smell hits my nose, I gag, almost throwing up.

"Excuse me," I say to the barista, "I ordered an espresso, but I don't think it's good." I hand her back the cup. She apologizes and remakes it. Not wanting to be late, I take the new drink with me to the car, but when I try to drink it, it tastes and smells just as bad as the last one.

What a shame…I really liked that coffee shop. Maybe my school will have a coffee shop on campus. Otherwise, I'm going to need to get up early, so I can go to the restaurant at the hotel.

Not wanting to risk getting sick on my first day of school, I forget the coffee and just eat the croissant while I mess around on my phone, checking social media. A few of my friends in Italy have started classes and have posted about upcoming performances. I no longer have Alex as a friend, but he's tagged in a few posts.

A picture of my mom at a charity function from last night pops up on my feed, and the feeling of loneliness overtakes me. My friends and family are all in another country going about their lives, while I'm over here. Sure, the restaurant kept me busy this summer, but I need something more. Something for me. Kostas doesn't understand that because when we got married, his life pretty much stayed the same. My life, on the other hand, completely changed, and going to school means holding onto that last piece of myself I haven't handed over to my husband.

Feeling overly emotional, I put my phone away.

We arrive at school, and Tadd opens my door for me. When I get to the first building, I pull out my map to see where my Theatre class is located, but Michael grunts out, "This way," and nods toward the first hallway.

"You know where all my classes are located?" I ask, confused.

"It's our job, ma'am," Tadd says. Of course. Kostas said they knew my schedule. He probably made them scour the campus and map out where and when each of my classes are.

When we get to the door that reads Theatre, Michael opens it for me. As I step in, I notice they're following me, so I halt in my place.

"You're not, like, coming in here with me, are you?" There's no way I'm going to sit in my classes with them literally standing guard next to me.

"It's our job, ma'am," Tadd repeats. Another student walks up, and since we're blocking the doorway, I move out of the way.

"You can wait outside," I tell them, trying to keep calm.

"You'll have to take that up with Mr. Demetriou, ma'am," Michael says with zero emotion.

Pulling my phone out of my purse, I dial Kostas. He answers on the first ring. "Talia."

"Kostas, they're trying to go in my class with me," I whisper-yell, not wanting to cause a scene, as if two two-hundred-pound men in the performing arts building aren't already standing out.

"That's their job." Jesus, is that the answer of the day?

"Kostas!" I screech, letting my frustration get the best of me. "You can't do this! It's so embarrassing. I'm a grown-ass woman. I don't need a babysitter in my class, let alone two!" When the phone remains silent, I fear I've crossed the line. Scared he's going to tell the men to bring me home, not allowing me to go to school after all, I change my tone.

"Kostas, please," I beg. "Can't they scope out the place and then wait outside by the door?"

"No."

"No?" I ask dumbly.

"No," he repeats.

No. That's it. Just fucking no. No conversing. No discussing. No compromising. Just *no.* Like he really is goddamn

God of the Underworld and has the final damn say in everything.

"Fine!" I hang up and throw my phone back into my purse. Stomping to the door, I swing it open, and my body-guards follow me in, knowing I didn't get my way.

I stalk down the aisle and find a seat a couple rows back, next to a girl who is flipping through the textbook for this class. I glance back and see Michael and Tadd have at least remained in the back, standing against the wall as if they're meant to blend in.

"I'm Penelope." The girl greets me with a soft smile.

"Talia."

"Did you see the performance schedule?" she asks, holding the syllabus up for me to see.

"Yeah, it's a good list. A couple of them I've performed back home, but a few are new."

"Home?" she questions.

"I'm from Italy. This is my first semester here."

"Italy is beautiful," Penelope gushes. "My family and I visited there last summer." She tells me about everything she saw and asks me questions about where I lived and went to school, until the professor enters the room and introduces himself. He runs through the performances and when the auditions will be held. I take notes, jotting down the ones I'm interested in. Because it's a senior level course, the only requirements are that we participate in a minimum of three performances, either by acting or as part of the stage crew. The first audition is for Macbeth. I already know I'm going to try out for the role of Lady Macbeth.

The rest of the morning goes smoothly. Michael and Tadd escort me to my creative writing class and once again remain in the back. The professor gets straight to it, going over the different types of poetry and assigning us homework: to create a poem of our choosing. I meet a couple of people in this class who seem really nice and ask me to join them for lunch.

The afternoon consists of my Lit and History of Art classes. They're not as fun as my morning classes, but they fly by, and before I know it I'm back in the car heading home. My classes are Tuesdays and Thursdays with Theatre practice on Fridays. That gives me the other days to get my homework done.

As I'm walking toward the parking lot with Michael and Tadd flanking me, my brother steps into view from out of nowhere.

"Phoenix!" I'm about to throw my arms around him for a hug when Michael yanks me back. "Hey," I shriek at the same time my brother hisses, "Get your hands off her."

"Back up," Tadd commands.

Phoenix reaches behind him, for what I assume is his gun, and before he can even pull it out, Tadd has him on the ground with his hands locked behind his back.

"Stop, please," I whisper, hating the attention we're drawing from the students walking by. "I know him. He's okay."

Tadd stands, bringing Phoenix up with him. "He's not on the approved list, ma'am."

"I'm her fucking brother, asshole. I don't need to be on any fucking list."

Tadd steps toward him. "You do if you want to go anywhere near her."

In fear he'll take out my brother, I move forward, only Michael is still holding me back. "Okay, okay," I say in a placating tone. "I'll speak to Kostas tonight and get you on the approved list." I silently beg Phoenix not to argue. The last thing I need is to give Kostas a reason to kill my brother.

Phoenix looks like he wants to say something, but when I shake my head, he closes his mouth.

"I'll see you soon," I tell him.

"All right." He nods once and then takes off in the opposite direction than we're heading.

By the time we're pulling through the entrance to the hotel, my blood is boiling. Damn Kostas and his need to control everything and everyone. Not sure when he'll be home, and not wanting to be here when he arrives, I opt to go for a swim in the pool to cool off. I can bring my homework with me and work on it by the pool. But when I step through the door, and am hit with a cold glare from Kostas, I know I'm not going anywhere. Setting my purse and books on the table, I shoot him what I hope is an equally pissed off expression.

"Welcome home, *wife*," Kostas greets as I stalk past him to the bedroom to change. Deciding a shower is in order, I strip down and go straight to the bathroom. I can feel Kostas behind me, but I ignore him, focusing on the temperature of the water. Once it's hot enough, I step in, only to find Kostas is also naked and following me in.

Doing my best to ignore him, I grab the body wash and squeeze some onto a loofah. But like the tyrant my husband is, he won't be ignored. Gripping the curve of my hip, he turns me around to face him, backing me against the shower wall. The loofah falls to the ground as he pins my hands above my head with one of his own. "I asked how your day was, *wife*," he seethes.

When I still refuse to answer, he leans in and bites down on my bottom lip. I screech out in pain, trying to push him away, but he's too strong, and I'm at his mercy. I'm *always* at his mercy.

"Want me to tell you how my day was?" he asks, clearly

as a rhetorical question, since he doesn't wait for an answer before he continues. "It started with my wife screaming at me over the phone while I was standing in an important business meeting." My eyes go wide. Shit, I didn't think about why he was being so short over the phone. "Apparently it's more *important* for her to fit in than to be safe." His icy-hot gaze bores into mine. "Not even an hour away from here and you're already forgetting whose *wife* you are." His grip tightens on my wrists, and with his other hand, he lifts me up by my ass. My legs wrap around his torso, and then he roughly drives into me.

Everything inside me clenches.

"You." *Thrust.* "Are." *Another thrust.* "My goddamned wife."

My eyes remain locked with Kostas's as he fucks me hard and deep, reminding me who I am. Who I belong to. And by the time we're both coming, I'm screaming out the name of the man who owns every single part of me.

"Add Phoenix to the approved list," I tell Kostas after the waiter sets down our plates of food.

Kostas's jaw clenches. "You're going to want to rethink how you speak to your husband, *anóito korítsi.*" *Foolish girl.* "Otherwise, I'm going to be forced to remind you again who you belong to, but you aren't going to be screaming my name in pleasure this time."

Not wanting to argue with him, I take a calming breath and try again, this time nicer. "Can you please add my brother to the list of approved people who can speak to me?"

Kostas glares my way but nods. "It's already been done."

"Thank you."

"How was your first day of school?"

"It was good. The first performance in my theatre class is *Macbeth*. Guess which part I'm trying out for." I bat my lashes playfully, and Kostas chuckles.

"Let me guess, Lady Macbeth," he answers dryly.

"Yep. I think I'll make a great Lady Macbeth. She's strong and ambitious. Determined."

Kostas barks out a laugh. "She's cunning and ruthless and manipulative. She repeatedly questions her husband's manhood until she pushes him to the edge, forcing him to commit murder. Then she can't handle it and takes her own life." Kostas puts his fork down and stares at me with a mixture of humor and seriousness. "You know what would've saved her life? If she had let her husband handle shit."

I roll my eyes. "You're such a caveman."

"Doesn't Lady Macbeth have to kiss Macbeth in that play?" Kostas asks thoughtfully.

"I don't know." I shrug. "If she does, it's only for pretend. It's a stage kiss. It's not real."

Kostas lets out a growl. "I'll be damned if my wife is kissing another man, staged or not."

"Caveman," I repeat.

"Careful, *Lady Macbeth*. You will hate the outcome if you drive your husband to the edge and he's forced to commit murder." Kostas's lips curve into a wicked grin as fear shoots through my veins like some deadly hit of a drug I want no part of.

Any other man and I would take his threat as a joke, but with Kostas, I have a feeling he's being dead serious.

chapter
thirty

Kostas

THERE ARE TWO THINGS THAT RILE MY WIFE UP. One, telling her no. The other, her motherfucking raging hormonal period time. This morning, the stage is set for a nuclear meltdown. For once, I'm eager to send her ass to school so I can get a moment of fucking peace.

"Say it again," she seethes, her face turning red.

I scrub my palm down my face in frustration. "You're just mad because you're on your period." She had Tadd and Michael run her by the drugstore after school yesterday, so I know this is half of her problem.

"What did you say?" Her voice is deceptively calm, but I can see the figurative claws coming out.

"I'm saying it's why you're being irrational."

She picks up a vase and heaves it at me. I don't even have to duck out of the way because she throws like shit. My wife's favorite things to throw are vases, so I keep having them replenished in our home. It crashes behind me and her chest rises up and down with fury.

"I am not being irrational, Kostas. I'm not being hormonal. You're being a psychopath!" She's too pissed to cry. Nothing but rage ripples from her. Normally, I like to pin her down and fuck the anger out of her, but she's on the rag and isn't into it.

I stalk over to her and grip her jaw, smushing her cheeks so her lips pucker out. "You married me knowing I was a psychopath. Don't act surprised now, Mrs. Demetriou."

She hisses like a fucking cat. "I'll be Lady Macbeth, and I'll kiss him! It's what my grade requires me to do!"

Just thinking about her kissing that motherfucker makes me see red. I'd been proud when she auditioned for the part and got it, but the moment she reminded me she'd have to kiss the guy, I wasn't having any of it.

"And I told you what I'd do if he kissed you," I bite out, rubbing the tip of my nose against hers and pinning her with a hard glare.

"You can't cut off his lips, you fucking freak!" she cries out, her emotions finally winning out over her anger. Tears well in her pretty blues and I hate that I caused them, but I won't back down on this.

"I will. Tell your teacher you can pretend to kiss him. But I won't have him taking what's mine," I tell her simply.

"You're impossible," she snaps. "I'm leaving."

"How long is this Theater practice?" I ask, not releasing her pretty face.

"Two hours." She rolls her eyes. "I know the drill. Come straight home. Don't pass Go. Don't collect two hundred dollars. Just come back to the dungeon so my psychopathic husband can put me back in my cage."

"Get over yourself," I grumble, letting her go. "I swear, I ought to put you in a cage one week out of every month."

Her lip curls up in fury. "I hate you."

"Mhmm."

"You can't keep me pressed under your thumb forever," she threatens, her lip wobbling slightly. "I won't stand for it. You know this, Kostas."

I grip a handful of her blond hair and kiss her pouty lips that keep spewing so much hate today. She doesn't kiss me back, which really fucking pisses me off.

"You'll stand for it because you have no goddamn choice," I bite out and press a soft kiss to her forehead. "Have a nice time at practice."

She pulls away and glowers at me for a moment before turning on her heel and stalking off. I should go after her, yank her back into the room, and make passionate love to her so she'll calm down…period be damned. But I have a meeting with my father and I don't have time to pacify her like usual.

"Don't wait up for me," she sasses over her shoulder.

"S 'agapó, ómorfi gynaíka mou." *I love you, my beautiful wife.*

The door slams before I even get the words out.

I'll let her cool off and then I'm going to spend all weekend teaching her how to behave. A little duct tape. Some rope. Naked and at my mercy. It'll be hard to be pissed when she's had countless orgasms.

Sometimes I think Talia likes to fight with me just so we can make up.

We're really fucking good at making up.

Father was in his bedroom when I arrived, laid up in his bed. For a man who months ago ruled with an iron fist he is weak now. So fucking weak. My mother made him that way. I helped him dress, along with his live-in nurse, and then wheeled him down to the dining room where his cook had made a fantastic lunch spread. An hour passes before we finish our meal and get down to whatever it is Father called me here for.

"How's married life treating you?" he asks, his features hardened.

"Splendid." He doesn't need to know that Talia pushes every fucking button I have, but I secretly like it. Our fighting is foreplay. Father definitely doesn't need to hear about that.

"Hmmm," is all he says. "Where's your brother?"

I pull out a phone and check for any texts.

Aris: *On my way. Sorry I'm late. Selene's mouth needed to be punished.*

Rolling my eyes, I set my phone down on the table. "He'll be here soon."

One of Father's servants walks in with a tray, bringing us some cookies and coffee. While she busies herself with setting everything out, I scroll through my phone checking on emails. I fire off a text to Talia.

Me: *I miss you even when you piss me the fuck off.*

I smirk, imagining the way her nostrils will flare and her blue eyes will darken with anger.

"The wind is fucking horrible," Aris calls out as he strides into the dining room looking disheveled. "Tropical storm coming through?"

He and Father discuss the weather while I stare at my phone. The servant brings out a plate of lunch for Aris.

After ten or fifteen minutes of them gossiping about the weather like two old fucking men, I let out a huff and set my phone down. My gaze finds Aris and I notice his bitch literally got her claws into him. His neck is red where she scratched him. Selene is a skank, but Aris seems quite taken by her. When he catches me staring, he flashes me a lazy grin.

"Where's Niles?" Father demands, dragging my attention his way.

I grit my teeth. For someone who has to have a nurse twenty-four-seven, he sure is a demanding motherfucker. "He's hiding like the rat he is."

Aris snorts. "His son sure as hell isn't."

Father lifts a brow at me in question. "Phoenix sniffing around?"

"I married his sister. It's not unheard of for annoying brothers to stick their noses where they don't belong." I level Aris with a glare that makes him bark out a laugh.

"Can we shake out information from him?" Father asks, his shrewd eyes narrowing at me.

"He doesn't know anything," I grit out.

Father blinks at me before shaking his head. "He does. And you could get it out of him. But you won't. Why is that, my son?"

"Father, you're out of line."

"Me?" He scoffs. "You're the one acting like a piece of ass is more important than this family."

"Enough!" I roar, slamming my fist down on the table. "She is my wife. And just like you respected my mother, I will respect her. He's her brother. I'm not going to torture answers out of him. We'll find Niles another fucking way."

Aris smirks as he watches our exchange.

"Talia is a distraction. She makes you soft," Father growls. "You're not fit to lead."

I rise from my seat and sneer at him, motioning at his wheelchair and the fucking salmon-colored afghan blanket in his lap. "Too bad you don't make those decisions anymore."

"Kostas Angelo Demetriou!" Father bellows, but I'm already storming away from him.

Father can meddle all he wants, but I know what the hell I'm doing. I have men all over sniffing out Phoenix's moves, hunting for Niles, and following every Galani roach left all over Crete. Just because I don't blab to my brother or my father every damn time I do something doesn't mean I don't spend all goddamn day piecing together the puzzle that is my life.

I climb into my Maserati and zip down the streets, anger buzzing through my veins. By the time I reach the hotel, it's ten minutes after when Talia gets out of class. Her not texting me back means she's super pissed. I shut off the car and dial a local flower delivery company. Women like flowers and Talia is no exception. Once the flowers are ordered, I text her again.

Me: I'm sorry, zoí mou.

I'm still staring at my phone when Tadd calls.

"Boss," he grunts out, his breathing heavy. "We've got a problem."

A chill races down my spine.

"What kind of problem?" I growl.

He curses. "A big one."

"Where. Is. My. Wife?"

A long pause.

"We don't know. She left the auditorium to go to the bathroom and never came back."

I pull up the tracker I have on her phone. "It shows she's

on campus. She's pissed, Tadd. We fought. Find her ass wherever she is hiding and call me. Check the campus coffee shop or the library. I'm on my way."

Without wasting a second, I haul ass to her school and dial Aris.

"Hey," he grunts in greeting.

"You heard from Talia?" I demand, pressing my foot down on the accelerator.

"Not since dinner the other night with Selene. Why? She pissed at you again?"

I don't have time for his taunting shit.

"Can you call her and see if she answers?"

He sobers up. "Is she missing?"

"Went to the bathroom and never came back."

"Fuck," he hisses. "She wouldn't just leave. Phoenix?"

I knew adding him as an approved person was a bad idea. "I don't know. Call him. Find him."

We hang up, and I try dialing her number. It rings and rings. Next, I call Adrian and send him to the airport since that's where she first ran off to.

Fuck.

As soon as I pull into the parking lot, I throw my car into park and take off running toward the building. Tadd greets me with a worried expression. Michael is nowhere to be found.

"Where's Michael?" I demand.

"Checking the school again."

"And you're sitting out here with your thumb up your ass?"

He frowns. "I was waiting for you."

If I wasn't worried about my damn wife, I'd cut this lazy dumbass's throat.

"Go get in your fucking car and find my wife," I snarl. "Your neck depends on it."

He gives me a clipped nod and runs off. Michael comes out of the building holding a young woman by her arm. Her eyes are wild when she sees me.

"Tell him," Michael barks at the girl.

She flinches and stammers, "I, uh, before rehearsal, she was crying. She was upset."

I already fucking know that. I pissed her off.

"And?" I snap.

"Uh," she whimpers. "She kept saying she just needs to see her mom."

My blood runs cold. She wouldn't just bail on me. Not now. Not with all the people who could hurt her. She knows better than this. Right?

"She seemed really upset," she says, "and then she grabbed her purse to go to the bathroom. Never came back. I thought she went home for the day."

I turn my glare on Michael. "You were to watch her every move. What the fuck were you two doing?"

"Jesus, boss," Michael grunts. "We didn't follow her into the bathroom. We stayed in the auditorium. The bathroom was just outside the doors."

I'll deal with these two pussies later once I've found Talia.

I *will* find Talia. I always do.

I pull the tracker app back up on my phone to check it again. "It still shows she's on campus." What the fuck? Did she leave her phone here? "Go check every damn classroom, every bathroom. That phone is somewhere on this damn campus. Find it. Find her."

My phone rings, and I answer it on the first ring. "What?"

"I asked Selene if she's spoken to Talia," Aris grits out. "Fuck. She's worried about her. She said last night in the middle of the night, she called asking to borrow some money. I didn't even know Selene left my villa to meet her with the money." And I didn't know Talia left ours. Fuck.

"Money for what?"

"Selene said she seemed as though she had her mind made up about something. She lent her the money and didn't think much of it until I called."

"So you're saying she willingly left me?" I growl into the phone.

Aris sucks in a sharp breath. "You and I both know we can't go on that assumption."

The line goes quiet before he lets out another heavy sigh.

"Some of the men at the hotel said they heard Estevan Galani finally recovered from what you did to him on your honeymoon and is here in town." Aris huffs. "What if…"

My blood turns ice cold.

I knew I should have killed that motherfucker.

"If he has her," I rumble out, "he's a dead man."

"Kostas, if he has her, she's a dead woman."

Fuck.

Fuck.

Fuck.

I have to find her.

Her life may depend on it.

To be continued in the epic conclusion of the
Truths and Lies Duet...
Stolen Lies

playlist

Head Above Water by Avril Lavigne

Complicated by Avril Lavigne

I'm a Mess by Bebe Rexha

Broken-hearted Girl by Beyoncé

Reason to Stay by Brett Young

Never be the Same by Camila Cabello

Consequences by Camila Cabello

The Scientist by Coldplay

Let it Go by James Bay

In Case by Demi Lovato

i hate u, i love u by Gnash

Desire by Meg Myers

Stay by Rihanna

Back to You by Louis Tomlinson

Bad Things by Machine Gun Kelly and Camila Cabello

Love on the Brain by Rihanna

Rock Bottom by Hailee Steinfeld

The Monster by Eminem

So Good by Zara Larsson

Remind Me to Forget by Kygo & Miguel

Him & I by G-Eazy & Halsey

Bad Blood by Taylor Swift

Mad by Ne-Yo

I'm a Mess by Ed Sheeran

acknowledgements from
NIKKI ASH

Bret, thank you for spending hours at Starbucks with me while I write all the words. To my children, thank you for simply being you. You are my inspiration in everything I do. Kristi, thank you for taking me under your wing and showing me what a true friend looks like. You are such a special person, on the inside and out. Nikki Ash's Fight Club reader group. In this crazy world, you guys are my safe place. Thank you! Thank you to all of the ladies who have my back. Stacy Garcia, Ashley Cormier, Brittany Ridge, Andrea Hebda, Tabitha Willbanks, Shannon Voyles, Kaylee Ryan, Lisa McKay, and Kristi Webster. I can't imagine doing any of this without you guys. Emily A. Lawrence, thank you for editing this book. Stacy Blake, thank you for making the book so pretty! Ena and Amanda with Enticing Journey, thank you for keeping me sane! To all of the bloggers who take time out of their day to share their love of books, thank you for everything you do. And a huge thank you to the amazing readers. There are so many books out there for you to read. Thank you for taking a chance on me. It's because of you, I get to continue to do what I love—write books.

acknowledgements from
K WEBSTER

Thank you to my husband… I love you for always being there no matter what. You're the best!

A big ol' thank you to Nikki Ash! I love when we collaborate! We come up with the best, most intricate stories, and I love it! Thanks for using your summers to play with me! Love ya, lady!

A huge thank you to my Krazy for K Webster's Books reader group. You all are insanely supportive and I can't thank you enough.

A gigantic thank you to those who always help me out. Elizabeth Clinton, Ella Stewart, Misty Walker, Holly Sparks, Jillian Ruize, Gina Behrends, Rosa Saucedo, Ker Dukey, and Nikki Ash—you ladies are my rock!

Thank you so much to Misty Walker for being the best friend a girl could ask for! Love you!!

Thank you so much, Wendy Rinebold, for proofing this book! You're a star, lady!!

A huge thanks to my Greek friend Pauline Digaletos who looked over our Greek words and phrases to make sure we did them right. You're the best!!

A big thank you to my author friends who have given me your friendship and your support. You have no idea how much that means to me.

Thank you to all of my blogger friends both big and small that go above and beyond to always share my stuff. You all rock! #AllBlogsMatter

Emily A. Lawrence, thank you SO much for editing this book. You rock!!

Thank you, Stacey Blake, for being amazing as always when formatting my books and in general. I love you! I love you! I love you!

Lastly but certainly not least of all, thank you to all of the wonderful readers out there who are willing to hear my story and enjoy my characters like I do. It means the world to me!

about
NIKKI ASH

Nikki Ash resides in South Florida where she is an English teacher by day and a writer by night. When she's not writing, you can find her with a book in her hand. From the Boxcar Children, to Wuthering Heights, to the latest single parent romance, she has lived and breathed every type of book. While reading and writing are her passions, her two children are her entire world. You can probably find them at a Disney park before you would find them at home on the weekends!

Reading is like breathing in, writing is like breathing out.–
Pam Allyn

Contact Nikki Ash

Facebook: facebook.com/authornikkiash

Twitter: twitter.com/authornikkiash

Instagram: instagram.com/authornikkiash

Amazon: amazon.com/author/nikkiash

Website: www.authornikkiash.com

Nikki Ash's reader group:
www.facebook.com/groups/booksbynikkiash

Subscribe to Nikki Ash's newsletter:
bit.ly/NikkiAshNewsletter

about
K WEBSTER

K Webster is a *USA Today* Bestselling author. Her titles have claimed many bestseller tags in numerous categories, are translated in multiple languages, and have been adapted into audiobooks. She lives in "Tornado Alley" with her husband, two children, and her baby dog named Blue. When she's not writing, she's reading, drinking copious amounts of coffee, and researching aliens.

Keep up with K Webster
Facebook: www.facebook.com/authorkwebster
Blog: authorkwebster.wordpress.com
Twitter: twitter.com/KristiWebster
Email: kristi@authorkwebster.com
Goodreads: www.goodreads.com/user/show/10439773-k-webster
Instagram: instagram.com/kristiwebster

books by
NIKKI ASH

All books can be read as standalones

The Fighting Series
Fighting for a Second Chance (Secret baby)
Fighting with Faith (Secret baby)
Fighting for Your Touch
Fighting for Your Love (Single mom)
Fighting 'round the Christmas Tree: A Fighting Series Novel

Fighting Love Series
Tapping Out (Secret baby)
Clinched (Single dad)
Takedown (Single mom)

Imperfect Love Series
The Pickup (Secret baby)
Going Deep (Enemies to Lovers)
On the Surface (Second chance, single dad)

Stand-alone Novels
Bordello (Mob romance)
Knocked Down (Single dad)
Unbroken Promises (Friends to lovers)
Through His Eyes (Single mom, age gap)
Clutch Player

Co-written novels
Heath (Modern telling)
Hidden Truths
Stolen Lies

books by
K WEBSTER

Psychological Romance Standalones:
My Torin
Whispers and the Roars
Cold Cole Heart
Blue Hill Blood

Romantic Suspense Standalones:
Dirty Ugly Toy
El Malo
Notice
Sweet Jayne
The Road Back to Us
Surviving Harley
Love and Law
Moth to a Flame
Erased

Extremely Forbidden Romance Standalones:
The Wild
Hale
Like Dragonflies

Taboo Treats:
Bad Bad Bad
Coach Long
Ex-Rated Attraction
Mr. Blakely
Easton
Crybaby
Lawn Boys
Malfeasance
Renner's Rules
The Glue
Dane
Enzo
Red Hot Winter
Dr. Dan

KKinky Reads Collection:
Share Me
Choke Me
Daddy Me
Watch Me
Hurt Me

Contemporary Romance Standalones:
Wicked Lies Boys Tell
Conheartists
The Day She Cried
Untimely You
Heath
Sundays are for Hangovers
A Merry Christmas with Judy
Zeke's Eden

Schooled by a Senior
Give Me Yesterday
Sunshine and the Stalker
Bidding for Keeps
B-Sides and Rarities

Paranormal Romance Standalones:
Apartment 2B
Running Free
Mad Sea
Cold Queen

War & Peace Series:
This is War, Baby (Book 1)
This is Love, Baby (Book 2)
This Isn't Over, Baby (Book 3)
This Isn't You, Baby (Book 4)
This is Me, Baby (Book 5)
This Isn't Fair, Baby (Book 6)
This is the End, Baby (Book 7 – a novella)

Lost Planet Series:
The Forgotten Commander (Book 1)
The Vanished Specialist (Book 2)
The Mad Lieutenant (Book 3)
The Uncertain Scientist (Book 4)
The Lonely Orphan (Book 5)

2 Lovers Series:
Text 2 Lovers (Book 1)
Hate 2 Lovers (Book 2)
Thieves 2 Lovers (Book 3)

Pretty Little Dolls Series:

Pretty Stolen Dolls (Book 1)
Pretty Lost Dolls (Book 2)
Pretty New Doll (Book 3)
Pretty Broken Dolls (Book 4)

The V Games Series:

Vlad (Book 1)
Ven (Book 2)
Vas (Book 3)

Four Fathers Books:

Pearson

Four Sons Books:

Camden
Elite Seven Books:
Gluttony
Greed

Not Safe for Zon Books:

The Wild
Hale
Bad Bad Bad
This is War, Baby
Like Dragonflies

Made in the USA
Las Vegas, NV
12 June 2021

24634789R00167